SHADOWS
OF
JUSTICE

A TOPHER DAVIS THRILLER

BRIAN
COPELAND

BLACK
ODYSSEY
MEDIA

WWW.BLACKODYSSEY.NET

Published by
BLACK ODYSSEY MEDIA
www.blackodyssey.net
Email: info@blackodyssey.net

SHADOWS OF JUSTICE. Copyright © 2025 by BRIAN COPELAND

Library of Congress Control Number: 2024916891

First Trade Paperback Printing: May 2025
ISBN: 978-1-957950-65-5
ISBN: 978-1-957950-64-8 (e-book)

Cover Design by Ashlee Nassar of Designs With Sass
To the extent that the image or images on the cover of this book depict a person or persons, such person or persons are merely models and are not intended to portray any character in the book.

10 9 8 7 6 5 4 3 2 1

Manufactured in the United States of America

Distributed by Kensington Publishing Corp.

The authorized representative in the EU for product safety and compliance
Is eucomply OU, Parnu mnt 139b-14, Apt 123
Tallinn, Berlin 11317, hello@eucompliancepartner.com

Dear Reader,

I want to thank you immensely for supporting Black Odyssey Media and our ongoing efforts to spotlight the diverse narratives of blossoming and seasoned storytellers. With every manuscript we acquire, we believe that it took talent, discipline, and remarkable courage to construct that story, flesh out those characters, and prepare it for the world. Debut or seasoned, our authors are the real heroes and heroines in *OUR* story. For them, we are eternally grateful.

Whether you are new to Brian Copeland or Black Odyssey Media, we hope that you are here to stay. Our goal is to make a lasting impact in the publishing landscape, one step at a time and one book at a time. As always, we welcome your feedback and kindly ask that you leave a review. For upcoming releases, announcements, submission guidelines, etc., please be sure to visit our website at www.blackodyssey.net or scan the QR code below. And remember, no matter where you are in your journey, the best of both worlds begins now!

Joyfully,

Shawanda Williams

Shawanda "N'Tyse" Williams
Founder & CEO, Black Odyssey Media

For the 280,031 African American women who disappeared in the United States in 2023, and their families.

May they find closure.

(Source: Black and Missing Foundation)

ONE

KRISTEN PROMES RUBBED her lower back as she watched the gaggle of children splash in her Olympic-sized pool. Her back had been bothering her for three days now, which surprised her. She was only four and a half months along and thought that those issues wouldn't start until she was a little later in her pregnancy. That's how it had been with Taylor, her first. She didn't have back problems with that gestation until she was at six months. It was an inconvenient day for this as there were over a hundred guests at the house.

The sun was hot this Fourth of July as the annual Promes Barbecue was in full swing. It was her husband, Tom's, favorite day of the year. He had made sure that anybody who was anybody in the city of Pleasanton was there. She spotted the mayor at the outside bar having drinks with her dad, Morgan Duffy. The fire chief chatted up Congressman Whitlock as they watched their kids get butterflies delicately drawn on their cheeks by the face painters Tom had hired. Steve Chambers, who owned the local BMW dealership, stood at the grill as the caterer piled his plate high with ribs, chicken, and hot links. Tom said that the event was good for business and that, as usual, he was right. She knew that you could never have too many friends in the real estate business. Her father had taught her that. He'd spent his life in the property game.

"Look at you! You're positively glowing!" came a voice from behind her.

Kristen turned to see Sheila Douglas, little Whitney's mom from Taylor's preschool. Kristen didn't much care for her. Since first becoming a mom four years ago, she'd discovered that every organized children's activity had a "queen bee." In her circle, it was Sheila Douglas. Sheila was the Room Mom for the class. She took it upon herself to coordinate the field trip the kids took to Knowland Park Zoo and the reception for the dance recital at the girls' ballet class. Sheila was only invited because Tom hoped to "buddy up" with her husband, Roland. Roland Douglas was on the zoning commission, and Tom needed some commercial lots the Duffy firm had optioned rezoned for residential development.

"Why, thank you!" Kristen said. "I sure don't feel like I'm glowing in this heat."

"The thermometer in my Mercedes read 102 degrees, and that was over an hour ago," Sheila said. "It's definitely warmer than that now."

"Good thing global warming is a hoax, or it would be really hot," Kristen joked.

Sheila laughed.

"Well, regardless," she said, "this pregnancy definitely agrees with you."

"Tell it to my lower back," Kristen said.

Sheila laughed again.

The cell phone in Kristen's pocket vibrated. She pulled it out and looked at the incoming number.

"Excuse me, Sheila," she said. "I need to take this."

Kristen pressed the answer icon and put the phone up to her ear.

"Just a minute," she said. "Let me get someplace quiet."

She walked around the pool, past the bouncy house filled with yet more kids gleefully jumping up and down as they laughed, squealed, and hollered. It was nice seeing the little ones having such a good time. She went through the patio door of her family's McMansion. Kristen hated that word, but it really was apropos. All the stucco monstrosities in their Colby Hills development fit that description: large, overbuilt structures that aspired to be something greater than they actually were.

Kristen walked through the kitchen and past Katrina Long, her housekeeper and nanny. Katrina was a slight woman in her late thirties who wore a black-and-white maid's outfit to work. Kristen always smiled when she saw it, thinking that her attire resembled something more out of a lingerie shop than a work uniform.

Katrina, carrying a silver tray of puff pastry hors d'oeuvres, nodded as Kristen walked past her and into the office that Tom kept at home. Kristen closed the door and plopped down behind Tom's neatly arranged desk. He was such a neat freak. Overly organized about everything. Sometimes, it drove Kristen nuts. *Love the man, love his faults*, she thought.

"Sorry," she said, putting the phone up to her ear. "Had to go inside. It's really loud out there."

"No problem," said Julie Wolfer.

Kristen and Tom met Julie and her husband, Jack, during a Lamaze class when they were both pregnant with their daughters, and they immediately hit it off. Julie's daughter, Hope, was born eighteen hours after Taylor, and the children had been inseparable ever since. So had their parents.

"What time you getting here?" Kristen asked. "You're about the only thing that makes this madhouse bearable."

"That's just it," Julie said. "I can't make it. My head is stuffy. My throat is sore. I'm congested. I just want to lie on the couch with a box of Kleenex and die."

"That's awful. Is it COVID?"

"No. I took a rapid test, and it came up negative. I tested Hope too. She's fine. Jack's out of town on business, and I'm not up to driving, so, unfortunately, we're not going to make it this year."

"Shit," Kristen said. "Taylor will be so disappointed. She was really looking forward to hanging out with Hope today."

"I'm sorry," Julie said. "I'd put her in an Uber and send her over, but she's a little young for that."

"Ya think?" Kristen laughed. "Tell you what? Why don't I come over and get her? She can spend the night. That way, you can get some rest."

"I really don't want to be a bother…"

"What bother? You're only ten minutes away, for God's sake."

"You sure?" Julie asked.

"Pack a bag for Hope. Let me fight my way out of here, and I'll see you in fifteen," Kristen said.

"Kristen, you're an angel."

"I've been told that before," she said, laughing. "See you soon."

She ended the call just as Tom walked in. Tom was tall and handsome with sandy-brown hair and chestnut-colored eyes. Strong, sloped shoulders indicated the physique of a man who never missed a daily gym workout.

"There you are," Tom said.

He walked over to Kristen and gave her a peck on the lips. "How you feelin'?" he asked.

"Lower back is killing me, and this heat isn't doing me any favors."

"I'm sorry, honey," Tom said. "The day will go by quickly. I just came in to get the maps with those parcels I want Roland to rezone for us."

"I'm glad you're getting some business done," she said. "Julie's got a bug or something. I'm going to pick up Hope. She's gonna spend the night if that's okay with you."

"Of course," Tom said. "Tell Julie I said to feel better."

"I will," Kristen said.

"Hurry back," Tom said. "I can't handle this mob by myself."

"I have complete confidence in you," Kristen replied, giving him another peck on the lips.

She left the office and made her way through the throng of guests to the front door. She reached into the little bowl they kept on a table next to the door and extracted the keys to her Rav4 hybrid. Even though it was starting to get up there in miles, Kristen loved the car and the fact that the electric vehicle's reduced emissions might, in some small way, help alleviate the extreme temperatures they'd been seeing lately. She tucked the keys into the pocket of her shorts and went out the door.

She had no way of knowing it would be for the last time.

TWO

IT WAS ANOTHER Pleasanton scorcher as I sat in the Electronic News Gathering, or "ENG" truck as we call them, with Stu Simons, my cameraman. The truck's AC gave us a respite from the noonday heat if we were judicious in our usage. It would run down the battery if we left it on too long. That was the last thing we needed. Whatever could go wrong had gone wrong that morning.

My alarm hadn't gone off at five as scheduled, so I had to scramble to the station in San Francisco from my home across the bay in Castro Valley. Then the first ENG truck we were assigned had mechanical problems on the Bay Bridge in the morning commute traffic, and we had to wait two hours for a replacement to be delivered to us. This, of course, made us get to the Pleasanton site later than every other news organization in the Western world, resulting in a parking spot four and a half blocks from our destination—the perfect start to the perfect day.

My name is Topher Davis, and for years, I've been an investigative reporter for Channel 6 in San Francisco, where I've reported on everything from political corruption to robberies to homicides. Stu, my producer, Mandy Lang, and I are now working under a different arrangement with the station. Following our reportage on a series of cop killings a few months back, we had the full resources of the station but were given a lucrative contract that gave us the independence to cover any story we deemed fit. I was enjoying the autonomy, even though there were times like this when there was something that I wasn't thrilled about covering but had to. This was a story that had captivated the nation. You do what you have to do.

A soccer mom in nearby suburban Pleasanton had left her home on the Fourth of July to run an errand and never returned. Her disappearance caught the media by storm. In the ten days since she vanished, the number of news vans in front of her home had swelled from just a few to dozens from media outlets across the country and as far away as the UK. Every station in the San Francisco Bay Area broadcast market was there, as well as radio, print, and social media reporters, bloggers, and true crime podcasters from our area and beyond. The media circus included the four major broadcast networks and cable news channels CNN, MSNBC, and FOX NEWS. PBS and even the BBC had gotten in on the act. Print journalists were adequately represented by the *Associated Press*, the *San Francisco Chronicle*, the *San Francisco Examiner*, the *East Bay Times*, the *San Jose Mercury News*, the *Sacramento Bee*, the *Los Angeles Times*, *The New York Times*, *The Atlanta Journal-Constitution*, *The Philadelphia Inquirer*, the *Orlando Sentinel*, *The Washington Post*, *USA TODAY*, and several alternative weeklies I'd never heard of. The story had devolved into entertainment and gossip with the *National Enquirer*, the *Star*, *People Magazine*, and *Us Weekly* present. *The Today Show* and *Good Morning America* were there, as were *NBC Dateline*, ABC's *20/20*, and CBS's *48 Hours*. There were even documentary filmmakers from *Netflix* and *HBO* in attendance.

Had I followed my initial instinct and passed on it, I would have been conspicuous by my absence. I was one of the only African Americans on the air in this broadcast market, and I've always believed that my lived experience as a Black man gives me a unique viewpoint on news coverage. I can see the world through a lens most of the other reporters can't. That's what I like to tell myself, anyway.

Mandy jumped into the back of our news van and quickly closed the door. The heat had turned her face into a dewy mess. Short brown bangs lay pasted to her forehead, held in place with perspiration. Beads of sweat streaked along tracks that ran from her temples to her chin and dripped onto the white blouse she wore. She'd only been out there ten minutes. Mandy had been with me since she was a college intern. Now, in her thirties, she was the best field producer in town and. . . one of my best friends.

"What's the deal?" I asked.

"Just a minute," she said, opening the small plastic cooler Stu had stocked with icy Evian water and placed in the back of the van. She pulled out a frosty bottle and downed it. How she did that without getting the requisite brain freeze, I have no idea.

"Goddamn, it's hot!" she exclaimed. "It's a hundred and six out there."

She grabbed a small hand towel from a backpack she'd brought and furiously mopped her brow.

"They're finally making a statement in about ten minutes," Mandy said. "You'd better get ready."

I opened my portable makeup bag, pulled out a compact of Mac powder, and used it to cover the perspiration shine on my nose and forehead. When I finished, Stu handed me a wireless stick mic.

"Fresh batteries in this?" I asked.

"Of course. When have I ever left you in the doggone lurch?" he said in his Odessa, Texas, twang.

"The way this day has been going, a dead mic would be par for the course," I said.

"It ain't gon' die on ya," he promised.

"Plus," Mandy added, "I'll be standing right beside you with a backup."

"And I'll have the camera right behind her," Stu said, hoisting his television camera on his shoulder. "Extra batteries are in my pocket."

I nodded, opened the vehicle door, and my little caravan began pushing through the media morass. A fleet of white ENG trucks sat in fortification of an army of tripods supporting television cameras. Hordes of reporters squeezed in where they could, pointing stick mics in the direction of a wooden podium that stood in front of the porch of the missing woman's home. Print photographers focused their lenses and prepared to fire off digital volleys when the time was right.

Much to the consternation of neighbors, the press had been camped out 24 hours a day for over a week in the event some titillating bit of information should trickle out from the command center that was the Promes's home. The press had nicknamed the encampment "Camp Kristen" in a nod to "Camp O.J.," the similar media circus that had spent a year parked in front of a Los Angeles County courthouse, covering the O.J. Simpson double murder trial a generation before.

"Camp" wasn't an inaccurate description. There was an almost festive feel about the whole thing. Food trucks offering everything from tacos and burritos to sandwiches, Indian food, and organic ice cream lined the perimeter, serving an ever-growing crowd of spectators, onlookers, and rubberneckers desperate for a glimpse of the action taking place in this ordinarily sleepy neighborhood.

My compatriots and I were able to wedge our way into a spot between a correspondent from *The Today Show* and a reporter from the Oakland FOX affiliate. We were about fifteen feet from the porch behind a row of steel barricades erected to keep the mob from charging the house itself.

Soon, an impressive-looking law enforcement officer walked out the front door of the home and approached the podium. He was a tall six-footer in a dark uniform covered with police commendations on the right breast. The sun gleamed off the bright silver stars that adorned the epaulets on his shoulders. His frame was muscular. His hair was black and wavy. His face, that of a teenager. Despite being in his early forties, he looked more like a high school kid playing dress up than Pleasanton's new chief of police.

He was followed by a professional-looking man in his midthirties who I recognized from news reports as Tom Promes, the missing woman's husband. He stood behind the chief, flanked on his right by a paunchy, balding, sixty-something Morgan Duffy, Kristen Promes's father. Duffy's baggy, bloodshot eyes indicated the poor guy hadn't slept in days. On Tom Promes's left, I recognized Skyler Duffy, Morgan's wife and Kristen's mother. Skyler stood a petite five feet. Brown hair with blond highlights was held tightly in a bun at the back of her head. Like the chief, she looked much younger than her age. I could tell that she'd had cosmetic work done, not unlike a lot of similarly aged women *and* men who populated the area. It was good work. Practically undetectable. She dabbed at her eyes with a white handkerchief. Tom Promes put a comforting arm around his mother-in-law's shoulder and pulled her close to him.

"Good afternoon," came a booming voice from the podium. "I'm Courtney Lane, the Chief of the Pleasanton Police Department."

A whir of camera shutters clicked in my ears from all directions—a symphony of castanets.

"With me," Chief Lane continued, "are the husband and parents of Kristen Promes."

More faster clicking and whirring.

"I'm here today to update you on where we are with our investigation," he said. "Kristen Promes left her home at this address at approximately 12:40 p.m. on July fourth during a family barbecue to pick up a friend's daughter for a playdate. When the friend called several hours later to inquire why Mrs. Promes hadn't arrived from what should have been a ten- to fifteen-minute drive, her family became concerned. Around 4:30 p.m. Mrs. Promes's husband, Tom, and her father, Morgan Duffy, drove the route that Mrs. Promes would have taken. Approximately one mile northwest of here, they found her Toyota Rav4 SUV parked along a residential side street near Bernal Avenue. Mrs. Promes was not inside, but her phone, keys, and wallet containing cash and credit cards were on the driver's seat. Mr. Duffy immediately notified the Pleasanton Police Department, which opened an investigation. We are asking for information from the public. If you saw Kristen Promes or a green Toyota Rav4 SUV in the vicinity of Bernal Avenue between 12:40 and 1:00 p.m. on the afternoon of July fourth, we're asking that you call the Pleasanton Police Department at your earliest convenience. Mrs. Promes is approximately five feet, two inches tall and weighs about one hundred forty pounds. She has blond hair and blue eyes. She is approximately four-and-a-half months pregnant and was last seen wearing a light blue cotton maternity blouse, white shorts, and brown leather sandals. We need any information you might have. Even the slightest detail could be important."

Sweat had formed at Chief Lane's hairline and rolled down his face and into his eyes. He blinked in discomfort a few times and then pulled a white handkerchief from his pants pocket and swiped his forehead.

Returning his attention to the crowd in front of him, he said, "I have time for a few questions."

Hands bolted into the air amid a chorus of men and women shouting, "Chief! Chief!"

"Yes," Chief Lane said, pointing at a forty-something woman holding a reporter's notebook.

"Shelley Burton, *USA Today*," she said. "Do you have any solid evidence that Kristen Promes was taken from her vehicle involuntarily?"

"I'm sorry," Chief Lane said. "I'm not at liberty to divulge any information on that subject."

Lane pointed to a young male reporter holding a stick mic.

"Charlie Frank, *NBC News*," he said. "Has the family received any kind of a ransom demand?"

"Not at this time," Chief Lane replied.

"Chief!" I bellowed.

"Yes?" he said, pointing at me.

"Topher Davis. Channel 6," I said. "Since Mrs. Promes's vehicle was found in a residential neighborhood, is it correct to assume that there may have been civilian surveillance and doorbell cameras on the street? And if so, has your department canvassed the area to retrieve any available video footage?"

"Our officers have canvassed the area for surveillance video," he said.

"A follow-up," I quickly added before he could recognize another reporter. "Did your department obtain any video footage?"

"I'm not at liberty to divulge that information at present," he said.

That's how it went for the next twenty minutes in the blazing heat. Reporters asking questions, and the chief was "not at liberty" to answer them. I hate it when they do that. Why even bother taking media questions at all if you aren't going to provide meaningful responses?

He thanked us for our attention to the matter and left the podium. Mason Duffy followed. Tom Promes, his arm still firmly around Skyler Duffy's shoulder, was right behind. Suddenly, the mother of the missing woman broke free of his arm and bolted to the podium mic.

"I'm Kristen's mom," she said, tears streaming down her face. "Whoever has my daughter, I beg of you, please. Please bring her back to us safely. Kristen, we love you, and we miss you."

Tom Promes walked to the podium and again put his arm around her. She buried her face in his chest. He hugged her tightly for a moment in a futile attempt to provide comfort and then guided her back into the house.

"The hell she must be going through," Mandy said softly in my ear.

"Every parent's worst nightmare," Stu said. "If this happened to one of my girls . . ." His voice trailed off as he shook his head.

"Let's get out of this heat," I said.

We again waded through the crowd and returned to our ENG truck, where Stu climbed into the driver's seat and cranked up the air-conditioning. Mandy opened the sliding door and took a seat in the rear. I opened the passenger-side door and was just about to plant myself in the seat when I felt a hand rest gently on my shoulder.

I turned to see an African American woman in her late forties. She wore a sweat-stained white tee shirt with the logo for ThriftyMart, a regional grocery store chain, emblazoned across the front. She was thin and of medium height with a haggard look about her. Dark circles underscored puffy, red eyes. Like Skyler Duffy, she wore her hair in a bun, but it was loose. Defiant strands of stray follicles pointed in all directions. She clutched an eight-by-ten photo in a gold, metal drugstore frame.

"Mr. Davis?" she asked.

"Yes?"

"My name is Josie Walker, and I need your help."

THREE

I LOOKED AT THE framed photo in my hand. It was of a pretty, young African American woman in her late twenties. The picture looked like a studio shot—baby blue background with perfect lighting. The woman was pretty with dark, sable skin, long, beaded braids, and brown piercing eyes. Just the faintest hint of a tiny scar was visible under her right eye.

"That's my daughter, Danica," Josie Walker said. "I've always loved that picture of her. She gave it to me last Mother's Day. She had a photographer friend take it. I told her she should have had him fix the scar under her eye. You know, photoshop it out or something. Danica liked it. She said it gave her face character. She got it falling off her bike when she was nine. Three stitches. I suppose it could have been worse."

Mandy handed Josie Walker a bottle of Evian from the cooler as she sat in the rear of the ENG truck. Josie placed the bottle against her cheek, like a makeshift ice pack, before opening it and taking a large swig.

"Thank you," she said. "I've been standing out there for three hours."

"Why?" I asked. "It's like Dante's Inferno out there."

"I was waiting for you," she said. "I figured that since it was a press conference, you'd turn up sooner or later. I tried you at your television station several times but couldn't get past the receptionist on the phone. She took my number and said she'd give you the message, but I never heard back."

"Sorry about that. I get a lot of viewer calls."

"I went down there too. Security wouldn't even let me past the front door."

"What exactly can I do for you, Ms. Walker?" I asked.

"I need you to find my daughter," she said, taking another drink of water. "She's missing."

"This sounds like a matter for the police," I said. "I'm just a reporter."

"But you're covering this missing white girl. Nobody's talking about my Danica. Not the press. Not the police—nobody."

"Why don't you tell us what happened?" Mandy asked.

"I'm Josephine Walker," she said. "I go by 'Josie.'"

"It's nice to meet you, Josie," I said.

"Likewise," she said, taking a larger gulp of Evian. "I live in East Oakland with my daughter, Danica, and her son, D'Vante," she said. "He's thirteen."

Mandy pulled a reporter's notebook from her backpack, flipped it open, and began to take notes.

"Danica had him when she was in high school. She got pregnant her sophomore year and had to drop out. Up until then, she was a straight-A student. Honor Roll and everything," she said, shaking her head with regret. "She and Rodney, that's D'Vante's father, were supposed to get married after he graduated that summer, but . . . He's in jail."

"What did he do?" I asked.

"When Danica got pregnant, he was trying to get some money together for a crib and baby things. You know, clothes and stuff."

She took another sip of Evian.

"Go on," I said.

"He agreed to be the lookout for some neighborhood boys robbing a convenience store. Such a stupid thing to do. I told him I could help him find work."

Josie Walker again shook her head. More regret. She took a more voluminous swig from the bottle of water.

"Rodney is a brilliant young man," she continued. "Such promise. He was on the Honor Roll too. Star center on the basketball team. Got a four-year free ride to play for Stanford and everything. Planned on being a software developer."

"What happened?" Mandy asked.

"A clerk got killed. Rodney wasn't even in the store when it happened. He just stood outside to give them a signal if the police or anybody showed up. Later, when they arrested everybody, they charged him in the killing too."

"California's felony murder rule," I said.

Under that law, all participants are equally culpable in the commission of a crime that results in a death.

"Yep," she said. "Twenty-five to life in San Quentin. He'd just turned eighteen years old. What a waste."

She took another drink of water. Between the liquid and the air-conditioning, I could see that she was beginning to cool down.

"I got Danica a job working with me at ThriftyMart. I'm a manager there. Been there since I was sixteen," she said. "Started out as a courtesy clerk and worked all the way up. It's gone pretty well," she said, proud of herself. "I was able to buy a house when Danica was in kindergarten. All mine. Well, mine and Wells Fargo's."

She brushed at her loose strands of hair. They refused to cooperate.

"Danica and I have been raising D'Vante by ourselves. We were getting along okay. Making ends meet, but Danica wanted a better life, ya know? More for herself and her son. She thought she could do better. I thought she was right."

More water. This time, draining the Evian bottle. Mandy took the empty one from her and replaced it with a fresh bottle from the cooler. Josie Walker eagerly took it, thanked her, and then cracked open the top to take another large drink.

"Danica got her GED and enrolled at San Francisco State. Pre-law. She always thought that what happened to Rodney wasn't right. I mean, she thought he should be punished, but a life sentence for watching the door from outside? No way they'd have given a white boy that much time. They'd say he 'made a mistake' and cut him deal so they didn't 'ruin his life.'"

I couldn't argue. In all likelihood, that's precisely what would have happened.

"So," Josie continued, "she wanted to be a lawyer to help people like him."

She stopped herself and cast her eyes down at her feet.

"I don't know why I'm talking about her in the past tense," she said. "She's not dead. I just don't know where she is."

"How long has she been gone?" I asked.

"About a month. She disappeared around the middle of June. The seventeenth."

"What happened?"

"Like I said, Danica's going to school. She's been taking classes year-round so she can graduate faster. She's hoping to get into the law school at Cal Berkeley. Her counselor at SF State told her that her odds would be better if she got an internship at a law office somewhere. He helped her get a job at a firm in San Francisco. Crane, Phelps, and Crane. She's their receptionist. She answers the phones, organizes their files, and sets up appointments. Stuff like that. She quit ThriftyMart and works at the firm after school and between classes. She also works weekends doing hair at Braids Salon in downtown Oakland on Telegraph."

"Tell me about June seventeenth," I said.

"Well, I keep D'Vante during the day. Like I said, he's thirteen. We didn't want him to be a latch-key kid. Too much devilment for him to get into in our neighborhood, and we do not want him to end up like his father. He's off for the summer, mostly. He's in day camp at Lake Merritt for a few months until August. I work nights. When Danica gets off at the law firm, she rides BART home and takes over so I can start my shift at the store. On that day, she called to say that something came up and she'd be a little late coming home. Maybe an hour or so."

More water. Thirsty woman.

"That's the last I heard from her," she said. "I called her cell phone, and it went straight to voicemail. After a few hours, it said that the mailbox was full."

"What about the law office?" Mandy asked.

"She hasn't been in since leaving work the night of the seventeenth," Josie said.

"Did you go to the police?" I asked.

"I called SFPD the very first night," she said. "They told me to wait 24 hours and then call back. Make sure she really was missing."

Most people think law enforcement won't consider a person missing for 24 hours. That's a fallacy created by four generations of television cop shows. They can look for somebody immediately if they deem it necessary and urgent, like they did in the Promes case.

"When she didn't come home the next day, I went to the station. The cops took some information and told me she probably just ran off with a man or something. Abandoned the family. I told them that there was no way she would ever run out on her son."

Josie Walker again shook her head in disgust. "They had me fill out a Missing Person's Report. Other than that, they didn't do a thing.

Nothing. I called every day for news or an update, and all they told me was that it was an 'open investigation.' I went to the papers and the TV news. I even went to the radio news station. Nobody was interested. Nobody cared. I had some flyers printed with her picture, and some neighbors helped me hand them out around her college campus and at the law firm. D'Vante built a website. Only thirteen years old, and he knows how to build websites. Isn't that something? I would get some billboards put up, but I don't have that kind of money."

It seemed like you couldn't drive down the street without seeing a billboard with Kristen Promes's smiling face. Money can buy a lot of attention, especially when a pretty white woman disappears.

"D'Vante asked if he could start something called a GoFundMe to raise some billboard and reward money. I told him if he thought it would help, go ahead. I guess he feels like he needs to do something. I don't understand how that stuff works anyway. He raised over a thousand dollars, though."

Her eyes moistened. She wiped them with the back of her hand.

"This rich white girl goes missing, and the whole damned world goes crazy. My girl disappears, and I can't even get the police to look for her. It's not right," she said. "That's why I came to you."

Mandy put a hand on Josie's back and rubbed it in a circle.

"We'll look into it," Mandy said. "At the very least, we can get some information out on TV."

Josie's hopeful eyes looked at me for confirmation. My gaze was fixed on Mandy, my eyes saying, "What the hell are you getting me into?"

"When was the last time you physically saw Danica?" Mandy asked.

"The morning of the seventeenth when I got home from work. She was getting D'Vante breakfast."

"Did you see her leave the house?" I asked.

Josie Walker nodded.

"Do you remember what she was wearing?"

She scratched her head as her eyes drifted upward, looking for answers.

"She was in her tan slacks and white work blouse, and she was carrying a San Francisco State windbreaker. It was supposed to be hot that day, but she thought it might cool down in the evening. You know how San Francisco is," she said.

Mandy wrote in her notepad.

"You say her last confirmed whereabouts were at the law firm?" I asked.

"I believe so. I think she was calling me from her desk. I could hear other phones ringing in the background."

"Since the firm is in San Francisco, that puts this in the jurisdiction of the SFPD, all right," I said.

"I already told you that I went to the police there. In Oakland too. She could have made it here by BART, but something happened to her on her way home. OPD isn't doing a damned thing either," she said, her eyes tearing up again in frustration.

"We have some connections in the San Francisco Police Department. Let me make a few calls and see what I can find out," I said. "Tell me, is there any place she might have gone on her way home? Maybe to see a friend? Or her father?"

"Believe me, I called every one of her friends I know. Nobody's heard a word from her since June seventeenth," Josie said. "As for her father, my husband was killed in a car accident when Danica was three. It was just the two of us until D'Vante came along."

She polished off her second bottle of water, and Mandy offered her a third, which she declined.

"I knew you'd help," she said with relief. "Danica and I have watched you on television for years. You help people."

"No promises," I said. "I'm just going to talk to my connections at the SFPD."

FOUR

AROUND ONE THIRTY, I sat at my usual table at The Cracked Egg, eating an egg white omelet with crab, avocado, and a side of honeydew melon. The doctor said my cholesterol was a little high and I should watch the yolks, cheese, and red meat for a minute. "The Egg," as we locals call it, is the best breakfast place in town. It's been an institution in the region for decades. About a dozen years ago, my brother-in-law, Jared Sloan, bought the place and renovated it in a 1950's motif. The restaurant now specializes in omelets, and it's become a cop hangout. Every morning, it's packed with law enforcement officers from all the surrounding jurisdictions, wolfing down eggs and consuming copious amounts of caffeine. It's also become my second home.

"More coffee?" Jared said, standing over me in the black, full-body apron that's the uniform for all The Egg's employees.

"Sure," I said.

"Lynn called and said to tell you that she's running late. She should be walking in any minute," he said, refilling my mug. Jared gave me an awkward, apprehensive look.

"What?" I asked.

"Well . . ."

"Come on. If there's something on your mind, spill it."

"I'm really supposed to let Lynn tell you this, but . . . well, you've been single for a while now and . . ."

"Absolutely not," I said.

"You haven't even let me tell you about her yet," he protested.

"I've had enough of the women you and my sister have been throwing at me," I said.

"Sylvia is a sweet lady, and we think you guys would really hit it off. She's a mortgage broker and—"

"No!" I shouted. "No more."

"It's just dinner. Lynn and I will be there too."

"I loathe blind dates," I declared.

"This will be different. You'll like this one," he said.

"I don't want or need a woman in my life right now, I said. "My last breakup ended with me throwing a butcher knife into her jugular."

"Breakups are messy," Jared said.

"Sophie and I are getting along just fine, thank you," I said. Sophie is my little white Bichon Frisé.

At that moment, Lynn rushed through the door, looking a little harried. I rarely see her like this. She's an SFPD homicide detective, and she's usually cool and calm about pretty much everything. We've always been close, but we've grown even closer since working a cop-killing case together a few months ago. She's a former Army Ranger and a good person to have at my side. It's nice to have a little sister who can kick my ass.

She made her way over to my table and gave Jared a quick kiss on the lips before plopping down in the empty chair in front of me.

"Sorry I'm late. I needed to make a hard copy of the file you asked for, and the damned printer at home is acting up," she said.

"Did you get it?"

She reached into the brown leather satchel she carried, pulled out a manila envelope, and placed it in front of me.

"I see you two are about to talk business," Jared said. "I'll leave you to it. Honey, can I get you anything?"

"Just a cup of chamomile tea," she answered.

"Coming right up," he said, walking away from the table.

I picked up the envelope, opened it, and removed its contents. Two pages.

"Is this it?" I asked.

Lynn nodded.

"Thin file," I stated.

Jared returned to the table and put a mug, a small silver pot of hot water, and a saucer with a tea bag and lemon wedges in front of his wife. He kissed her again and then went about his business.

I looked at the pages in front of me. Just the standard Missing Person's Report that Josie Walker filed. It contained Danica's name, vitals, places of residence, employment, and the last contact she had with her mother.

"This is it?" I asked.

"Afraid so," Lynn said, opening a tea bag and dropping it into her mug. She drowned it in hot water from the silver pot.

"Josie was right. They haven't done shit," I said.

"They have to prioritize," Lynn told him. "Triage. Do you know how many missing person reports are filed annually in our department?"

I didn't.

"Hundreds," she said. "A lot of them turn out to be misunderstandings. Somebody didn't call home, or they took off on their own for some reason. There are a lot of runaways. We look at the ones that seem the most dire. All departments do."

"What does law enforcement consider 'dire'?"

"Possible kidnappings. Foul play. Stuff like that."

"I see they have no problem pulling out all the stops when a woman like Kristen Promes goes missing."

"That case isn't in our jurisdiction. That's Pleasanton PD's. And that case is different. From what I understand, there are clear signs of foul play. That's dire."

"Does 'dire' mean that one life is more valuable than another?" I asked.

"Hey, don't pull that crap on me. You and your media friends are giving just as much, if not *more*, attention to the Promes case than you are to any of the other hundreds of open missing persons cases on every department's books."

She had a point.

"Touché," I said.

Lynn removed the tea bag from her mug, put it on the saucer, and replaced it with a lemon peel.

"I'm going to look into Danica Walker's disappearance. Will you help me?"

"I'm a homicide detective, Big Brother. We don't have a homicide here," she said.

"We don't know that. The woman vanishes without a trace. Doesn't call her friends. Her mother. Not even her thirteen-year-old kid. If that doesn't smell like foul play, I don't know what does."

Lynn contemplated as she drank from her mug, made a face, and then stirred a packet of Stevia into the tea.

Jared returned to the table and again refilled my coffee cup.

"Did you talk to him?" he asked Lynn.

"Not yet," she replied.

"I've already told Cupid here that the answer is No!" I said. "N. O. No! I'm not going on a blind date. Just leave me be. I'm fine."

"Every night, you go home to your dog, heat up a Lean Cuisine in the microwave, and then drink scotch while you watch Netflix. That's fine? *That's* the life you want?" she asked.

"Hey! *The Crown* is a great show!" I responded. "Yes. That's the life I want right now. In the future, who knows? What *I* know is that my fiancée left me, and then I took up with a sociopath. I no longer trust my judgment when it comes to women."

"That's why you have to trust us," Jared said.

"I met Sylvia at my spin class. I've known her for a while. She's solid, stable, reliable, and she's—"

"Housebroken?" I interjected.

"I was going to say 'fun,' smart-ass. We've socialized with her on several occasions."

"Socialized? You? When do *you* have time to socialize with *your* workload?"

"Jared and I socialize, don't we, honey?" she asked.

Jared gave the obligatory, "Of course, dear." Spousal nod.

"We've had dinner with her a few times. We even went to a concert with her. Bruno Mars," she said. "Sylvia was supposed to go with a couple of girlfriends, and they flaked, so she invited us."

"Great time," Jared added.

"If she's so wonderful, why's she single?" I asked.

"She got out of a long-term relationship about a year ago. She needed some time to heal," Lynn said. "Now, she's ready to jump back into the dating pool."

"Come on," Jared pestered. "Jump in with her. Like I said, it's just dinner."

"You guys are double-teaming me here."

"Okay. Tell you what," Lynn said. "You have dinner with Sylvia, and I'll do a little digging into your case. I'll start by checking her cell phone records and credit card activity."

"You're really going to resort to blackmail as a condition of helping me find a missing mom? A quid pro quo? Seriously?"

Lynn didn't answer me. Instead, she smugly smiled as she took another sip of her tea. I knew she was just busting my chops and would help me regardless.

"Fine," I finally said. "I'll go out with this . . . Sylvia. Happy?"

Jared smiled.

"Extremely," Lynn said. "Dinner is Saturday night at Shokumotsu. Eight o'clock."

"Fine," I surrendered. "Sushi at eight o'clock Saturday with you guys and God's gift to men."

"I also expect you to adjust your attitude by then," Lynn said.

"Yes, Auntie," I sighed.

I always take that tone with Lynn when I feel like she's reprimanding me the way our Auntie who raised us used to.

"Can we talk about the case now? Please?" I pleaded.

Lynn nodded.

"Good," I said. "I think that we should talk to the people at the law firm where she works since that's where her mother believes she was when they last spoke."

"Okay. We can do that. You said she usually took BART home when she got off work? Since it's a daily commute, odds are, she uses a Clipper card. Let me see if she used it that day, and if so, where she went."

"Sounds good. When do you want to go by the law firm?"

"Aren't you the eager beaver?" she said. "I've actually got a little time this afternoon. Will a couple of hours from now be soon enough for you?"

"Crane, Phelps, and Crane in the city. I'll meet you there."

FIVE

CRANE, PHELPS, AND Crane was located on California Street among the tall office structures in San Francisco's Financial District. The firm was a large one, occupying the entire tenth floor of the skyscraper across the street from the Merchant's Exchange Building. I was waiting in the hall outside of the reception area when the elevator door opened, and Lynn stepped out. She was wearing what I call her "interrogation clothes." Dark slacks. Blue blouse. Black blazer. The Armani blazer was a birthday gift from yours truly. The ensemble gave her the look of a professional who was not to be trifled with. Being taken seriously can be tough in the professional world when you're a woman, especially if that profession is police work.

"Thanks for doing this," I said.

"Hey, a deal's a deal," she replied. "Plus, it's my job."

"Did you get a chance to look into this at all?"

"Danica Walker used her Visa debit card at the salad place up the street around lunchtime on the seventeenth of June," she said. "No activity since then. None on the Mastercard she has either."

"That was fast. No subpoena or warrant required?"

"I called Juanita Parker. I cited 'exigent circumstances,' and she expedited warrants for me. Everything I needed," she said.

I knew and liked Judge Parker. She had recently been appointed to the bench from the DA's office. That's where Lynn got to know her. As for me, I met her when we were co-panelists at a symposium called Journalism and Legal Procedure at the USF School of Law a few months back.

"You called a Black woman judge?"

"Yep. I figured she'd be more sympathetic to the situation," Lynn said, proud of herself for her inspired thinking. "Once I had the warrant, my friend Stephanie Weisman over at Card Services quickly got me the debit and credit card info. I spoke to Josie Walker and got Danica's cell number. I tracked down her carrier and served them a warrant for her phone records."

"I know *that* can be a slog," I said.

Cellular phone companies are notoriously difficult when it comes to sharing consumer information. They always cite privacy. They've been known to fight subpoenas. There have been cases when they won't even give customers who've been carjacked GPS info when the robber still has their phone *in* the stolen vehicle. It's ridiculous. The customer has just been robbed at gunpoint, and the cellular firm is giving them the company line on privacy.

"Judge Parker happened to know somebody at the phone company she'd dealt with when she was at the DA's office," Lynn said. "No problem. They emailed the cell records over as soon as they got the warrant. My guys are sifting through them. What I can tell you right now is that there's been no cell activity since the seventeenth of June, just like on her plastic. We'll hopefully have some info on who she's been calling before that in about a day or so. Same goes for cell tower pings. That stuff's gonna take a minute to analyze."

"What about her Clipper card?"

"I got her Clipper card info from the Metropolitan Transportation Commission. The MTC records show her taking BART from the Coliseum station in Oakland at 6:53 a.m. and arriving at the Montgomery Street station a few blocks from here at 7:28 that morning."

"Return trip?" I asked.

"Nada," Lynn said. "No activity."

"Did the good judge sign off on a warrant for her financials?"

"Checking account with about four hundred dollars in it. A little over a grand in a custodial account for her son's college. Again, untouched since she went missing."

"Not good," I said. "Not good at all."

"Let's not jump to any conclusions just yet, Big Brother," she said. "But you're right. It doesn't look promising. You gonna keep her mother in the loop on any progress?"

"When I have something definitive to tell her, I will," I said. "I'm assuming there are street cams in this area with all of the finance taking place on this street and all."

"Way ahead of you. Street cam footage is being pulled from the city surveillance systems in the area as we speak. I have a couple of officers canvassing the street for civilian videos. ATMs and the like."

"Wow. You really want me to go out with this Sylvia woman, don't you?"

Lynn smiled and then gestured toward the office entrance. "Shall we?" she asked.

We opened the thick, double glass doors with the firm's name etched in a stylized font. I guess if you expect to do business in the Financial District, everything needs to be first class.

The outer office was done in dark brown wood. Dark leather couches with brass studs were stretched on opposite walls of the reception area. A slim desk with a clear glass top sat adjacent to the double doors. On the wall were three oversized color portraits. Each hung above a brass nameplate.

The first photo featured an older gentleman with a full head of thick, gray hair. I'd place him in his eighties. Lines of experience creased his face. His eyes gave the camera an inquisitive look as though they were searching for something. Justice maybe? He reminded me of a kind uncle. The nameplate below read STANLEY CRANE.

The next picture was of a similarly aged man. He too had the face of experience. His hair was thin and cropped on the sides. His shiny, bald pate prominent. He was much portlier than his partner. Well-fed and prosperous. His gaze, sterner. Less compassionate. THOMAS PHELPS read the name below.

The final portrait displayed the fresh face of a younger man. He appeared to be in his late thirties or early forties. He looked competent enough in the photo, but he didn't have the same look of wisdom that comes from having lived a lot of life. At least not as much as his partners. He wore a dark power suit with a red tie. His hair was dark brown and slicked back. To me, he looked more like a hedge fund manager than an attorney. The brass nameplate read STANLEY CRANE JR.

A thin, thirty-something strawberry-blond woman sat at the reception desk. She was clearly in distress as she juggled an incessantly ringing phone bank, putting callers on hold, transferring them, and taking messages. I pictured Danica Walker behind that desk, her textbooks in a backpack on the floor between her feet.

"May I help you?" the exasperated woman asked, putting a caller on hold.

Lynn flashed her SFPD shield. "I'm Detective Sloan, and this is—"

"Topher Davis!" she shrieked with excitement. "I watch you all the time!"

"Thank you! I appreciate that," I said with all the false modesty I could muster. Sincere insincerity comes with the territory.

"We'd like to speak to Mr. Crane, Mr. Phelps, or Mr. Crane Jr., please," Lynn said.

"Mr. Crane Sr. died a few years back."

"I'm sorry," I said.

"He was in his late eighties. Dementia. It was actually a blessing," she said, waving off my condolences. "Mr. Phelps is retired and living in Boca Raton. Mr. Crane Jr. runs the firm now," the woman said.

The few dark buttons on the phone bank lit up, and the ringing intensified.

"Ugh," said the woman. "I don't usually do this. I'm an associate here. This isn't my job. Our regular girl quit, and I'm just pitching in."

"You mean Danica Walker?" I asked.

"Oh," said the woman. "You know her?"

"We're looking for her," Lynn said. "How well do you know her?"

"Not very. She answered our phones. Ran errands. Got coffee. She was good. The best one we've had in this job, actually. Then she just quit coming to work. No letter of resignation. Not even a call or an email. She just stopped showing up."

"When was this?" Lynn asked.

"June seventeenth is the last day she worked."

"You're pretty sure about the date. Why?" I asked.

"The eighteenth was my birthday. I had to spend it chained to this desk covering for her. I'm stuck here until they find a replacement. I don't know why HR doesn't just call a temp agency. But hey, I'm a team player. Hang on a minute."

She returned to the phones and put the freshly blinking lines on hold.

"Has anybody been here to talk to you about her?"

"Anybody like who?" she asked.

"Like the police," I said.

"Why? Is she in some kind of trouble or something?"

"She's missing," I informed her.

A French manicured hand shot over a startled mouth. "Missing?" she said. "Oh my God. Like that woman in Pleasanton?"

"Her family has been distributing 'missing' flyers around here. You haven't seen them?" I asked.

"People are always trying to hand you postcards or leaflets when you walk down the street in this area. Like the panhandlers, you learn to ignore them," she said indifferently.

"Her family hasn't heard from her since the seventeenth of last month. We think that she talked to her mother from here that afternoon. Were you working then?" Lynn asked.

"Sure. I spent the day working on a brief for a civil suit that Mr. Crane Jr. is handling. I worked in the office I share with Natalie Shaw. She's another associate here. By the way, I'm Patricia Hart," she said, extending her hand.

"Nice to meet you, Patricia," I said, taking her hand. She gave me a gentle squeeze. "Tell me, did you talk to Danica that day?"

"I'm sure I did."

"What about?" Lynn asked.

"Oh, I don't remember. Probably just office stuff like usual. Transfer a call. Take a message for me. Things like that."

"Was there anything unusual about her demeanor that day?" Lynn asked. "Think hard. Was she in a good mood?"

"Come to think of it," Patricia said, "there was one thing. She was in a conference of some kind with Mr. Crane Jr. They were behind closed doors for about twenty minutes. I know because I went to his office to ask a question about the brief I was working on, and I bumped into her as she was on the way out. She seemed kind of . . . maybe 'frazzled' is the right word."

"Frazzled, how?" Lynn asked.

"Like she was upset about something."

"Do you think Mr. Crane Jr. fired her?" I asked.

"No. She came right back here to her desk and finished the day. When she stopped coming in, Mr. Crane Jr. was just as surprised as anyone. So, no. I'm sure he didn't let her go."

"Was she in the habit of not showing up on scheduled workdays?" Lynn asked.

"Not that I'm aware of," Patricia said. "You'd have to ask HR about that. I do know that her hours were flexible because she was in school full time."

"Is Mr. Crane Jr. available?" I asked. "We'd like to talk to him."

"No. He's in a deposition across town all day," Patricia said. "He should be in tomorrow, though."

She looked at the lights on the phone bank. "I'm sorry," she said. "I need to get back to these calls."

"We understand," Lynn said, removing the little leather case she keeps her business cards in from the vest pocket of her blazer. Another gift from yours truly. She took one out and handed it to Patricia.

"Would you please give him this and tell him I need to speak with him at his earliest convenience?" she asked.

"Sure thing," Patricia replied, taking the card and putting it on top of a stack of mail on the desk addressed to Stanley Crane Jr.

"Thanks," Lynn said. "My cell number is on there. Please tell him that he can call me any time. Day or night."

"Will do. Nice meeting you, Mr. Davis. Like I said, I positively love your reports."

"That's very kind of you," I said. "Thanks for watching."

Lynn and I left the office, walked back to the elevator, and pressed the down button.

"Ooh! I can't believe I get to ride in the same elevator with *the* Topher Davis," she shrieked, dramatically putting the back of her right hand against her forehead. "I think I may faint!"

"Shut up," I said with a laugh. "So, I have fans. Sue me."

"Well, we're in a lawyer's office, so this would be the right place for it."

"What do you think?" I asked.

"I don't know. The fact that she worked a normal day and then stopped coming in without any kind of notice . . ." Lynn said. "I want to know what she and Mr. Crane Jr. talked about that upset her so much."

"Me too. We know he didn't fire her. You don't can somebody and then let them return to their desk. Not at a place like this. There's too much damage a disgruntled 'soon-to-be-former' employee can do. This is the kind of place that has security, and they stand over you while you clean out your desk and then unceremoniously walk you out of the building."

"I'll stay on him," Lynn said. "I'll give him a day or so to reply. If he doesn't, *I'll* get back to *him*."

The elevator doors opened, and we stepped inside and pressed the button for the underground garage.

"Shit," Lynn said as the elevator doors closed. "I forgot to see if they validate. Sorry, taxpayers. Let's be sure to connect later, Chris."

Lynn is the only one who still calls me "Chris." My given name is Christopher Robin Davis. When I was in college and trying to intern at a television or radio station, I noticed that putting "Topher Davis" instead of "Chris Davis" on an application got me more interviews. Lynn said it was because "Topher Davis" looks whiter than "Chris Davis" on paper. I can't prove she was right, but "Topher Davis" sure did generate a lot more interest.

We got to the garage, where Lynn hopped into the gray Ford Taurus she was currently using as an unmarked, and I jumped into the Black Beauty. The Beauty was a gleaming, black 1957 T-bird given to me by the grateful widow of a cop whose murder I'd recently helped solve.

We drove to the exit, paid the attendant the exorbitant twenty-dollar-per-fifteen-minute parking fee, and headed out. Lynn drove back to her office at San Francisco's Hall of Justice, and I pointed the Beauty west to my digs at our television station along the Embarcadero.

It was a warm day. A rarity in San Francisco, even in July. It was a mild, pleasant warmth as the bay breeze swept across the city—such a contrast to the inland oven that was Pleasanton. I put the soft top down on the Beauty and drove along the downtown back streets until I reached my destination. Market Street would have been a faster, more direct route to take, but the city, in its infinite wisdom, had closed the street to cars to reduce carbon emissions and encourage the use of public transportation.

Soon, I pulled into the gated lot of the San Francisco Broadcast Center on Front Street. I parked and used my card key to enter the building. As I walked in, I gave Steve Showers, our new security guard, a masculine nod. All right, as masculine as I could pull off.

Steve was a muscular former cop who'd recently been hired to man the entrance after a disturbed viewer tried to get into the studio with a .38 revolver. Fortunately, Charlie Wu, our weatherman, and our sports guy, Chris Hernandez, happened to be in the lobby then. These two buff guys were able to wrestle the gunman to the ground and subdue him until the SFPD arrived. The incident was the catalyst for two changes. First, Curtis, the septuagenarian security guard who had primarily acted as a station greeter, was gently nudged into retirement. Second, I realized that if I'd been in the lobby instead of Chris or Charlie, I'd never have been able to take on that potential mass shooter, so I started putting in more hours at the gym.

"There you are," Steve said as I approached his desk. "The boss has been looking for you."

"The boss" was Curt Weil, the station's general manager. We affectionately called him "Captain Queeg," after the eccentric captain from the "Caine Mutiny," because he often made decisions that were just . . . well, crazy. Weil wasn't technically my boss any more. Under the new contract I'd recently signed, I was an independent contractor and my own boss now.

I took the elevator to the third floor, looking out its window at the throng of tourists enjoying the sunshine along the Embarcadero. It was so nice outside, I wished that I was one of them. It had been awhile since I last visited the Ripley's Believe it or Not Museum. I stepped out of the elevator and entered Curt's outer office. Ethyl, Weil's matronly administrative assistant, tapped away at the keys on her desktop while simultaneously talking on her headset.

"Hi, Ethyl," I whispered. "Is the Man in?"

She pointed her thumb in the direction of Curt's office door. I walked over to it and gently knocked.

"Come in," came a gruff voice from behind the door.

I opened it to find Curt reviewing a stack of papers on his desk.

"Oh," I said. "Hope I'm not disturbing you."

"Not at all," he said, his tone shifting from authoritative to solicitous. "Have a seat."

I sat on the couch adjacent to him. He reached under his desk, pressed a button, and the office door closed. There's always been something about that device that creeps me out.

Curt laid his papers on the desk, walked over to the couch, and sat beside me. He was a short man. Five-foot-five on his best day. A large painting of Napoleon hung on the wall above us.

"How are you?" he asked.

It's amazing how obsequious he'd become since I signed my new deal. It wasn't that long ago that he had prepared to let me go. Curt used his GM position as a bully pulpit in every sense of the word. Especially when it came time for contract negotiations. His signature move was to yell, scream, and then flip his desk over, leaving his office floor strewn with an array of papers, writing instruments, and work accoutrements for poor Ethyl to clean up. Weil knew better than to pull that stunt on me. I don't like bullies and I won't be intimidated by them. Plus, it didn't hurt that I'd just helped Lynn crack a big case that was a ratings bonanza, and every other station in town was vying for my services. Corporate had ordered Weil to keep me at all costs. My new autonomy had its perks.

"You know me," I answered. "Grinding away like always."

"Take a look at this," he said, handing me a few pages of white paper held together by a staple.

I took the papers and thumbed through them. It was a list of Emmy Award nominees for the San Francisco Bay Area broadcast market.

"Take a look at page 2," he said.

I did as he requested, and I found my name. Twice. I was nominated for Best Investigative Reporting and Broadcast Personality of the Year.

"You did one hell of a job on that cop-killing case," he said.

"Thanks."

"The ceremony is in about six weeks. I hope you have your tux ready."

"I always do," I said.

"Good work, Topher. Good work," he said. "Speaking of which, I was just looking at the overnights. We're killing it with this Kristen Promes coverage. The viewers are just eating it up. Your reports are beating everything else on the air with this stuff. Every single quarter hour."

In terrestrial broadcasting, ratings are measured by the quarter hour. The goal is to keep them watching, or in the case of radio, listening, for as much of each fifteen-minute period as possible. Keep their attention for eight minutes and you get credit for the whole fifteen.

"The people can't get enough of it," he said.

"I'm glad you're happy, Curt."

"Happy?" he asked. "I'm over the moon. By the way, I ran into Mandy in the lunchroom. What's this I hear about you looking for some Black girl?"

"Well," I said, "there is an African American woman from East Oakland who's also gone missing. There's been zero coverage, as far as I can see. Her mother has asked for my help."

I emphasized the words "African American." Something tells me that back in the day, the word "colored" was part of his vocabulary.

"That's good," he said, feigning interest. "Just keep your eye on the Promes ball."

He averted his gaze from me to the big picture window that framed the Bay Bridge behind his desk.

"I've got a daughter about her age," he said, a faraway look glazing over his eyes. "You know . . . She even kind of looks like the Promes woman."

His focus returned to me.

"For me, and for that matter, for a lot of people, this feels personal," he said.

"A lot of people have daughters who look like Danica Walker too," I said, my tone clipped. "If they were aware of her case, it would also be personal to them."

"Of course. Of course," he said, trying to placate me. "I just want you to stay focused. The Promes story is big."

"The Promes story is big because *we* made it one."

"Be that as it may," he said, "we live and die by the ratings book. You know that."

"Yeah, I know that. More people can relate to a well-off white mom disappearing from the suburbs than a poor Black one from East Oakland."

"I didn't say that."

"You didn't have to," I said.

He exhaled a heavy, frustrated breath and got up from the couch. He walked over to his desk and picked up a white mug of coffee with the word BOSS stenciled on its side in bold, black lettering. He sipped and quickly put it down. Then he pressed the intercom button on his desk.

"Ethyl, this damned coffee is cold," he roared.

"Right there!" came the frantic response.

Within seconds, there was a knock at the door. Curt pressed his secret button, and it opened. Ethyl rushed in with a fresh, steaming BOSS mug, set it on Curt's desk, picked up the old one, and exited the room without saying a word. Curt again pressed his button, closing the door.

"Is there a way you can cover both stories?" he finally said to me.

"That's exactly what I plan on doing."

"Okay. Just make sure that you don't shortchange Promes."

"Don't worry," I said. "I'll provide the copious amount of coverage you and the viewers want."

"Your cynicism is showing," he said.

"Yes," I replied. "It most certainly is."

SIX

THAT NIGHT, I did my segment on the Promes press
conference during the *SIX O'CLOCK NEWS* show. Not much to
report other than the police chief's appeal for the public's help.
Katie Robards, the show's co-anchor, did a brief Zoom talk-back
with the author of a book on stranger abductions and human
trafficking. The writer talked about what the Promes family felt
(helplessness and despair) and what they could expect to feel
over the days ahead (more helplessness and despair along with a
possible tinge of hope if there was any communication from the
kidnapper or kidnappers). Although it wasn't expressly revealed at
the press conference, the idea that Kristen Promes's disappearance
might be a kidnap-for-ransom plot was not out of the realm of
possibility. Her father, Mason Duffy, had been the real estate king
of the valley for decades. He was a very wealthy man. I was no
slouch in the net worth department myself, and Duffy could buy
and sell me a hundred times over. When the author finished his
analysis, Katie tossed back to me where I did my first story on
Danica Walker.

"This is a story that you probably haven't heard much about," I said into the camera. "In fact, I'll bet you haven't heard anything about it at all."

I paused for effect.

"Danica Walker is the missing twenty-nine-year-old mother of a thirteen-year-old boy. She's a San Francisco State University college student and a receptionist at the law firm of Crane, Phelps, and Crane in the Financial District."

The photo of Danica that Josie had given me earlier filled the screen.

"Danica Walker disappeared on the evening of June seventeenth, sometime after getting off work at the law firm. Please take a good look at this picture," I said off camera in voiceover. "She's African American, with brown eyes. She stands about five feet, six inches tall, and weighs approximately one hundred twenty-five pounds. She wears her hair in long, beaded braids and has a faint scar under her right eye from a childhood accident. According to her mother, Danica Walker left home that morning wearing a white blouse, tan slacks, and a San Francisco State University windbreaker."

The camera returned to a close-up of me.

"If you have any information regarding Danica Walker's whereabouts, or if you've seen Danica Walker on, around, or after the seventeenth of June, please call the number below."

Lynn's office number appeared in chyron on the lower third of the screen.

"Like Kristen Promes's family, Danica Walker's loved ones miss her and want her home safely too. Your information and cooperation are vital in helping to solve this case."

I then threw it to anchor Phil Wagner, who introduced Charlie Wu with the weather. Charlie reported that San Francisco would remain mild as a ridge of high pressure combined with an onshore flow blanketed the city. The high pressure over the inland valleys of the East Bay would produce what could be "record-setting temperatures over the next few days," Charlie said.

Great. More time broiling in the sweltering Pleasanton sun while we staked out the Promes house.

After the show, I went back to my dressing room, washed off my TV makeup, walked out to the Black Beauty, and took the Bay Bridge toward home. My home was a custom-built house in Palomares Canyon in Castro Valley, about twenty-five miles southeast of San Francisco. I love where I live. Castro Valley is an unincorporated area that's a mix of small-town life, suburban homes, and rural properties. I chose to build my house in the latter. It was close to Castro Valley Boulevard with its stores, shopping, and restaurants, yet near enough to the freeway on-ramp, making it convenient to commute to any place I needed.

The house is large. Too large for one person, really. It's a four-bedroom ranch-style home with a den and family room, complete with a pool table and bar cart. Those entering the front door step into a spacious living room with a black leather couch and a matching love seat on an off-white area rug covering a portion of the freshly stained, black hardwood floors. An antique coffee table, also black, sits between the couch and the love seat. Soft, overhead lighting illuminates the room at night. Sunshine bathes it from a skylight above during the day. The kitchen, with its shiny silver, top-of-the-line appliances, culinary contraptions, and black marble countertops, is fit for a professional chef. The original thought was that my former fiancée, Sarah, and I would hire professionals to use it to prepare lavish dinner parties. The best-laid plans of mice and men . . .

In the last month, I'd had a few rooms redecorated. I needed a change. When I initially built the place, it was for Sarah. An early wedding present. Upon its completion, she decided that marriage to me wasn't in her future and moved on. I haven't heard a word from or about her since. It's strange how somebody can be a daily part of your life, and then, suddenly, they're just . . . gone. No contact.

Lately, it's just been me and Sophie rattling around in that big, empty showplace all by ourselves. Nighttime is the worst. The hollow sound of my solitary footsteps echoing as they traverse the hardwood floors is sometimes more than I can bear. Lynn and Jared keep pushing me to get another girlfriend. I've already tried that, with deadly consequences. My "palate cleanser" as I now refer to her, was the catalyst for the redecoration. She lived here briefly, and I don't want a trace of her in my home. I don't want another girlfriend. Hell, I'm more inclined to get another dog. I've been seriously thinking about it, but I'm afraid Sophie might get too jealous. She likes being the lady of the house.

I parked the Black Beauty in my four-car garage, shut the door with the remote, and entered the house through the kitchen. As I walked in, Sophie greeted me at the door, tongue hanging out and tail wagging furiously. Bichon Frisés are very needy dogs and prone to separation anxiety. She hates it when I'm gone. As usual, she put her front paws on my pant leg, and I picked her up. She was filthy. She had spent the day running around and playing in the dirt that covers some of my three-acre property. On a white dog, the dirt really shows. I made a mental note to make an appointment with the groomer.

Upon being picked up, Sophie immediately began licking my face. Unconditional love. I think the meme is true that says, "I want to be the person my dog thinks I am."

I exchanged my designer suit for denim jeans and a San Francisco Giants T-shirt and swapped out my Kenneth Cole shoes for a pair of black, high-top Converse All Stars. I put Sophie's leash on and took her for a thirty-minute hike around the property before heading back to the house and feeding her the gourmet dog food she loves. Afterward, I opened the freezer, pulled out a fettuccini alfredo Lean Cuisine, and popped it into the microwave. Four minutes later, I grabbed a fork and plopped down on the living room couch in front of my sixty-four-inch "smart" TV. By then, Sophie had finished eating and lightly snored at my feet as I picked up the remote. My God, Lynn was right. My home life had become tedious and routine.

I clicked on CNN, and the network was announcing breaking news. Kristen Promes had been found.

SEVEN

LAKE DEL VALLE is a storage reservoir that's part of the Del Valle Regional Park, about ten miles southeast of Livermore. It's half an hour from Pleasanton on the eastern edge of the Bay Area. It's enjoyed as a recreational area where you can enjoy boating, camping, and fishing. When I was a Boy Scout, we'd sometimes pitch tents there on weekend overnights.

At dusk, a father and his nine-year-old son were climbing through one of the brushy, wooded areas near the lake, looking for a good spot to catfish, when they came upon what appeared to be wisps of human hair peeking from just below the surface of the dirt. Upon closer inspection, they discovered a dismembered, decaying human right arm lying a few feet away. Coyotes or bobcats had begun digging up what appeared to be a shallow grave. Father and son quickly went to where they could get cell phone reception and called the Livermore Police Department. Soon, the area had been cordoned off with yellow tape and designated a crime scene. I haven't a clue how CNN scooped us on this. It was practically in my backyard.

I grabbed my phone from the coffee table and called Mandy. She answered on the first ring.

"Hey, Topher," she said before I could utter a word, "I've already heard. I called Stu, and he's on his way to my house with an ENG truck. We should be by to get you in about half an hour."

"Okay," I said. "Call me when you're five minutes away, and I'll be out front."

"Copy that," she said, hanging up the phone.

I grabbed the little black makeup bag I keep at home as a backup for breaking stories, changed back into my "on air clothes," and soon, Mandy was back on the phone telling me that she and Stu were out front. I set the burglar alarm, locked the front door, and closed it over Sophie's whines. I love that dog, but sometimes, her separation anxiety gets on my last nerve.

The white ENG truck soon pulled up in front of me, and I got in on the passenger side.

"What do we know?" I asked.

"CNN broke the story. One of the officers in the Livermore PD has a brother-in-law at the network. He was their source. We don't know a lot more than what's already been reported. A kid and his dad found her in a shallow grave near the water's edge."

"Are they sure it's Kristen Promes?" I asked.

"Well," she said, "CNN isn't the only news agency with connections. My old college roommate works as a dispatcher for Livermore PD. Off the record, she told me that nothing is certain, of course, until they check DNA and dental records. It's going to take a few days for an autopsy report, but the corpse is female, about Kristen's size, and was wearing the type of maternity top Kristen was last reported being seen in. The critters got to the body's right arm, but the left one was still connected to the torso. There was a three-caret diamond and emerald wedding set on her left hand, just like the one Kristen Promes wore. They're pretty sure it's her."

"Three carets," I whistled. "Guess that knocks out robbery as a motive."

About forty-five minutes later, we were at the crime scene. Camp Kristen had now migrated to the new location. The horde of trucks and reporters from the Promes home now crowded around the perimeter of the area where the body had been discovered. We found a spot next to the CBS affiliate, and Stu parked just as two men dressed in white loaded a sheet-covered stretcher into the back of a coroner's van. Mandy hopped out of our vehicle and talked to one of the officers standing guard in front of the yellow crime scene tape. Five minutes later, she was back.

"Nothing he could tell me other than the Livermore chief will give a press conference as soon as they're ready to make a statement," she said.

"Well, when the hell will that be??" I asked.

"Hey, don't shoot the messenger! Your guess is as good as mine," she said, shrugging her shoulders.

"Sorry. It's just frustrating how the cops are playing things so close to the vest in this case," I said. "Think we can get an interview with the father and son who found the body?"

"Not right now. Livermore PD has them behind closed doors down at the station."

"Any chance your friend in dispatch may have something new for us? Anything at all?"

"It doesn't hurt to ask," she said.

Mandy pulled out her cell and dialed. "Hey, Sharon," she said into the phone. "Me again."

A beat.

"Yeah, we're here at the scene now," she said. "Anything new?"

Another beat.

"Of course, it's still off the record," she said.

Like my sister, Lynn, Mandy is generally unflappable. That's why it was surprising to see her mouth drop suddenly and her skin turn ashen.

"Oh my God!" she said, her face pinching into a grimace, her free hand now covering her mouth. She caught her breath, took a moment to compose herself, and then said into the phone, "If you can do it without getting yourself in trouble . . . Please keep me posted."

She clicked off.

Stunned silence.

"What is it?" I asked.

"It's horrible," she said, still trying to maintain her composure.

"What, Mandy?"

"Well . . . It isn't confirmed," Mandy said, obviously shaken despite her best effort to present otherwise.

"Spit it out," I said. "What's wrong?"

"My friend Sharon says there's a rumor that the baby Kristen Promes was carrying wasn't with the body," she said. She had a sudden desperation to gulp air. Her eyes filled with tears.

"Somebody cut that baby out of its mother's womb," she said, brushing at her eyes and again trying hard to reclaim her usual air of professionalism.

"Jesus," I said.

I put an arm around Mandy's shoulder and pulled her close to me for momentary comfort. It was hard seeing her this way. As I said, this woman doesn't easily get the wind knocked out of her.

"They're looking for the baby's body, but so far, they've come up empty."

"There's a lot of acreage up here," I said. "They sending in the cadaver dogs?"

She nodded as tears again filled her eyes.

Mandy and I have been through a lot together. She's been with me at fatal car accidents where the victims were so mangled they were barely recognizable as human beings. She's seen decomposing bodies from drug overdoses that had been in rancid-smelling apartments for days. She's even been to murder scenes where the victim was so filled with bullet holes they appeared to be more colander than person. All that, and I've never once seen her lose her composure. Until now. No matter how much human tragedy you witness as a reporter, you can always put a wall around it. For the sake of your sanity, you can compartmentalize and put it out of your mind . . . unless a baby is involved. No matter how hard we try, there's something innate in even the most jaded journalist that won't allow us to harden ourselves when the crime victim is an infant or a child. I understood Mandy's tears. I remained stoic. I'd cry later, in private, when I got home.

Since there wasn't a lot for us to do there, Stu rigged the lights, handed me a stick mic, and had me do a live stand-up in front of the crime scene tape. I only reported what we knew for certain: a woman's body had been found by fishermen. There was no positive identification of the remains, but they reportedly matched the general description of Kristen Promes. I didn't mention the wedding ring or the missing fetus. The Livermore police chief would hold a press conference when there was something definitive to release publicly. Until then, law enforcement had designated the place where the body was found to be a crime scene, and they were combing the area looking for potential evidence. I reported that we'd update viewers if any significant developments came in.

***

Mandy, Stu, and I sat in the back of the truck playing penny ante poker with the crew from Channel 8 until the sun came up. At about seven, we got word that the chiefs of police of Livermore and Pleasanton were going to make a joint statement since the case now traversed both their jurisdictions. A small podium was erected near the entrance to the park, and the Livermore chief spoke into the mic. Pleasanton's young chief, Courtney Lane, stood at his side, eyes cast downward, his hands reverently folded in front of him.

The Livermore chief was a stark contrast to Chief Lane. Whereas Lane was thin and athletic, Livermore's top cop was portly and out of shape, his gut hanging slightly over the belt that strained to support his radio, taser, Glock and ammunition. He had bright red hair, freckles, and scarlet skin that looked like it burned at the mere hint of sunlight. He must have spent a small fortune on sunscreen working in the hot Livermore sun. July in Livermore makes Pleasanton look like Anchorage.

"I'm Liam O'Reilly, Livermore's chief of police. Courtney Lane, the chief of the Pleasanton department, is here with me."

Chief Lane nodded to the reporters.

"At approximately seven thirty p.m. last evening," he continued, "a pair of fishermen discovered human remains buried in a shallow grave near the eastern shore of Lake Del Valle. They immediately notified law enforcement, and a team was dispatched, designating the area a crime scene. Some of the remains had been scattered by the animals occupying the region, but we're confident that, working through the night, we've recovered most of the body."

A voice rang out above the scribbling of pens on notepads and the clicking of SLR cameras.

"Tammy Sanchez, Telemundo. Was it the body of Kristen Promes?" a reporter shouted.

"I'll let you take this," O'Reilly said to Chief Lane, who switched places with him in front of the microphone.

"Based on artifacts found with the remains, a member of the Promes family was able to positively identify the body as that of Kristen Promes."

Pandemonium ensued as reporters all began yelling at once, doing their best to "out shout" each other. The chiefs stood silent until the press settled down.

Once the din subsided, a loud woman's voice shouted above the crowd.

"Cindy Simons, ABC News. Chief, can you tell us what artifacts led to the positive identification of the body as being that of Kristen Promes?"

"We are not at liberty to divulge that information at this time," Lane said. He'd repeated those words so often that now, they came out as rote. They were withholding the discovery of Kristen's wedding band. And they were keeping the missing baby a secret.

"Since this crime now covers two jurisdictions, Chief O'Reilly and I have formed a joint task force between our departments to solve this crime," Lane said.

"And solve it we will," O'Reilly said, leaning into the mic. "Whoever did this can be damned sure of that."

"We will not be taking any more questions," Lane said, "but we *will* provide you with some information. Chief?"

Chief O'Reilly resumed his position at the podium.

"As I said, the decedent's remains were scattered about the area by the indigenous animals in the region. We won't have a cause or a time of death until an autopsy is completed. The Alameda County Coroner's Office will work as expeditiously as possible to determine the relevant information and return Ms. Promes's remains to her family. The Promes and Duffy families are currently in seclusion. They are requesting privacy, respect, and your prayers as they deal with this unfathomable loss."

"Is it true that her baby was cut out of her womb, and if so, have you found the remains?" came a male voice from the sea of reporters.

So much for keeping secrets.

"Again," Chief O'Reilly repeated, "we will not be answering any more questions at this time. Thank you."

Both chiefs walked away from the podium over the cacophony of ongoing press inquiries. Lesson number one as a reporter: never take "no" for an answer.

Stu broke down the camera and tripod and then returned to the van. Mandy and I followed. We'd received all the information we would get.

Once inside the vehicle, Stu strapped into the driver's seat and shook his head.

"This is so goddamn gruesome," he muttered.

I was a bit taken aback. Stu was a devout Southern Baptist. Utterances like this were not common from his lips. Again, babies.

My cell rang as he navigated the ENG truck through the glut of similar vans in the confined area. Lynn.

"Hey," I said. "Have you heard the news?"

"Who in the Western world hasn't," she replied. "The question is, have you?"

"What are you talking about?"

"They just found Danica Walker's body."

EIGHT

SAN FRANCISCO'S GOLDEN Gate Park is one of the most visited parks on earth. An urban oasis comprised of twenty-four miles of foliage, trails, and gardens, with a few museums thrown in for good measure. Acres of nature in the middle of centuries of "progress." Unlike in Livermore, where I had been kept at a distance from the goings-on, at Golden Gate Park, thanks to a healthy dose of nepotism, I was allowed behind the yellow crime scene tape. Also different from the Livermore site was the conspicuous absence of the media throng. Our crew was the only one in the area—just another random San Francisco homicide.

The cordoned-off perimeter encompassed the wooded part of the park in the rear of Robin Williams Meadow. For decades, the late comedian was a regular performer at San Francisco's annual Comedy Celebration Day Festival on that site. For that reason, the city's Recreation and Parks Department posthumously named the area after him. The meadow was a large section of neatly maintained greenery fronting a bushy, wooded area in the rear. Having covered Comedy Day back when I was a feature reporter,

I recognized the spot as the designated parking place for the press and performers during the event.

It was a dirt clearing with thick bushes, shrubs, and tall eucalyptus trees on both sides. The right side of the clearing had a thicket much denser than the left, and it was there that the action was centered. I watched as the crime scene technicians sifted and brushed soil from uncovered remains.

"How do you know it's Danica Walker?" I asked.

"911 dispatch got a call around ten last night from someone who said that they'd seen your report and if we wanted to find Danica Walker, we should check the area surrounding Robin Williams Meadow," Lynn said. "The information was passed along but . . . not quickly acted upon."

"Let me guess, triage," I said, rolling my eyes.

"We had a stabbing fatality and two fentanyl overdoses in the Tenderloin, a shooting in the Mission District, and a multicar injury accident at Valencia and Duboce Streets last night," she snapped. "Add to all that the fact that we're short-staffed with about seventy-five vacancies in the department right now, so yeah, we were a little busy. Feel free to put in an application for one of the open jobs if you'd like. I'll be happy to put in a good word with the higher-ups for you."

I held up both hands in surrender.

"I came in early this morning to look at the progress on another case I'm working on when I saw the 911 call info. I had dispatch get me the recording, and when I listened, it sounded legit. I came out here and started poking around. It didn't take me long to find her."

Lynn shook her head.

"I wonder how many people picnicked in that meadow or jogged through this clearing over the last month while she was lying here," she said.

"Do they know where the call came from?" I asked.

"Burner cell. Sounded like a teenage kid to me when I listened to it. We're trying to see if we can nail down the cell tower the caller pinged off, and we're using the cell number to possibly find some info on the phone's point of sale."

I watched closely as more of the body was excavated from its hiding place—another shallow grave.

"How long do they figure she's been here?"

"Coroner says about three or four weeks from the looks of things. That would mean she was probably killed around the time she disappeared."

"Cause of death yet?" I asked.

Lynn pointed to the dead woman's neck. It was ringed with a thin, reddish-black line.

"Ligature marks. We won't know for sure until the autopsy's done, but from the look of it, I'd say she was garroted."

I peered over the shoulders of the evidence techs to get a closer look. Even though she had apparently been dead longer than Kristen Promes, Danica Walker's remains appeared to be in much better shape than the description of Kristen's body released to the press. Danica was still in one piece. Fewer critters in Golden Gate Park than at Lake Del Valle, I guess. There was also less decomposition. I could make out her features as the soil was gently brushed from her face.

Danica Walker's eyes were closed. She looked almost peaceful . . . as though she were sleeping. Her long, black, beaded braids rested neatly on her shoulders. She was still wearing her work clothes and her San Francisco State windbreaker. A modest gold locket, centered with a small chip of diamond, hung around her neck on a gold chain.

Even in death, she was an attractive young woman with high cheekbones, hollow cheeks, and full lips. She was "model pretty," depending, of course, on your standard of beauty. She probably could have made some law school money posing for print ads. She probably could have done a lot of things. Possible futures never to be explored. The price of the finality of death.

"Her eyes are closed. If she were garroted, they'd be open and bulging out, wouldn't they?"

"The murderer closed them postmortem," Lynn said. "Probably somebody she knew who couldn't stand being stared at after killing her."

I watched one of the forensic techs use a small brush to remove a clump of dried soil from her forehead. As he did, an image began to come into view. It was a scar, caked thick with dried blood and dirt. First, the beginnings of what looked like a circle appeared, and then, there were the five points of a star.

"What the hell is that?" Lynn asked.

"Looks like a pentacle," I responded.

"You mean a pentagram?"

"Without the circle, yes. With the circle around the five-pointed star, it's called a pentacle. It's considered a sacred symbol in some faiths. I did a story on it once. Wiccans, pagans, and . . . Some Satan worshippers use it. Despite some popular misconceptions, Wiccans and pagans are peaceful religions," I said.

"And Satan worshippers?" Lynn asked.

"I guess it depends on the sect. There are extremists and fanatics in every faith."

"Based on what you know from your prior research, do you think this murder could have had something to do with devil worship? Human sacrifice, maybe?"

"I suppose with the aforementioned fanatics, anything's possible."

"Great," she said. "A case straight out of *The Exorcist.*"

The techs continued to brush soil from the body. I noticed what appeared to be slash marks across Danica's stomach.

"What the hell is that?"

Lynn examined the wounds.

"Jesus. Was she garroted and then stabbed for good measure?" she asked.

The crime scene techs finished their work and gently placed the corpse in a body bag that they then put on a stretcher and gently placed it in the back of the coroner's van.

"No useful tire tracks, I suppose."

"With all the parking, hiking, and cycling here over the course of a month? Not a chance."

"I guess I should probably go with you for the notification," I said. "Josie did reach out to me."

Lynn nodded. She was deep in thought.

"We need to reconstruct the rest of Danica's last day. Find out what happened between the time she left the law office and the time she ended up here with a demonic symbol carved into her forehead."

"Sacred symbol," I corrected.

"Whatever."

"I'm guessing by your reaction that you haven't seen this type of thing before," I said.

She shook her head.

"Guess I need to find out if there are any satanic cults on the department's radar in the area," she said.

"It could also just be some lone nut sending a message," I said. "Or 'autographing' his work."

"Somebody out to make a name for himself," she said, staring at the coroner's van as the techs closed its rear doors.

"You mean, like the Zodiac Killer?"

"San Francisco does have a reputation for attracting wannabe comic book villains."

"That it does," I agreed. "So, what's first?"

"It depends on whether Danica is the only one marked up like this or if there are others. Like I said, there are none that I'm aware of, but I *do* want to know about groups in the area using this . . . 'pentacle' you called it?"

"That's right."

"I still want to talk to 'Mr. Crane Jr.' to find out what that little tiff he and Danica had was all about," she said.

"I think we'd better head over to Josie Walker's as soon as possible. I'd hate for her to hear about this some other way," I said. "Can you keep this development quiet for a minute? Based on what we've seen in coverage of this case so far, I don't think keeping the press from covering it will be a problem."

She pursed her lips and again nodded her head.

"Shall we take your car or mine?" she asked.

NINE

WE ENDED UP taking both our vehicles. I hopped into the Black Beauty, pulled out my iPhone, and punched the work address Josie Walker had given me into the Waze app. Once the route had been mapped out, I fired up the Beauty's engine, and Lynn followed as we caravanned through the Haight Asbury District to Highway 101. We followed it to I-80 and across the Bay Bridge. The app took us to Highway 880 and through downtown Oakland to the 98th Avenue exit across from the Oakland Coliseum. Soon, we were approaching the East Oakland ThriftyMart grocery store. The midday heat was upon us, and the parking lot was mostly full. We found a pair of adjacent spaces and parked.

The store was designed with a stone façade, slant roof, and glass architecture of the mid-twentieth century. It was the standard look for grocery stores of its kind in the area, although there had been periodic updates and minor remodels over the years. Renovations usually took place when the building changed hands. This particular location had been through several iterations over the decades. It had begun life as a Lucky store in the mid-1960s before being acquired by Safeway about twenty years later. Since then, it had been a FoodMaxx, then a Lucky's again, switching to a Grocery Outlet, and finally, its current residency as a ThriftyMart.

ThriftyMart was a small discount grocery store specializing in meat and poultry, which was a little closer to their expiration dates than some other stores. Their pantry staples consisted primarily of off-brand canned goods, generic boxes of rice, macaroni, highly sweetened sugar cereals, and a colorful array of "fruit-flavored" sodas. There was also an ample supply of fresh fruits and vegetables that didn't stay crisp in your refrigerator quite as long as produce from the larger chains.

The clientele consisted mainly of families on federal and state food assistance, seniors on fixed incomes, and the working poor. The chain carried plenty of sugary, processed foodstuffs. The kind of sustenance that is cheap, filling, and a major contributor to obesity and type 2 diabetes. Eating healthy is expensive. If you want organic or locally grown, you need to go to one of the high-end grocery store chains or farmers' markets in the ritzy Rockridge area of Oakland. ThriftyMart offered what the financially challenged could afford: food that would sate their hunger before eventually killing them. That was the chain's business model as they strategically opened their locations in predominantly low-income, Black, and Latino communities. God Bless America.

Automatic glass double doors bookended both sides of the building, and we walked to the pair closest to where we'd parked. When we got in range of the sensors, the doors didn't open. A sign that appeared to have been made from part of a brown cardboard box was pasted inside the entrance door. In a neat black felt marker was written the message *THIS DOOR CLOSED. PLEASE USE OTHER ENTRANCE.* We were seeing this more and more in the Bay Area.

Since the COVID shutdown, there has been a spike in shoplifting and petty crimes due to several factors: lost jobs, financial desperation, and lax prosecutions by short-staffed district attorneys' offices whose focus was more on reducing mass incarceration than dealing with "quality-of-life" crimes. Having only one way in and one way out of stores made it easier to monitor some shoplifters. I say "some" because there were reports of thieves so brazen, they'd fill a shopping cart with merchandise and then walk right past the check stands and out of the store with it. It had gotten so bad that smaller items like batteries, bars of soap, and underarm deodorant were under lock and key in many places to keep them from being stolen in bulk and then resold on Amazon and eBay.

We made our way to the other set of doors and walked in. It was busy, and I could see why the lot was so full. There were a dozen check stands, but only three were manned. Customers stood in long lines that stretched across the common walkway area and into the aisles.

"You think *your* workplace is understaffed," I said to Lynn.

The store's one saving grace was its enticing aroma. ThriftyMart stores baked their own bread on-site, and its scent wafted throughout the building. It was one of the few twenty-first-century amenities the chain offered.

Though we hated to slow down the already tortoiselike pace of the line, we interrupted a teenage African American courtesy clerk furiously stuffing two-liter bottles of grape soda and an enormous bag of off-brand potato chips into large, reinforced plastic grocery bags. Even though ThriftyMart was a privately owned white corporation, its nonunion, underpaid staff was nearly 100 percent Black. It gave the owners PR bragging rights as "a major employer of people of color."

"Excuse me," Lynn said to the courtesy clerk.

"S'up?" the young man said, not looking up from the task at hand.

"Can you please tell me where we can find Josie Walker?"

"The manager?" the kid said, brushing a bead of sweat from his forehead with the back of his hand as he finally looked up at us. "Who messed up?"

"It's nothing like that," Lynn said. "We have some personal business."

"She's in the office. It's behind the double doors at the end of aisle three," he directed us, pointing to his left.

"Thank you," Lynn said.

"Sure," he replied, stuffing a chuck roast into another plastic bag. The meat lacked the vibrant red color of newly butchered beef, instead presenting a dull, brownish tint. I hoped the shopper would cook or freeze it that night. If not, I sensed food poisoning in their near future.

We walked down aisle three past rows of dented cans of soups, stews, and chili and through a pair of black rubber-lined doors. Inside was a large storage area constructed of unfinished plywood and piled high with boxes of canned goods. We walked around the boxes, past a time clock and two restrooms, one marked GUESTS, the other EMPLOYEES ONLY, and eventually found a cramped little office with no door. Inside, Josie Walker sat at a paper-covered desk, laser-focused on an inventory list. She was so engrossed in what she was doing that she didn't hear us enter.

"Josie," I said softly.

She snapped out of her work trance and looked up. It took her a moment to mentally switch gears before her eyes registered recognition.

"Oh, Mr. Davis. What brings you here?" she asked. She then looked at Lynn.

"Josie, this is my sister, Detective Lynn Sloan of the San Francisco Police Department."

"Hello," Josie Walker said.

"Nice to meet you," Lynn replied.

"San Francisco police? Has something happened?" Josie asked.

Lynn and I looked at each other. Death notifications are never easy, and this one was going to be brutal.

"We have some news about Danica," I said.

Josie looked at me with anticipation. I hated this. In the next few words, I would change this woman's life forever.

"She's been found," I said.

Josie's face lit up with excitement.

"Thank God," she said. "Thank God. Did you bring her home?"

I looked at the floor. It was covered with dirty Formica.

"What is it?" she asked.

I took in a deep breath of air.

"She's all right, isn't she? Tell me she's all right," Josie pleaded. "Tell me she's all right."

I slowly exhaled. "I'm sorry, Josie."

Her eyes immediately filled with tears. "Are you telling me she's dead? My Danica is dead?"

"We're sorry for your loss, ma'am," Lynn chimed in.

Josie's tears began to drip from her eyes and run down the contours of her face. I noticed that she had the same high cheekbones as her daughter.

"Oh God!" she screamed. "No! No!!"

I'm rarely at a loss for words, but I just didn't know what to say.

"Oh God!!" she wailed, the tears coming faster. "D'Vante. What am I going to tell D'Vante? His mother is gone. His mother is gone!"

She opened a desk drawer, pulled out a travel packet of tissues, and ripped it open. Then she violently snatched a few and began wiping the sadness from her eyes.

"What happened?" she asked.

"We're not exactly sure yet," Lynn said. "We found her body buried in Golden Gate Park."

Josie's tears increased their flow. "Her . . . body," she said. "Buried? Dear Lord. Someone . . . killed her?"

"It looks that way," I said, modulating my voice to the gentlest tone possible.

"Who?" Josie demanded angrily as she stabbed at her eyes with tissues. "Who killed my baby?"

"We don't know," Lynn said in a soft voice. "We're looking into it right now. We will do everything in our power to find the person responsible and get justice for Danica."

"Josie, when we found Danica, she wore a gold locket around her neck. Do you know anything about it?" I asked.

Josie sniffled and then blew her nose. She threw the used tissues in the wastebasket next to her desk, snatched a few fresh ones from the packet in front of her, and resumed dabbing at her eyes.

"She bought it from the mall jewelry store while working here. The first paycheck she got after D'Vante was born," Josie sniffed, again wiping at her nose. "She has his baby picture in it."

"You find the bastard who did this!" Josie said, breaking down again and looking at me. "Promise me that you'll find him, Mr. Davis."

"Josie, . . . I—"

"Promise me. I know that if you promise me, you'll do it. On TV, when you promise to stay on something, you always keep your word," she said. "Promise me."

Lynn and I looked at each other. My sister's eyes seemed to warn, *"Don't do it."*

"Promise me you'll find out who did this," Josie begged again. "That you'll find the person who took D'Vante's mother."

I took in and released another lungful of air.

"I promise," I said.

Lynn gave Josie the number of the San Francisco Coroner's Office so that she could arrange to retrieve Danica's remains once the autopsy was completed. Lynn and I walked through the store and out to the parking lot. Once we were outside, Lynn looked at me and shook her head.

"Why in the hell did you promise her that?"

"I don't know," I said. "There was just something in her face . . . her voice."

"And what will you tell her if we *don't* find the killer? What do you think will be in her face and voice then?" she scolded.

"I have the utmost faith in our sleuthing abilities," I said.

"I swear to God," she said. "It's just like Auntie used to say about you."

Auntie was our mom's older sister. She took on the burden of raising the two of us after our mother was killed when we were children.

"Which thing Auntie said?" I replied. "There were so many."

"Sometimes you don't have the good sense to come in out of the rain."

She was right, but sometimes, it was a character flaw that served me well.

"We're just gonna have to solve it, that's all," I said.

"Oh yeah," Lynn said. "That's all. Just like that. Easy peasy."

"Well, we know one thing for certain."

"What's that?"

"Since her gold and diamond locket was still around her neck, robbery wasn't the motive."

Lynn stared daggers at me as her cell rang, and she clicked it on.

"Sloan," she said into the phone. "Yeah, we just notified the mother."

A beat.

"They found what??" she said, apparently shocked. "Are they sure? Okay. I'm gonna swing by there. I'm already in the East Bay. Keep me posted if anything else comes up."

She clicked off the phone.

"Get in your car," she said. "We're going to Livermore."

"What is it?" I asked.

"That was Roger Murray in the coroner's office. They wanted me to know that Danica Walker was pregnant."

"Pregnant?"

"Yep. They figure about three months."

"They determined that from the size of the fetus?" I asked.

"That's just it. There is no fetus."

I thought for a moment.

"The slash marks across her belly."

"The baby was cut from her womb," Lynn said. "Postmortem."

TEN

"**I** THINK OUR CASE and the Kristen Promes case might be connected," Lynn said.

We were sitting in Chief Liam O'Reilly's office in the Livermore Police Department. O'Reilly sat behind his desk, his fingers tented under his chin as he listened intently. Chief Lane stood beside him, sipping from a white coffee mug with the word "*CHIEF*" boldly emblazoned on both sides in a black M*A*S*H-style lettering. Rank has its privileges.

"So," Chief Lane said, "we've got two dead mothers-to-be with their babies ripped from their bodies."

"That's about the size of it," I said.

He sipped from his coffee mug. "Not something we see every day, I'll grant you, but I don't know if it's enough to say that we're dealing with the same killer," he continued.

"Got anything else? Any other details that resemble our murder?" O'Reilly said.

"Hard to tell," Lynn replied. "There was a gold and diamond locket on the body. That knocks out robbery as a motive. We heard your vic's hand still had the enormous rock she called a wedding ring. You guys have been so tight-lipped about your case. What have *you* held back?"

The two chiefs looked at each other. Lane nodded.

"Are there any strange markings on the body you discovered," O'Reilly asked. "Anything out of the ordinary?"

"You mean like a five-pointed star with a circle around it carved into the vic's forehead?" I asked.

Both chiefs looked stunned. I thought Lane was going to drop his coffee mug.

"Your body has that symbol?" O'Reilly sputtered in surprise.

"The coroner says she was already dead when the carving was made," Lynn added.

"Shit," Lane said, shaking his head. "Shit. Shit. Shit."

He took a large swig from his coffee mug as if trying to wash the taste of what he'd just heard from his mouth.

"At least she didn't have to sit through the pain of that torture," he finally said. "Thank God for small favors."

"I take it Kristen Promes has the same postmortem marking on her forehead?" Lynn asked.

"You got a cause of death?" O'Reilly shot back.

"Nothing official yet. The autopsy isn't completed," Lynn said.

"Unofficial then," O'Reilly stated.

"It looked to me like she'd been garroted. Maybe a guitar string or a piano wire was the murder weapon. Easy to carry, easy to dispose of."

"Garroted," Lane said, shaking his head before taking another sip of his coffee. "Same as our body."

"So, we're looking for a serial?" I asked.

"Maybe," Lane said. "What's it mean? That marking?"

"It's a sacred symbol for pagans, Wiccans . . . and Satanists," I said.

"Satan worshipers," O'Reilly said, shaking his head. "Great."

"Keep in mind that even though their beliefs are a little out there, they generally aren't known to be violent," I added.

"I'm a good Catholic boy," O'Reilly said. "As far as I'm concerned, they're *all* dangerous."

"Let me guess," I said. "You were a kid during the Satanic Panic of the '80s when we were scared into believing there was a human-sacrificing Satanist around every corner just looking for a kid to grab to offer up in tribute to the devil."

O'Reilly didn't say anything. He didn't have to.

"I'm a good Catholic boy too," I said. "Just because the killer used satanic symbolism doesn't necessarily make him a member of that church any more than being a Mormon makes you a polygamist."

"Keep in mind that it might be a member of an extremist group of some kind. Take a charismatic leader, add a group of easily indoctrinated followers, just add water, and voilà, instant cult," Lynn said. "Have you had any known activity by those who dabble in the occult in this area?"

"Not that I'm aware of," O'Reilly said.

"Nothing I've heard about in Pleasanton either," added Lane. "Chief O'Reilly and I are both looking into it."

"So, what now?" I asked.

"I'd suggest we form a task force: your offices and mine. Let's share all the information and work it together," Lynn said.

"Do you really think that's necessary?" Lane asked.

"My brother was talking about the Zodiac Killer earlier. You know one of the reasons he was never caught? He committed his murders in different jurisdictions. Law enforcement agencies couldn't get their dicks out of the way long enough to cooperate with each other by sharing evidence and information," she said. "The left hand never knew what the right hand was doing. That enabled the killer to slip right through both."

Chief O'Reilly stroked his chin and then turned to Chief Lane.

"I think she's right," Lane said.

O'Reilly thought for a moment and shrugged his shoulders before slowly nodding his head.

"Okay," Lynn said. "Let me clear it with my captain. If you guys don't mind, I'd like to take the lead on this."

"Why you?" Chief Lane asked. "Shouldn't it be me or Chief O'Reilly? Kristen Promes is our case."

"How many homicides have you personally solved?" Lynn asked.

Chief Lane looked at the floor. Lynn turned to O'Reilly.

"You?" she asked.

"Two," he replied.

"I've got over thirty solves," Lynn said. "I don't mean to brag, but, gentlemen, I do this shit for a living."

"I've got some damned good homicide detectives of my own," Lane snapped.

"So do I," O'Reilly added.

"I'm sure that you've got some great detectives. It's just that San Francisco has the unfortunate distinction of dealing with a lot more homicides than you do down here. I've just worked them more often, that's all," Lynn said. "I meant no disrespect to your departments or your officers. I just have a little more experience with this kind of thing."

She took a beat.

"How about I work the case? I report directly to the two of you, and you will be the face of the investigation for the media."

O'Reilly again stroked his chin in thought. Lane scratched his head.

"The Kristen Promes case is international news. You've got the goddamned BBC on your doorstep, for Christ's sake. You handle all that. Take all the credit for anything we find. You'll be internationally famous."

Nothing wins the day like vanity. Show me a police chief who doesn't like a television camera, and I'll show you a Pegasus giving birth to a unicorn.

"What about Mr. TV over here?" O'Reilly said, gesturing in my direction.

"It's not my first rodeo either," I said. "Lynn and I have worked unusual cases together before."

"Oh yeah," Lane said. "Those cop murders a few months back."

"All I want is access," I said. "Crime scenes, evidence . . ."

"And to be the first one on the air with anything new," Lane said, draining his coffee mug before setting it on O'Reilly's desk.

I smiled.

"I won't report anything without your say-so," I said. "Believe me when I say that I won't do anything that will compromise this investigation."

The chiefs looked at each other again.

"Okay," O'Reilly said. "Our three departments will work this together, but I don't want that publicized. Nothing on television about the task force, the satanic stuff, or the connection between the two murders. The last thing we need is the public panicking because there's some devil-worshipping psychopath on the loose. We don't want to ignite a *new* Satanic Panic."

"Agreed," Lynn said.

"They won't hear it from me without your stamp of approval first. Scout's honor," I stated, raising my right hand in the Boy Scouts' three-fingered pledge.

"Okay," O'Reilly said. "Where do you want to start?"

"You got a lead suspect?" Lynn asked.

"Well, you know that the spouse is always the first one we look at in a case like this," Lane replied.

"I assume you've interviewed him?"

"Of course," Lane said. "The first night his wife was reported missing."

"All right, we'd also like to talk to Mr. Promes. I also want to see who Danica Walker was involved with romantically. I want to know who fathered that baby."

"All right," O'Reilly said. "Anything else?"

"It might also make sense to pay a visit to the Church of Satan. It used to be headquartered in San Francisco," I suggested.

"Let me guess," O'Reilly said, "You did a television segment on them once."

I shrugged. "I'm a reporter. I get around," I said. "It was a background piece. A feature story for Halloween."

"Thought you said they weren't violent," Lane remarked.

"I don't believe they are," I said. "But maybe they can point us to somebody who is."

"You guys got any street cam footage from the day the Promes woman disappeared?" Lynn asked.

Lane shook his head. "Unfortunately, we don't. There's a camera on the corner of that section of Bernal Avenue, but it isn't in working order, and Public Works has been dragging their feet about fixing it."

"Any home surveillance video from the surrounding streets?" I asked.

"Nada," said Lane. "The most common home surveillance video recorders these days are those Ring attachments for the front door. Whoever did this was smart enough to use a scrambling device. Knocks out any video from a camera connected to Bluetooth, and that includes Ring."

"You can get the damned scramblers on Amazon for fifty bucks," O'Reilly said. "They should be illegal."

"Okay," Lynn replied. "I'll see if there's any street cam footage from the area of the law office where Danica was working. Maybe

I'll have better luck. I also want to talk to anybody from that Fourth of July barbecue you think might be of interest. Is there a guest list or something?"

"I think Tom Promes has one. I'll see that you get a copy," Lane chimed in.

"All right then," Lynn said, "if we are dealing with a serial killer here, let's see if we can stop this bastard at two murders."

"Two murders that we *know* of," I threw in. "It might be a good idea to see if there are other pregnant women who've gone missing over the last several months."

"I was thinking the same thing," Lynn said. "I also want to see if there's any kind of connection that Danica and Kristen had in life. Anything or anyone in common."

"Looks like we've got our work cut out for us," O'Reilly added.

"Not to mention the damned media nonsense we're dealing with," Lane said before quickly looking at me. "No offense."

"None taken," I said.

"Why don't we conduct all of our future powwows over Zoom? Might help keep the media from finding out we're coordinating on this," Lane suggested.

"My department has an encrypted video chat that's secure," Lynn said. "Why don't we use that?"

"Sounds good to me," O'Reilly agreed.

Lane did as well.

"Okay, now, let's go catch us a killer," O'Reilly expressed.

As Lynn and I walked through the Livermore Police Department's visitor parking lot, she looked at me and shook her head.

"What?"

"When were you ever a 'good Catholic boy'?" she asked.

"Hey! I was an altar boy. And Auntie did put us through Catholic school from kindergarten to high school."

"And when exactly do you go to mass *now?*" she asked.

"I go," I protested.

"When? Christmas or Easter?"

"I went with you and Jared to midnight mass on Christmas Eve," I said indignantly.

"That was *five years* ago."

"See?" I replied. "Good Catholic boy."

Lynn just shook her head, hopped into her unmarked, and sped west on I-580 back toward San Francisco.

I followed her as far as Castro Valley, then exited and headed to my home in Palomares Canyon. I'd been up about forty hours and was about to drop.

ELEVEN

I WAS AWAKENED AFTER dark by the *I Love Lucy* ringtone on my cell phone.

"Hello," I croaked.

"God, you're still in bed?" Lynn said.

"What time is it?"

"You're holding a phone. Look at it."

I pulled my iPhone away from my ear and glanced at its face. 6:15.

"Why in the hell are you calling me at 6:15 in the morning?" I barked.

"It's 6:15 in the *evening*, doofus. Have you been asleep all this time?"

"After I left you, I came home and napped for a few hours," I said. "What's the big deal?"

"That was *yesterday*."

"Yesterday??" I said, bolting upright in bed.

"Do you mean to tell me you've been out for over 24 hours?"

"Apparently so. I was too tired to sleep, so I took a Lunesta. I guess my body needed rest more than I thought."

"You're getting old, Big Brother," she smirked.

"Shut up."

"Get your behind out of bed and get dressed."

"For what?"

"It's Saturday."

Silence.

"Saturday," she repeated.

More silence.

"Shokumotsu? My girlfriend, Sylvia? Ringing any bells?"

"Oh shit. Is that tonight?" I asked.

"In an hour and forty-five minutes."

"Lynn, it's been a long couple of days and—"

"Uh-uh. You promised me you'd have dinner with Sylvia if I worked the Danica Walker case for you. I'm holding up my end of the deal, and you'd better believe you'll hold up yours."

I groaned.

"So, get your lazy ass out of bed, shower, shave, put on something *nice*, and splash on some Old Spice," she demanded, drill instructor-like. The Army Ranger in her was now on full display.

"I haven't worn Old Spice since high school. I'm into Armani now."

"Ooh la la," she mocked. "Put some on and get your tail down to the restaurant."

"Okay," I growled.

"And," she said, "behave as though you actually *want* to be there. Sylvia is a friend. *Don't embarrass me.*"

"No promises," I said as I hung up the phone.

I'd slept for over twenty-six hours. I guess I was more tired than I'd thought. Maybe Lynn's right, and I am getting old. I headed to the bathroom to shower when I suddenly remembered Sophie. She had been trapped in the house for over a day. I went into the living room, where I expected a mess of epic proportions, but found her patiently lying on the rug next to the front door—no pee or dog poop in sight. The poor girl had been holding it, waiting for me to let her out. She's such a good dog.

She let out a pained yet excited bark when she saw me.

"I'm sorry, honey," I said, scratching behind her ear with one hand while opening the front door with the other.

Once the door was open, she flashed out of the house like Mercury. She ran to one of my American Beauty rosebushes in front of the house and did her business, which I dutifully cleaned up.

Note to self: Get a doggie door.

While Sophie relieved herself, I filled her dish with water and prepared her gourmet dog food. Ten minutes later, she was back in the house, happily nibbling away at her dinner while I showered, shaved, and debated stopping by the drugstore to buy some Old Spice just to piss off Lynn. No time. Armani would have to do.

I applied a spritz to my right wrist, rubbed it against my left, and then gently caressed my face with both. A little goes a long way.

I put on my chocolate Armani suit and a silk, sky-blue dress shirt, sans tie. I slipped on my brown wingtip Ferragamos, realized they were a little too "matchy-matchy," and opted for my black Kenneth Coles instead. I walked through the kitchen and past Sophie, who was now contentedly sleeping on her plush dog pillow, and through the side door into the garage, where I climbed behind the wheel of the Black Beauty. I turned the key in the ignition, and she started right up. The engine purred. It was a 300-horsepower symphony. God, how I love that car. Though she doesn't have all the bells and whistles my former Lexus did, the Beauty is a far superior machine, in my estimation. I've always had an affinity for the classics.

Twenty minutes later, I pulled into the parking lot at Shokumatsu. I found an empty spot right next to Lynn and Jared's car. Lynn had left her unmarked at home in favor of Jared's new metallic gray Mercedes SUV. Apparently, business at The Cracked Egg was very good.

Shokumotsu was a relatively new Japanese restaurant in Danville, about twenty minutes from my house. I like to visit Danville for the diversity. That would consist of me when I was within the city limits. According to the latest census, the city is 0.9 percent Black. You'd need a microscope to find people of color. It's a tony, well-to-do city comprised of professional athletes, the rich, and the nouveau riche. The people are nice. It has a historic landmark. Eugene O'Neill wrote a few of his better plays there. It's just not a city that will be confused with the Rainbow Coalition anytime soon.

I entered the restaurant to find a typical Japanese eatery décor. Linen-covered tables and high-end restaurant chairs were in much of the room. There were also individual, semiprivate nooks walled with bamboo. Each was equipped with a vibrant Japanese cloth that could be pulled closed for seclusion. There was a long, L-shaped bar, its seats filled with diners watching a battery of Japanese sushi chefs chop, slice, and roll various pieces of brightly colored fish and deep-green seaweed.

I recognized the faint sound of a Japanese shamisen playing softly in the background. The shamisen is a box-shaped instrument consisting of three twisted silk strings played with a pick resembling a spatula. The paramour of a psychologist friend of mine makes guitars, and between them, they'd taught me quite a bit about stringed instruments.

"Topher . . ." I heard in a loud whisper.

I looked to the far corner of the restaurant to find Lynn, Jared, and a stunning redhead seated on colorful pillows in one of the private bamboo nooks. Lynn motioned me over, and I approached their little Japanese enclave.

"You're actually on time," Lynn said. "It is the age of miracles."

I turned to the redhead. "Besides being a cop, my little sister fills in for Big Ben when he goes on holiday."

"Call me your 'little sister' again, and I'm sending *you* on holiday."

The redhead giggled. She had a cute laugh. "Lynn told me you were funny," the woman said.

"Oh, he's a laugh riot," Lynn remarked, her words dripping with sarcasm. "Topher, this is my friend Sylvia McNamara. Sylvia, my brother, Topher Davis."

"Oh, everybody knows Topher Davis," Sylvia said, extending an exquisite hand with long, red-lacquered nails that lightly scratched the back of my hand.

I took her hand and cupped it in both of my own. She was simply extraordinary—lush red hair, green eyes, and porcelain skin. Thick, pouty lips with just a hint of rose-colored lipstick that complimented her fiery locks. How in the world was this goddess still single?

"I'd kiss your hand," I said, "but I'm afraid it might break."

"I'm sturdier than I look," Sylvia said with a smile.

I lowered my lips and gently touched them against the back of her hand. It was like kissing a piece of fine silk.

Lynn darted a glance at Jared, and they both smiled.

"Please, sit," Sylvia invited.

I slowly sat on the empty pillow beside her. I'd recently recovered from some cracked ribs suffered during another case Lynn and I had recently worked. I was mostly healed, but movement in some positions was still a little uncomfortable.

"Are you okay?" Sylvia said, noticing my grimace.

"Old football injury," I said. "Kicks up sometimes."

Lynn rolled her eyes.

"Sake?" Jared asked, lifting a large white ceramic sake decanter from the center of the table. I'd been mostly off the booze of late. After the breakup with Sarah, I hit it pretty hard for a while. Then

I had decided to reduce my alcohol consumption some. However, this was a special occasion.

"Sure," I said.

Jared grabbed four neatly stacked sake cups, filled them, and handed one to each of us. The porcelain was hot to the touch.

"*Kanpai*," he said, toasting in Japanese as we all clinked cups before downing the hot rice wine as though we were drinking shots of tequila.

"So," I said to Sylvia, "my sister tells me you two take spin classes together."

"I'm not really a gym rat or anything. I just do a little spinning to help keep up my wind," she said.

"Please," Lynn said with a smile. "She's got a tush you could bounce a quarter off of."

"And me with no change," I said as Jared refilled my sake cup. Sylvia giggled again. It was a sound I could get used to.

"In time, you'll see that the more you drink, the more charming I become," I told her.

Lynn looked at me as if to say, "*Seriously?*"

Sylvia and I made small talk for a while, and it was easy. She was one of those people you meet, and you feel like you've known them your whole life.

The waiter set steaming bowls of miso soup before us and then took our dinner orders. We chose an assortment of sashimi, California rolls, and shrimp tempura for the table. Once the waiter left, Sylvia excused herself to go to the ladies' room. When she was out of earshot, Lynn whispered to me.

"See?" she bragged. "I knew you two would hit it off."

"She sure is pretty," I said. "I'll give her that."

"Pretty? *That's* your takeaway?" Lynn exclaimed. "Chris, I swear sometimes you have the depth of a kiddie pool."

"I'm a guy," I said with a roughish smile. "What do you want from me?"

Sylvia returned to the table, and to Lynn's delight, we continued to get to know each other until the waiter brought our food. It was a kaleidoscope of variously hued pieces of fish served on a giant wood platter that had been carved into the shape of a boat. Like the rest of us, Sylvia declined silverware and, with apologies to the rain forest, opted for wooden chopsticks. I was becoming more smitten by the second.

"Say," Lynn said, "don't you have that Emmy Awards thing coming up in a few weeks?"

"Ooh, the Emmys," Sylvia cooed.

"How'd you know about that?" I asked.

"The *Chronicle* printed a list of all the nominees," she said before turning to Sylvia to add, "My brother is up for two awards."

"It's the *Regional* Emmys," I clarified. "Just awards for television work done in San Francisco and the surrounding areas. It's no big deal. A story Lynn and I worked on together a few months back got nominated for a couple of them."

"Jared and I are going. Hey," Lynn said to me, "you get a guest ticket. You should bring Sylvia."

Sylvia looked at me, her emerald eyes glowing with anticipation. I could do worse. A lot worse. What the hell? Why not?

I turned to Sylvia and said, "It's on the 31st. Are you free?"

"I'll make myself free!" she exclaimed.

"It's going to be a blast," Jared said. "We're dressing to the nines. Black tie. Stretch limo. The whole nine yards."

"Prom night, the sequel," I said, sipping from my sake cup.

"That sounds amazing," Sylvia gushed. "I have a red sequined gown that will knock your socks off," she said with a sly smile. "And maybe a few other things."

I could feel my cheeks get warm.

"The Emmys. How exciting is *that*?" Sylvia said, barely able to contain her excitement.

"Oh, it's not that special. Really. Just a big self-congratulatory party," I said.

We all began to fill our small plates with pieces of fish from the serving dish in the center of the table. I opted for some yellowtail sashimi to start. That's how I was taught to tell if a sushi place is any good. If the yellowtail is fresh, you can trust that everything else will be as well. I dipped the triangle of fish into some wasabi-infused soy sauce and popped it into my mouth. It melted like butter. This place was excellent. Looking at the faces around the table, I saw that my sentiment was shared.

"I hear your job is pretty interesting," I said to Sylvia, pinching another piece of yellowtail between my chopsticks. "You're a mortgage broker?"

"Yes," she said. "My days consist of trying to get Jews to give my clients home loans."

I choked on my yellowtail and quickly downed another cup of hot sake to dislodge it from my windpipe. I looked at Jared. He was about to put eel-loaded chopsticks into his mouth when he stopped short, suspending the fish midair. Lynn had the same look on her face Auntie used to get when I'd break wind in church.

"I'm sorry?" I finally managed to get out.

"Mortgages from the Jews," she said as if explaining the facts of life to a five-year-old. "They control the banks, you know?"

"No," I said, "Actually, I don't 'know.'"

"Sure, you do," she insisted with a giggle that had suddenly lost its cuteness. "They've controlled banking in this country since the beginning. You know how it is. You're in the media, for God's sake. The Jews control your industry too."

"The . . . Jews . . . control . . . the . . . media," I said slowly, silently praying that she was kidding.

"They control everything. We might as well be living in Israel. You know, our businesses are alike. We just play their little Jew games and work their system. It's the only way to survive," she said, crunching on a piece of tempura shrimp in her mouth.

"Oh, Lynn," I said suddenly, "I've got to give you that case file in my trunk. Come get it from me before I forget."

Lynn, looking as though something creepy was crawling up her leg, excused herself from the table, gave me her right hand for support to help me pull myself to my feet, and followed me out into the parking lot. Once we were far enough from the restaurant's front door that I was sure we couldn't be heard, I turned to her.

"What the actual fuck??"

"I don't know," Lynn said, shaking her head. "I don't know."

"You don't know?" I sputtered. "You said you'd been friends for years."

"Well, spin-class friends. We pedal side by side on stationary bikes and make small talk. In all the years I've known her, I've never heard anything remotely like that come out of her mouth. I just don't know," she repeated.

"Some detective you are."

Lynn stared at the ground, still shaking her head in disbelief.

"I'll tell you what *I* know," I said. "There is *no way* I'm taking Eva Braun in there to the Emmys or any place else."

"I understand," Lynn said, nodding her head. "I'm sorry."

"And you were afraid *I* might be an embarrassment."

My sister is a tough-as-nails ex-Army Ranger with two tours in Afghanistan under her belt. She's one of the few women homicide detectives in the entire San Francisco Police Department. She's a trained interrogator with the best built-in bullshit detector I've ever seen. In short, she's rarely at a loss for words. Yet, she silently continued to cast her eyes downward, looking at the asphalt parking lot.

"Well, I'm out of here," I said.

"What'll I tell Sylvia?"

"Tell her that the Jews said I have to work," I scoffed.

"I'll take care of it," she said.

"Damned right you will," I retorted. "Now, do you finally understand why I hate blind dates?"

I left Lynn standing in the parking lot as I hopped into the Black Beauty and sped away. The rise in anti-Semitism in this country is getting downright scary. It's like people have no compunction about spewing their ignorance and saying "the quiet part" out loud, even on a first—and, in this case, last—date.

As I got on Highway 680 toward home, I turned on the Beauty's vintage AM radio for some local news. That was one of the few modern upgrades I planned to make to the car—a new stereo system with Bluetooth. When I reached for the volume knob, I heard the *I LOVE LUCY* ringtone go off in the vest pocket of my jacket. I'd also need to add a hands-free phone device to the Beauty.

"Hi, Mandy," I said, holding the phone with one hand and the steering wheel with the other.

"Sorry to interrupt your date," she said.

"It's not a problem. Trust me."

"Hey," she said, "is that the T-bird engine I hear in the background? Are you driving and talking on the phone?"

"At least I'm not texting."

"Topher . . . you know better than—"

"I'm putting in a hands-free device as soon as I can," I said, cutting her off. "I swear. Just don't tell my sister. I don't need another $250 ticket."

"That's really dangerous, you know," she reprimanded. "That old car doesn't even have airbags. You're gonna wrap yourself around a pole."

"I know. I know. I'll put airbags in too," I said. "Is that why you called? To break my balls over cell phone road etiquette?"

"No, I called to let you know that tomorrow morning, we have an exclusive on-camera interview with Julie Wolfer," she said, self-satisfied.

"Why do I know that name?"

"Kristen Promes's best friend. The one she was on her way to see when she disappeared. The last known person, other than her husband, known to have talked to her alive."

"Wow. Every media outlet in the Western world must be trying to get to her. How'd you pull that off?" I asked, impressed.

"Girl's got mad skills," she said.

"In what regard?"

"Julie Wolfer is my cousin."

"And you planned on telling me this when?"

"When it became necessary. The Promes and Walker cases are definitely linked. My sources in the San Francisco and Alameda County Coroner's Offices confirmed that both women were garroted with a wire of some sort and had pentacle carvings on their foreheads," she said. "It just became necessary."

"What time tomorrow?"

"Julie says they will try to slip out to church in the morning, and then she'll come home and fix brunch. We're invited."

"Lovely," I said. "Nothing says Sunday brunch like a double homicide. She know how to make eggs Benedict?"

TWELVE

"**I** JUST FED THE girls and got them down for a nap, so we shouldn't be disturbed for a while," Julie Wolfer said as she held court at the head of her walnut dining table.

Places were set for Stu, Mandy, and me. Julie Wolfer sipped coffee from a cup and saucer from the same herringbone china set on which she served the food. She had put out quite the spread: fresh fruit, pastries, waffles with butter and warm maple syrup, sausages (both pork and vegan, as she'd forgotten to check our dietary preferences), pork and turkey bacon, scrambled eggs, home-fried potatoes with grilled onions, and eggs Benedict with freshly made hollandaise sauce.

Every time I eat breakfast out someplace that isn't The Egg, I feel like I'm cheating on Jared, but this is work related, and the eggs Benedict looked scrumptious, so I rationalized it.

"You have both girls here, Jules?" Mandy asked, loading her china plate with fresh fruit and turkey sausage.

"Tom thought it would be the best way to keep Taylor away from the media for the time being. She and Hope are besties. Being together makes the most sense for them both right now," she said.

"I can't believe she's gone," Julie said with a sniffle as Mandy gently rubbed her back in a circular, clockwise motion.

Stu had two plates. The first was piled high with eggs, pastries, and pork bacon. A second plate contained waffles smeared with copious amounts of butter and swimming in a pool of syrup. It was a heart attack on a plate. I've never understood how the man could consume the kind of food that he did and still be alive. His breakfast made me feel a little less guilty about the hollandaise sauce covering the eggs and English muffins on my own plate.

Stu ate like a Hoover vacuum cleaner, sucking the dirt off an area rug. Once he'd all but licked his plate clean, he removed the cloth napkin he'd shoved down the front of his shirt and set it on the table next to his empty dishes.

"Do you mind if we shoot the interview in the living room? I think the natural light might be better there," he said.

"Whatever you'd like," Julie replied.

Stu got up from the table and headed into the living room, where he'd stowed his gear.

"Nobody knows the girls are here," Julie said. "I'd appreciate it if you would keep it that way."

"The public won't hear it from us," I assured her.

"Thank you," she said.

"So," I said, "you and Mandy are cousins?"

"Yes. Our moms are sisters," she said.

Julie turned to Mandy.

"How's Aunt Stacy?" she asked.

"As cantankerous as ever," Mandy said. "Still nagging me to find a man, settle down, and start pumping out babies. Thanks for setting that precedent."

Julie grinned a sheepish grin.

"We lived next door to each other, so we grew up more like sisters than cousins," Julie explained. "Wherever one went, the other followed. That's how Mandy became a cheerleader in high school."

I turned to Mandy and laughed. "You? A cheerleader?"

Mandy put her face in her hands in embarrassment.

"Go, Pioneers!" Julie shouted, raising a fist in the air.

"Thanks, Cuz," she said, glaring at Julie. "Don't think I haven't forgotten I owe you for that one."

"Well," Julie said, "because of you, I spent every chilly February Saturday morning of my childhood sitting at a card table in front of Safeway in a Girl Scout uniform selling Thin Mints."

"Hey! Mom said it built character," Mandy laughed.

"I can't stand those damned cookies to this day." Julie paused and drew in a deep, tortured breath. "Kristen and I talked about the day when our girls would join the Girl Scouts. We suffered, so why shouldn't they?" she laughed. "We were gonna be troop leaders."

Julie started to tear up. She caught herself and brushed the moisture from her eyes with her napkin.

I reached into the pocket of my sport coat and handed her a fresh pack of travel-sized tissues. Lynn and I always carry them. In this line of work, you see a lot of tears.

She took the pack, opened it at the top, and removed a baby blue Kleenex.

"Thank you," she said, gently wiping the corners of her eyes.

"Thank you for agreeing to talk to us," I said.

"I'm really not sure what else I can tell you. I've already told the police everything I know."

"Sometimes, when you repeat a story, you remember more details. Little things you may have forgotten previously. In a case like this, even the tiniest thing can sometimes be of major importance," I told her.

That was something I learned from Lynn. Like I said, the master interrogator.

"Okay," she replied. She removed another tissue and dabbed at her eyes. "Sorry. Been holding it back. I don't want the girls to see me like this."

"Understandable," I said. "You just go ahead and let yourself feel whatever you feel."

Stu poked his head back into the room. "Okay," he said, "I reckon we're about ready to start."

The three of us got up from the dining room table and followed him into the living room, where he'd focused the lights and camera on a brown antique love seat.

"Herringbone china. An early twentieth-century love seat," I said. "Are you an antique collector?"

"My tastes are . . . eclectic. If I see something I like, I buy it. Drives my husband nuts. He keeps threatening to call that show *Hoarders* on me," she said with a faint smile. She wiped at her eyes again. "My mascara must be a mess."

"Here," Mandy said, opening the makeup kit she'd brought in and removing a black mascara tube. She touched up her cousin's eyes and then took out a brush and smoothed a little powder on Julie's forehead to cut down on the glare of the lights.

I reached into my own makeup bag, removed a compact, and did the same.

Mandy said, "Jules, you just forget we're here. Ignore us. All your focus should be on Topher. Look at him. It's just a conversation between the two of you."

"Okay," Julie replied.

"All right," Mandy said. "In three . . . two . . . one . . ."

She pointed to the love seat, and Stu began rolling video.

"So," I said, "how'd you and Kristen Promes first meet?"

The hint of a smile creased her face. "It was in a Lamaze class. I was pregnant with my daughter, Hope, and she and Tom were expecting Taylor. In between our breathing exercises, Kristen kept cracking jokes. We're practicing cleansing breaths, and she's going, 'When do the drugs kick in?'"

She emitted a soft giggle.

"Kristen kept making me laugh, and by the end of that first class, we were joined at the hip. Our husbands liked each other too. They started playing golf together."

"Your husband's name is Jack?"

"Yes," she said, nodding her head. "Jack Wolfer."

"How's he handling all this?"

"Okay, I guess. He sells computer security software so he's on the road quite a bit. He's in Phoenix right now. Please keep that to yourself. We don't want reporters hunting him down. He offered to come home and stay with me and the girls, but I told him to continue with his work and avoid this circus. I feel like I'm a prisoner in my own home with all these trucks and cameras everywhere."

"Well," I said, "you could slip out to church this morning."

She held up her hand to block the camera.

"This part isn't for TV, okay?" she pleaded.

"All right," I agreed.

"The Montesanos next door have a gate that opens into our backyard. Then they snuck us into the back of their garage, and we hid under a pile of blankets in their SUV. Thank God it hadn't heated up outside yet. They drove us right past the jackals out there. We didn't go to our own parish. We drove out of town to a little church in Stockton, where we figured we wouldn't be recognized. Real 'cloak and dagger.'"

She pointed to the white turban she wore covering her hair. "This and a pair of dark glasses helped too. I felt like Taylor Swift hiding from the paparazzi."

The turban she wore looked good. It was a nice complement to the white sundress she wore. She was a thin, stylish woman, the kind who could put on a potato sack and still look like she'd just stepped off the cover of *Vogue*.

"When church was over, the Montesanos brought us home the same way. No one was the wiser. Please don't tell anyone. We may need to repeat that routine. At least by taking them to church, the girls can have some sense of normalcy," she sighed. "If such a thing is even possible right now."

"Don't worry," I said. "Your secret is safe with us."

Julie removed her hand from in front of the camera lens.

"Let's talk about the day of Kristen's disappearance," I suggested.

"Okay," she said.

"I understand that she and Tom were having their annual Fourth of July barbecue?"

"It's quite the social event around here," Julie replied. "People look forward to it all year. Anybody who's anybody in Pleasanton is there."

"But you weren't."

"I woke up feeling lousy. Sore throat. Slight fever. At first, I thought it might be COVID, but I took a rapid test, and it came back negative."

"Where was your husband?"

"Jack was gone as usual. Atlanta that day."

"So, you were home alone?"

"Just me and Hope. I couldn't go to the barbecue. It still worked out, though."

"How do you mean?"

"Kristen's birthday was coming up on August 1. Tom was going to surprise her with an early present. A new Tesla. Her Rav4 was starting to get up in miles. Tom had just closed a big real estate deal and wanted to do something extra special for her. I was supposed to call her and say that I had car trouble and ask if she'd come get me and Hope. When she returned home, this shiny new Tesla was supposed to be sitting in the driveway. Tom would make a big show out of giving it to her in front of all the barbecue guests. Everything is always a production with that guy."

"A real showman, huh?"

"Show-off is more like it. He always has to find some ostentatious way of letting everybody know how well he's doing."

"So, you were already scheduled to call Kristen for a ride, but you got sick?"

"Yeah. Before I could call her, Kristen called me to ask where I was. When I told her we weren't coming, she offered to come and take Hope for the night so I could get some rest. Tom's surprise would have worked out after all. I was still able to get her out of the house so that he could slip the Tesla into their driveway."

"But she never showed up at your place?" I asked.

Julie shook her head, sniffled some more, and wiped at her nose with a fresh tissue.

"It's a ten-, fifteen-minute drive from her house to mine. After about forty-five minutes, I called, and Tom said she'd left awhile ago. I tried calling her cell, thinking maybe she'd had car trouble or something, but it went right to voicemail. After about an hour, I called Tom again."

"And what was his demeanor like?"

"Demeanor?"

"You know. His affect? Was he nervous? Scared? Did he seem like . . . Tom?"

"Well, he was worried, of course. He and Mason jumped into his car and drove her usual route to my house."

"That would be Mason Duffy, Kristen's dad?"

"Yeah," she said, uncrumpling a wad of tissue from her hand and using it to dab her eyes again.

"I can't believe she's gone," Julie said as tears dripped from her eyes and down her cheeks. "Why would somebody do something like that to her? She was the nicest woman on the planet. 'Walking Sunshine,' we used to call her. If only I hadn't let her come over here."

Mandy reached into the frame and patted her cousin's hand.

"You've got to stop thinking like that," Mandy said.

"What else am I supposed to think? If I hadn't lured Kristen over here, she'd still be alive."

"But," I said, "you were supposed to get her to come over here anyway. The Tesla, right?"

"That's true," Julie conceded.

"Either way, she'd have been on that route," I said.

"I guess so."

"So, it isn't your fault," Mandy said.

"This is the first I've heard about the new car," I remarked. "Did you mention it to the police?"

She thought for a moment.

"I don't remember. There was so much going on," she said. "Tom bought it. It's silver with black leather interior. Kristen had a thing for silver cars. She said they reminded her of the DeLorean in *Back to the Future*." She half smiled. "It was her favorite movie."

She wiped her eyes again and then lowered the tissue out of the frame.

"Tom had a big red bow for the roof and everything."

"You saw the Tesla?" I asked.

"I helped Tom pick it out. We got it from the dealership here in town. He wasn't sure which model she'd like best, so he asked me to tag along."

"The press has been staked out at the Promes house since the night Kristen was first reported missing. I don't recall seeing any video of a silver Tesla in the driveway."

"Tom must have put it in the garage before the media storm started," she said. "Lots of those cars are being stolen lately. It's an epidemic."

"Have you talked to Tom much since the tragedy?"

She shook her head.

"He called and asked if Taylor could stay with us when he and Mason first called the police. He saw the media blitz coming. Skyler, Kristen's mom, dropped her off.

"I called after they found Kristen's body. He was too broken up to talk. He asked me if I'd keep Taylor awhile longer. I said, 'Of course.'"

"How long is she staying?"

"As long as Tom needs her to."

"Has he been by to see his daughter since . . . ?"

"No. Too many reporters. They're watching my house because I was one of the last people to talk to Kristen alive. Like I said, Tom and Mason expected the press. They're a prominent family. Nobody expected it to be anything like this, though. It never occurred to us it would get this insane."

"The Fourth of July," I said. "Slow news cycle."

"May I please have a glass of water?" she asked.

"Sure," Mandy said.

She entered the dining room and returned with a full tumbler of water. Julie took a few dainty sips to regain her composure.

"So, has anyone told Taylor about her mother?" I asked.

"Tom did," Julie replied. "Over FaceTime."

She shook her head. "What a way to find out your mother is dead," she mused.

"How'd he break the news to her?"

"Tom told her that her Mommy was in heaven. That she loved her very much and that she'd always watch over her. She'd always be with her."

She let out a sob. "It was heartbreaking," she said.

"How's Taylor doing?"

"She's young. I'm not even sure that she fully understands."

I paused for a moment and looked into her eyes. Her grief was palpable.

"How are you?" I asked.

"I'm a lot of things right now. Sad. Confused. Angry. Guilty. Depends on the moment."

Mandy again patted her cousin's hand.

"It'll be okay," Mandy said. "It's going to be okay."

"My best friend was murdered," she snapped. "It'll never be okay again."

Mandy again patted her hand and then removed it, realizing the action's futility.

"I'm sorry," Julie said.

"It's okay, Jules," Mandy said. She had that helpless feeling of wanting to do something but having no idea exactly what.

I figured I'd gotten all I would get from Julie Wolfer for the moment.

"Thanks for talking to us," I said. "I know it wasn't easy."

"Anything I can do to help find the son of a bitch who did this, I'll do," she said, sadness turning to angry determination.

"Let's keep each other up to speed on anything we hear," Mandy told her.

"Okay," Julie said, nodding her head.

"Thanks for the brunch," I added.

"I was happy to do it. Cooking took my mind off things for a while. Gave me something else to focus on."

"I'll call you later, Cuz," Mandy said.

***

Stu, Mandy, and I headed out to the ENG truck.

"Poor thing's wracked with guilt," Mandy said.

I was climbing into the passenger seat when the familiar strains of the Desi Arnaz Orchestra brought my phone to life. It was Lynn.

"I was just going to call you," I began. "We're just finishing up an exclusive with Julie Wolfer. Turns out she's Mandy's cousin. We're headed back to the station. Thought you might want to view the raw footage before we edit."

"That's great," she said. "I'll meet you there."

THIRTEEN

LYNN STOOD OVER Mandy's shoulder as the three of us squeezed into one of the station's editing bays, reviewing Stu's footage at Julie Wolfer's home.

"That's it," Mandy said, hitting the stop button on the console. "Anything helpful?"

"Didn't know about the Tesla," Lynn said. "Wonder what Pleasanton PD knows about it?"

"Is it important?" I asked.

"Dunno," she replied.

Lynn pulled out her cell and dialed Chief Lane. After a few moments of pleasantries, she asked about the car. She listened intently for a moment, thanked him, and hung up the phone.

"Lane says that the car was in the garage when they first did a walk-through of the house. No red bow on the roof. Just a brand-new silver Tesla parked next to Tom Promes's Mercedes. Lane says it didn't even have plates yet. Still had the dealer's stickers in the window. He also says that Promes never mentioned it as being a birthday surprise for his wife," she said.

"Oversight or withholding information?" I asked.

"Withholding information about what?" Lynn said. "The car was there. It checks out that he bought it from the local dealer and told him he was purchasing it as a surprise birthday present for his wife. I think it's probably just an oversight."

"Their forensics people go over it?"

"They did their due diligence. It was clean. The thing barely had 50 miles on it. They did find the giant red bow in the trunk sealed in plastic. Guess he never got a chance to open it and put it on the roof," she remarked.

"Lane and O'Reilly tell you anything about how Tom Promes acted during their dealings with him?" I asked.

"As you well know, in cases like this, the spouse is always suspect numero uno. Lane says that Tom Promes was well aware of that fact and that, in the hours after the abduction, he was as cooperative and forthcoming with detectives as he could possibly be. Answered every question. Didn't ask for a lawyer. He just wanted his wife found," Lynn stated.

"Did Lane say how he's doing now?"

"He just lost his wife and unborn child to homicide. He's living in the center of a media firestorm. Lane says he's acting how you'd expect a man in his situation to act. Distraught. Overwhelmed. Beside himself with grief, while at the same time trying to hold it together so his little girl can come home soon," she said. "While people react to tragedy differently, Lane and O'Reilly think that his behavior during the whole situation has been appropriate. Plus, where's the Danica Walker connection? So far, there's no reason to believe that Tom Promes and Danica Walker ever met. They don't think he was involved."

"What else did the coroner have to say?" I asked.

"There was no surgical precision with the fetus removals," Lynn said. "The killer used a scalpel, but the procedures, if you can call them that, weren't done by someone with medical skill. No clean incisions—more like a butchering. Horrible."

"Thank God the victims were already dead when it was done," I said.

"Do you think Josie Walker knew about Danica's baby?" Mandy asked.

"I doubt it. I'm sure Josie would have mentioned it when she first asked for my help. She told me everything else."

"Any thoughts on who the father might be?" Lynn asked.

"Not a clue. Her son's father is doing a long stretch at Q. Josie never mentioned another man in her daughter's life. As far as she told me, Danica was all about work, school, and raising her son."

"You know," Mandy said, "we don't necessarily tell our mothers about *every* guy we go out with. I sure don't."

"You think she could have had something going on with somebody Josie didn't know about?" I asked.

"There's a way to find out," Lynn said.

"How?"

"You said she worked part time at a hair salon?" Lynn asked.

"Yes. Place called Braids over in Oakland. Why?"

"Oh, Big Brother," she laughed. "I've been a woman a long time and there is one place where we talk about *everything.*"

"The hair salon?"

Mandy laughed and shook her head.

"Men," she said with a laugh.

"All right, let's take a trip out there tomorrow," I suggested. "It's Sunday. Am I at least correct in assuming that the shop is probably closed today?"

Mandy pulled out her iPhone, tapped it about a dozen times, and then showed it to me. It showed Braids with a customer review of four and a half out of five stars and the shop's hours. Sundays were designated as closed.

"Tomorrow is fine," Lynn said.

"Well," I responded, "I guess that means we're done for the day. I've got a pup at home who needs some attention."

Lynn and I firmed up our arrangements to visit Braids the following morning. I hopped into the Black Beauty, and though it was still warmer than usual, it was pleasant enough for me to let the top down. I was lucky to be headed home to the East Bay early in the day, so I was going against the traffic of suburbanites headed to the city for a Sunday afternoon of recreation. The drive to and across the Bay Bridge was light.

Once I was out of the city, I immediately regretted the decision to let the top down. Without the breeze of San Francisco Bay, the temperature immediately jumped ten degrees as soon as I hit Highway 580 and drove through Oakland. It seemed to climb an extra degree for every mile I drove in the eastbound direction. Though the Beauty came factory equipped with air-conditioning, it was 1957 AC. It wasn't enough for scorchers like today. I made a mental note to look into a modern upgrade. Without one, I didn't know how I would drive in this heat. It was too hot to drive with the top down and an oven inside when the top was up. The fact that it was a black car didn't help the temperature situation either.

I eventually pulled into my Castro Valley garage, soaked to the bone with sweat. Sophie greeted me at the door with her usual tail-wagging enthusiasm. I scratched her gently behind the ear, and she immediately rolled over onto her back, demanding some tummy attention. I obliged. Once I'd given her some love, she followed me to my room, where I changed out of my wet broadcast clothes and into a cool shower. Once I was clean and dry, I put on a light cotton short-sleeved shirt and blue jeans. I slipped my feet into a pair of Italian leather sandals I'd picked up awhile back. The leather felt soft. Like an old wallet I'd been carrying in my hip pocket for years. The sandals were expensive but spending a little extra on good quality is always worth it.

As I left my bedroom, Sophie darted past me and into the family room. She quickly returned carrying a hamburger-shaped squeaky toy that she dropped at my feet. Her signal that she wanted me to take her outside to play fetch. Normally, I'd have done it, but it was now well over 100 degrees outside. Much too hot for dog or man to be out playing in the sun. I went into the kitchen, opened the cupboard, and removed a shrink-wrapped, bone-shaped rawhide chew from the shelf I keep for Sophie's things. I got her to exchange the hamburger for the rawhide and then led her to my den, where I sat at my desk. I fired up my MacBook Air while the pup sat on her pillow in the corner and happily gnawed away.

I did a Google search for murders that had some connection to satanic symbolism. I found nothing in the country in the previous ten years. I then looked for murder cases where a fetus was removed postmortem from the womb of its mother. The only case I could find went back thirty years. A very disturbed woman had been faking a pregnancy. When it came time to produce a child, she murdered a pregnant woman she knew, performed a bathroom Cesarean, delivered her victim's eight-month-developed fetus, and tried to pass the baby off as her own. Her ruse was quickly discovered, and she ended up with government-administered needles of lethal chemicals for her trouble.

I wondered if someone could be doing the same thing in the Promes and Walker cases. Could they be taking babies to either pass off as their own or sell on some black market somewhere? I quickly dismissed the idea. Kristen Promes was less than five months pregnant. According to the coroner, Danica Walker was still in her first trimester. Neither fetus was developed enough to be viable outside the womb. So, why go to the trouble of removing them? Trophies of the kills? Human sacrifices to the devil? Was it a sterile woman who was exacting "revenge" against women who were having babies when she couldn't?

The whole practice was risky for the murderer. Besides being gruesome and unnecessary, it added time to the commission of the crime. Dissecting a human uterus is not something you can do "lickity split." The longer the killer was with the bodies, the greater the odds they'd be discovered. There are no signs that the dissections took place at the burial sites. The coroner says they were butchered. There would have been a bloody mess. They would have had to have been done someplace where the killer or killers didn't feel rushed. Somewhere they knew they could take their time without fear of being interrupted.

I went back farther in time in my Google search and delved into Wikipedia as well. Although it had been decades, there had been cases of dead bodies found with pentacles or pentagrams marking them. Almost every single one was carved into the stomach. None on the forehead like our vics. Maybe that was because after cutting up the victims' wombs, there was no room to leave a signature on the torso.

I searched pentacles and pentagrams. Their usage was even more extensive than I had initially thought. They've been used over the centuries by everybody from Satanists to Wiccans to the Freemasons. They've been found on ancient Egyptian tombs and ancient Greek coins. They've been used as symbols of protection and perfection. Among Christians, the star's five points have been used to symbolize the five crucifixion wounds of Christ. In some pagan religions, its points represent the five elements: air, fire, water, earth, and spirit. Today, it's primarily associated with devil worship. Trying to figure out exactly what the symbol was meant to represent in this context was like looking for a specific grain of sand at the beach.

After about three hours, I called it quits for the day and turned off my laptop. Sophie had made a good dent in her rawhide bone, and the evening temperature outside had dropped to a point where it was at least tolerable. I took the dog and her squeaky hamburger outside and played fetch, all the while thinking about ways that the murders of Kristen Promes and Danica Walker could be connected—two very different women from two very different worlds yet suffering the same grisly fates. Maybe there was no connection. Maybe we were just looking for a random serial killer. If that was the case, that meant that there would be more mutilated mothers' bodies before this was finished.

FOURTEEN

AS USUAL, THE Cracked Egg was packed on Monday morning with law enforcement officers from all the local jurisdictions downing cups of hot coffee and scarfing Jared's famous omelets. There were deputies from the Alameda County Sheriff's Department as well as officers from Oakland, Hayward, and San Leandro. A few from Pleasanton and San Ramon were also sprinkled into the mix. Lots of police live in the area and start their days here. Few live in the cities they serve, and with good reason. Who wants to run into the perp they arrested last month for shoplifting when they're at Baskin-Robbins with their kids? Or bump into the parolee they helped lock up while at Farmers' Market with their spouse some Saturday afternoon? No cop wants to be pestered night and day by neighbors with problems or begged to "fix" tickets.

I walked through the restaurant, doling out waves and perfunctory "hellos" to various officers I knew. I found Lynn at our usual table sipping her traditional chamomile tea as Jared hovered over her.

"Hey," I said, pulling out the chair opposite my sister and planting myself in it.

"Good morning, brother-in-law," Jared said, brushing the sandy-brown hair from his eyes.

"Morning, Jared."

Jared looked at his feet and then at me, embarrassed. "Listen," he said, "about that scene at Shokumatsu—"

"Forget it," I said. "It's over."

"You know the whole thing was Lynn's idea, right?"

My sister glared at him. "Oh great," she said. "Throw *me* under the bus."

"Well, it was!" he protested.

I saw a few nights of couch slumber in Jared's future for that.

"It's okay. Really," I said. "Just leave my love life, or lack thereof, to me."

"We're just worried about you, that's all," Jared said. "We don't like the idea of you in that big house all by yourself."

"Hey, I'm not by myself. Sophie's there."

"You know what he means," Lynn said.

"Little Sister, after my last two relationships, my heart is just a great big hunk of scar tissue," I stated. "All I need is work, so let's get to it. Work and breakfast."

"Egg white omelet with Swiss and tomato? Honeydew melon on the side, hold the toast?" Jared asked.

"That sounds good," I said, "but let's make it jack cheese this time."

"I'll have it up in a jiff," he said as he kissed my sister on the top of her head in an act of contrition and walked off in the direction of the kitchen.

Lynn drifted off into another world, deep in thought. She'd been like that since we were kids, able to tune out the world around her and mentally go to another place and time to concentrate on a problem.

"And where exactly are you now, Space Cadet?" I asked.

"Huh?" she said, snapping back to the present. "Sorry, just thinking."

"About?"

"The case. I can't wrap my mind around this baby thing," she said. "What kind of maniac would do something like that? I've seen some sick shit since I started carrying this badge, but nothing as vile as this. This is beyond the pale."

"I know what you mean," I said. "I've covered some sickening stories myself. Heartbreaking stuff, but this . . . It really gets to you, doesn't it?"

Lynn squeezed the juice from a wedge of lemon into her cup and then placed it on a saucer. She opened two packets of Stevia, dumped them into the teacup, and slowly began to stir.

"I talked to Paul Marian, one of our criminal profilers. He went over the crime scene and autopsy photos. He got a few things from the crime scene pics, but not a lot. The Promes home is like the Cleaver house on *Leave It to Beaver*. It's one of those places that's so neat it doesn't look like anybody really lives there. It's like one of those houses professionally staged for sale."

She took another small sip of tea.

"The burial sites didn't tell him much either. Just that the graves were hastily dug, hence their shallowness. As for the way the wombs were carved up," she said, shaking her head in disbelief, "this wasn't done by anyone with any medical training or expertise. Those bodies were just slashed up quickly and violently. Cut into a bloody mess. Marian thinks we're looking for a woman."

"Funny, I had the same thought," I said. "Maybe a woman who can't have natural kids of her own and resents other women who can."

"Exactly. Maybe you should give up that television gig and come work for us," she said, raising her teacup again to her lips.

"Sometimes I feel like I already do," I quipped. "I'm just better paid."

She took a sip, smiled, and put the cup back on its saucer.

"He have any thoughts about the pentacles?"

"He's not sure," she said as Jared returned to the table with a steaming plate of breakfast for me.

"One egg white omelet with jack and tomatoes. Honeydew melon on the side," he said, sliding a white oval-shaped plate in front of me.

"That was fast."

"Premium service for family," he said. "Anything else?"

"Maybe some coffee?"

He gestured to one of his servers, who was refilling coffee cups at a nearby table, and directed him to ours. The waiter, a pimply-faced college kid around nineteen, grabbed an empty mug from one of the busboys, filled it, and set it in front of me.

"Thanks," I said to the kid.

"My pleasure, sir," he responded.

Jared always knew how to pick good staff. It was one of the reasons the place was always so packed.

"Anything else?" the kid asked.

"No, this is perfect, thank you."

The young man nodded and resumed making his way around the restaurant, filling half-empty coffee mugs.

"Nice kid," I said to Jared.

"Yeah. Jason Diaz. Just hired him. Conscientious kid. Studying sociology at Cal State. Going to school full time and working full time to help support his single mother and little sisters," Jared said. "They don't make many like him anymore. He's gonna go far."

I nodded. I felt for the kid. Working your way through school is not easy these days with tuition prices as high as they are now. I did it, but it was a lot cheaper back then. Our aunt Jessie raised us while working her way up from the secretarial pool to a highly paid executive position at one of the big multinational corporations in the city. She could have afforded to put me through San Francisco State, but she made me pay half the tuition and fees myself. She said I'd appreciate my degree more if at least some of the money came from my own pocket. She was self-made and wanted to pass that same drive on to me and Lynn. So, I worked at the mall selling shoes to get through school. Lynn went into the army, and then they paid for her education through the GI Bill when she got out.

"Well, if there's nothing else, it's back to the salt mines," Jared said as he left our table and began making his own rounds of the restaurant, checking on the satisfaction of customers and glad-handing dining police officers.

"So," I said to Lynn, "the pentacles?"

"Marian says the jury is still out on those. He's never seen this kind of signature on a body before. He's not exactly sure what it tells us about the perp. It could have something to do with Satan worship or human sacrifice. Or it could be something else."

"Like what?"

"A cult. A gang initiation. Some sick loner who's listened to too many serial killer podcasts. I'll bet you spent all last night researching devil worshippers, didn't you?"

"Not all night," I said, taking a bite of my omelet. It was bland, as egg whites tend to be. I grabbed the bottle of green Tobasco in the center of the table and doused the omelet in hot sauce. Then I took another bite. Perfect.

"Marian thinks there's also the possibility that it's none of the above, and the killer may just be trying to lead us down a rabbit hole of Satanists and occult enthusiasts," Lynn said.

"Brilliant way to throw law enforcement off the scent."

"Yeah," she said. "It's definitely a possibility. Either way, we're looking for a wacko."

"Does he think this 'wacko' is done killing?"

Lynn took another sip of her tea. "Probably not," she said, returning her teacup to its place.

I finished my breakfast, slipped a twenty on the table for Jason to help with his college fund, and followed Lynn out to the parking lot, where we jumped into her unmarked. Soon, we were on I-580 West, headed toward Oakland. Once we got there, we took the Lakeshore exit and followed it to Lake Merritt. It was already shaping up to be another warm day, and the lake was bustling with activity. Runners were plodding along the trail that surrounded the reservoir. The Cal Berkeley rowing team was going through its morning drills, the oarsmen and women rhythmically gliding through the still waters as the coxswain called out the repeated order to "row." A trio of young mothers talked as they wheeled their toddlers' strollers toward Fairyland.

Fairyland is Lake Merritt's small children's amusement park. It has been an Oakland institution for decades. Auntie used to bring Lynn and me there often when we were kids. We loved it, watching Popo the Clown's silly antics and playing in fairy-tale replicas of the Three Little Pigs' houses and Cinderella's pumpkin coach. Local lore has it that Walt Disney himself visited the place incognito in the 1950s when he was looking for ideas for building Disneyland.

We turned down one of the side streets directly adjacent to Fairyland and came across a triplex that had been converted into a commercial space. A UPS store sat on the corner, and a line of hot, uncomfortable people holding packages of varying sizes stretched outside the building and spilled onto the sidewalk in front. Next to the store sat a small Greek restaurant with the words GUS'S PLACE emblazoned across a sign above its glass door. We could see an older man, whom I assumed to be "Gus," wiping down tables and arranging chairs in anticipation of the lunch rush.

A small shop with a glass front was next to Gus's Place. Cursive gold lettering ran diagonally across a large picture window that read BRAIDS. A late-model Audi was pulling out of a space on the street directly in front of the salon, and Lynn quickly darted into it. Good parking karma in this part of town was rare.

We parked and walked in. Three stylists' chairs sat in front of large mirrors as a pair of hairdressers worked on customers. One of the stylists was an African American woman in her mid to late forties. She was rail thin with brown-lacquered nails and straight, jet-black, shoulder-length hair. In her chair sat a high school girl patiently enduring the tedium of having a new weave applied.

There was an empty stylist chair next to her, followed by a chair being worked by a much-younger Black woman. I'd have put her in her early twenties. She was applying hair coloring chemicals to a light-skinned woman who appeared to be biracial, her features an attractive blend of African American, Asian, and some other indistinguishable ethnicity.

In the rear of the shop, an eight-by-ten black-and-white photo of a grinning Danica Walker hung over a glass table covered with large white candles, notes, sympathy cards, and an assortment of different flowers—a makeshift shrine.

"Hi," Lynn said to the older stylist, "we're looking for the owner or manager."

"Who's asking?" came the woman's terse reply.

Lynn flashed her shield.

The woman stopped what she was doing and carefully inspected the badge. The teen in the chair also looked at the badge. Then at Lynn. Then the badge again.

"San Francisco PD? You're on the wrong side of the bay, aren't you?" the stylist said to Lynn.

She then scrutinized me.

"And you . . . You're that guy on television, aren't you? Topher-something, right?"

"Topher Davis," I said, extending a hand.

She again looked me over carefully before gripping my hand and giving it a weak shake.

"Sharice Jenkins," she said. "I own this place."

"This is my sister, Lynn," I said, concluding the formalities.

Sharice grabbed Lynn's hand with the same passivity with which she'd shaken mine.

"You have a very nice salon here," Lynn said, looking around and putting away her badge.

"Thank you. What can I do for you?" she asked. "Is this about what happened to Danica?"

"I'm afraid it is," Lynn said.

Sharice Jenkins looked at the floor and shook her head.

"Now, why would somebody do something like that to her?" she said, both disgusted and perplexed. "She was a nice girl."

"That's what we're trying to find out," I said. "We understand she worked here part time?"

Sharice nodded. "Saturdays. For about four years now. She came in here for years before that to get her hair braided. Then one day she noticed I had an empty booth and asked if she could try braiding hair. She'd been braiding the hair of some girls in her neighborhood. Said she was good at it."

Sharice smiled.

"She was great at it. She could do anybody's hair except her own. I'd braid hers."

She went back to working on her client's weave.

"It got so she was booked solid every Saturday. From eight o'clock in the morning when we opened until closing at five."

Sharice Jenkins looked at Lynn's coif.

"You ever thought about getting your hair braided?"

"Not really," Lynn replied.

"You should," Sharice said. "Some long black braids. A few beads for color. It would look good on you."

"I'll keep it in mind," Lynn said. "Did you know that Danica was pregnant?"

"Sure," said the girl in Sharice's chair. "We all did."

"And you are?" I asked.

"Cassandra Dearing. Cassie."

"So, Cassie," Lynn continued, "Danica told you?"

"Yep," Cassie said. "I was here one Saturday morning while she braided my sister Sandra's hair when Danica said, 'I hope I have a girl this time.'"

"Yeah," Sharice confirmed. "I was here that day shortly before she disappeared. Came out of the blue."

"Who was the father?" I asked.

"She didn't say," Cassie replied.

"Was she seeing anyone regularly? A boyfriend, maybe?" Lynn asked.

"She talked a little about a guy she was seeing," said the other stylist.

"That's Cynthia," Sharice said. "She's been here almost as long as Danica was."

"But I work here full time," Cynthia said. "This is my career. It was just a side hustle for Danica. She had school and some job in the city."

"At a law firm," I said.

"Yeah," Cynthia replied.

"What can you tell us about the guy she was seeing?" Lynn asked. "Did she mention a name?"

"She just called him Cuff Links," Cynthia laughed. "Said he always wore gold cuff links, so that was her nickname for him."

"Was Cuff Links the father of her baby?" I asked.

"I dunno. Maybe," Cynthia said. "He's the only guy she mentioned around here over the last year."

"Did he ever come in? You ever meet him or see a picture?" Lynn asked.

"No," Sharice said. "He never came in. We'd tease her about making him up. Since we never saw him, we used to say he was her imaginary boyfriend."

"That's right," Cynthia added. "We never laid eyes on him. We just heard about him."

"I was here one Saturday when he sent her roses. Remember?" Cassie said to Sharice.

"That's right. A beautiful bouquet. Three dozen long-stemmed red ones."

"Not cheap," Lynn said. "Sounds like Cuff Links had a few bucks."

"Maybe," Sharice said.

"Did anybody get a look at the card?" I asked.

"No card. Danica said she knew who they were from," Sharice said. "I always had the feeling that they were sneaking around."

"Sneaking around?" Lynn repeated.

"You know, on the QT. Like nobody was supposed to know," Sharice said. "She used to tell us how they'd meet at restaurants in the South Bay. San Jose spots. Places not too close to here. 'Out of the way,' as they say."

"And she would always tell us that it was late at night. 'Rendezvous,' she called them," Cynthia added.

"Sounded to me like she was his side piece," Sharice said.

"I thought the same thing," Cynthia agreed. "That the guy was married."

"Any idea how long this little romance had been going on?" Lynn asked.

"I want to say two, maybe three months," Sharice said. "At least that's when she started talking about him around here."

Sharice stopped working on Cassie's hair and glanced at Danica's picture on the wall above the shrine.

"She didn't deserve this," Sharice whispered. "She was special. She was going places. It shouldn't have ended like this."

"No," Lynn said in a soft voice. "It shouldn't have."

"Have you talked to Josie, her mother?" Sharice asked.

"Yes," I answered.

"How's she doing?"

"I guess about as well as can be expected."

"I need to call her," Sharice said. "Tell her how sorry I am and how special Danica was to all of us."

"I'm sure she'd appreciate that," I told her.

Sharice Jenkins brushed a hand over watery eyes and then returned to working on Cassie's hair.

"Life is so goddamned unfair," she said.

"That it is," I responded. "That it is."

Lynn and I rode back toward The Egg in silence.

"This one is really getting to you, isn't it?" she asked.

"Well, isn't it getting to you?"

She paused for a moment. "More than usual, Big Bro. More than usual."

"So, Danica was having an affair with a married man. Casanova's wife finds out and decides to take out her rival."

"It's a good theory," I said. "But if that's the case, how does the Promes murder fit in?"

"You always have to mess up my bingo card, don't you?" she said.

She was referring to when we were kids and playing bingo with Auntie. We placed our little wooden chips on our cards as Auntie called numbers. When Lynn yelled, "Bingo," I was so angry that I knocked the chips off her card before she could verify her win. I was seven, and my sister never let me forget it.

Lynn's cell rang. She pressed the hands-free button on her steering wheel, putting the call on speaker.

"Sloan," she answered.

"Hi, Lynn. Courtney Lane," came the reply.

"Hey, Courtney."

"What are you doing?"

"Just finished talking to Danica Walker's coworkers at her weekend salon gig."

"Get anything useful?" he asked.

"Sounds like she might have been having an affair with a married man," Lynn responded.

"Funny you should mention that," he said.

"Oh?"

"I've got a woman in my office right now who says that Tom Promes was playing around. Want to talk to her?"

"We'll be there in forty-five minutes."

Lynn clicked off the phone.

"I wonder if Tom Promes wears gold cuff links," she said.

FIFTEEN

"**N**OW, MS. HUNT, please tell Detective Sloan and Mr. Davis what you told me."

Bethany Hunt was a wispy young woman in her early twenties with short brown hair and bangs that covered her eyebrows. Her eyes were bluish grey, her skin pale. Almost milklike. A thin layer of bright red lipstick coated her mouth. She was uncomfortable as she fidgeted in the hard wooden chair she sat on.

We were in the Pleasanton PD interview room. I'm unsure why Chief Lane put her in there for our powwow. It was a mostly barren room with wooden chairs, a table, and hidden cameras. It's off-putting for most people, and that's the point. The uninviting environment can throw off your equilibrium. Criminal suspects tend to be a little more forthcoming when they're uncomfortable. That didn't apply in this case. As far as I knew, Bethany Hunt wasn't suspected of anything.

"But I just told you," Bethany said. "Can't you just tell them? I answered all of your questions."

Frustrated fingers with neatly trimmed unpolished nails ran through her short hair, brushing bangs from in front of her eyes.

"It's better if they hear it from you," Lane said. "They may have some questions of their own."

She sighed with the annoyed exhale of a seventh grader being told to finish her math homework.

"Fine," she said. "Where do you want me to start?"

"How about at the beginning," Lynn suggested with the patience of a parent.

Another sigh.

"About six weeks ago, Phillip, that's my boyfriend, and I were spending the weekend in Monterey. He's working on his master's in education at USF and hasn't had a lot of time lately. This trip was supposed to be his way of making it up to me."

"Go on," Lane said.

"We stayed at this little boutique hotel on Cannery Row— the Seaside Inn. Nice place. Small. Cozy. Close to everything. Not that anything is far away from anything in Monterey," she said. "May I please have some water?"

Chief Lane reached across the far end of the table where a half-dozen small plastic bottles of Crystal Geyser sat. He grabbed one, cracked open the top, and handed it to Bethany. She grasped the bottle and took a big drink, swallowing about a third of it.

"Thanks," she said. "I'm a little nervous. I always get cotton-mouth when I'm nervous."

"No reason to be nervous," I said. "You're among friends."

She cautiously smiled.

"Anyway, we're at the Seaside Inn at the front desk, and another couple stands behind us to check in as well. They were all lovey-dovey. Holding hands and kissing. Phillip and I figured they were newlyweds on their honeymoon or something. That's how they were acting."

She took a smaller sip from her water bottle.

"Don't get me wrong. I'm not a prude. I have nothing against public displays of affection. I think PDA is fine in its place. This was just excessive. I'd have told them to get a room, but that's just what they were standing there to do. So, we check in, go to our room, unpack our bags, and head to Fisherman's Wharf. We walked along the pier and browsed the little tourist shops. At the entrance of the wharf was this old Italian guy with an accordion and a little . . . spider monkey, I think they're called. A small audience of tourists surrounded him. The old man would play his accordion for the people, and then some in the crowd would hold up a dime or a quarter, and the spider monkey would run over, take the coins out of their hands, and drop them into a wicker basket at the old man's feet."

"Tell them what happened next," Chief Lane said.

"So, we're watching the guy play his accordion, and when he finishes, Phillip pulls out a quarter. The monkey takes it and drops it into the basket. The old man thanks us and then says what a lovely couple we are and asks if we'd like him to take our picture. We figure, what the heck, ya know?"

A larger drink of Crystal Geyser.

"I hand him my phone; Phillip puts his arm around me, we smile, and the old man takes a picture. When I look at what he shot, behind us in the background is the couple from the hotel, still making out."

She reached into her purse, pulled out her phone, tapped it a few times, and handed it to Lynn. Lynn looked at it and then gave the phone to me. In the foreground was Bethany Hunt, her boyfriend's arm firmly around her waist. The pair smiling like young lovers. Behind them was a man in a passionate embrace with a woman. The woman's back was to the camera, and you couldn't see her face, just the long, ponytail she wore in the back. The man's face was in full view. Tom Promes.

"I saw the guy on the news after they found his wife's body, and I knew I'd seen him before, but I couldn't place him. Then I remembered the picture. I found it on my phone, and I was right. Phillip told me to call the police, so . . . Here I am," she said. "I thought it might be important. Is it?"

"It may very well be," Lynn said, pulling out her own phone and bringing up a picture of Kristen Promes. She held it out for Bethany Hunt to see.

"Was this the woman he was with?" Lynn asked, showing her the photo.

Bethany looked at Lynn's phone.

"Nope," she said. "Definitely not her."

"You say it was six weeks ago?" I chimed in. "Was the woman pregnant?"

"No. At least she wasn't showing if she was."

"Believe me," Lynn said, "at almost five months, she'd be showing. Can you tell us anything else about her? Anything at all?"

Bethany shook her head and then drained the rest of her water bottle.

"No. Not really," she said. "She was just a woman."

"Was she Black, white, Asian?" I asked.

"Definitely white. Late twenties. Early thirties. Dark hair, as you can see in the picture. It was down on her shoulders when we were at the hotel. She must have put it in a ponytail before they went to the wharf. It gets windy down there."

"Would you mind if we took a copy of that picture?" Lynn asked.

"Help yourself," Bethany replied.

"Chris . . ." Lynn said, looking at me.

"Way ahead of you," I said as I Airdropped the picture on Ms. Hunt's phone to our phones.

"Did you hear the man call the woman by name?" I asked.

"You mean like Linda or something? Nope. Just a few terms of endearment. Honey. Sweetheart. Babe. You know, stuff like that."

"You didn't, by chance, get a look at their car? What were they driving?" Lynn inquired.

"Nope. Just saw them at the front desk and in that picture. To be honest, I didn't even see them at the wharf. Had no idea they were behind us until I saw them on my phone," she answered.

Lynn reached into her pocket and pulled out a card she handed the young woman. "Can you please do me a favor and call me if you think of anything else?" Lynn asked.

"Of course," Bethany said, taking the card and looking it over. "So, that *is* the husband of that murdered woman? And the woman he was with wasn't his wife?"

"It looks that way," Lynn said.

Bethany shook her head. "Cheating on his pregnant wife. That's a special kind of piece of shit."

"Never try to figure out why humans do what they do," I said. "You'll drive yourself crazy."

Bethany nodded.

"Can I go now?" she asked. "I promised Phillip I'd pick him up from the BART station after class today."

"Sure, Ms. Hunt," Lane said, "You're free to go. Thank you. You've been a big help."

"We'd appreciate it if you'd keep the information you gave us and the picture confidential for now," Lynn added. "We wouldn't want to do anything that would impede the investigation."

"Of course," she said, rising from her chair. "I hope you nail the son of a bitch."

Chief Lane escorted her out the door.

Lynn looked at me.

"Well," she said, "there's your motive."

"Yep. If you're a married man with a girlfriend, and your wife turns up dead, that's your ass," I said. "Scott Peterson 101."

"Maybe, maybe not," Lynn said, deep in thought. "How does this tie in with Danica Walker? It's apparent that both women met their demise at the hands of the same killer—"

"Or killers," I said.

"Or killers," Lynn repeated. "I can see Tom Promes killing his wife to be with his girlfriend, but why kill Danica? Bethany Hunt said that the other woman was a white woman, and there were no braids with decorative beads on the woman in the picture, so we know the affair wasn't with her. How does Danica Walker fit into all this?"

"Maybe she found out about the affair, and Promes killed her to keep her quiet."

"But we don't have any evidence that Danica Walker ever met Tom Promes. They traveled in different worlds. Hell, different universes."

"Maybe if we can find out who the mistress is, we'll find a connection," I said.

"Maybe," Lynn replied. "But we're still left with another problem regarding Tom Promes being the killer. He has an airtight alibi. He was at the barbecue at the time Kristen disappeared. A hundred people can vouch for his whereabouts."

"Ever hear of murder for hire?" I asked.

"Possible. But if it was a hit man, we still don't know why he'd kill Danica. And what about the pentacles? And the babies cut out of the wombs? Not your typical hit man's MO. A pro would want to get in and out as quickly and efficiently as possible. No time for impromptu hysterectomies."

"Maybe he hired cultists," I said. "Paid them to commit the murders and told them they could ritualize the bodies any way they wanted to."

Lynn shook her head in disgust.

"Having the mother of your child killed and her unborn baby carved out of her womb? Bethany was right."

"About what?"

"If Tom Promes did this, he is a piece of shit."

"Any thoughts on who the mystery woman in the picture might be?" I asked.

"Not a clue. You?"

"I got nothing. I'll take this picture back to the station and look at it on a bigger screen. Maybe there's something we're missing here."

Lynn drove me the twenty minutes it took to get back to The Egg, where I picked up the Black Beauty. Then she headed to her office at 850 Bryant Street. I drove to the station. Traffic was light across the Bay Bridge. We'd missed the horrendous morning commute. It was warming up, and the view of San Francisco from the bridge was crystal clear. Not a patch of fog in sight.

Half an hour later, I sat at my desk in the Broadcast Center, looking at the photo Bethany had given us on the large screen of my Mac desktop. I zoomed in on every inch of the picture and went over it five times. Not much in the closeup that I didn't see on my phone. Bethany and her boyfriend grinning in the foreground. Tom Promes kissing a woman. All that was visible was her ponytail. Nothing identifiable. You couldn't even see the woman's neck.

I zoomed out. About a dozen people were behind Promes and his paramour going about their own touristy business. An older African American couple walking hand in hand along the pier. A mother with two prepubescent boys, skipper's caps on their heads, entering a seashell store. A dark-haired white woman darting into the Old Fisherman's Grotto seafood restaurant. A middle-aged white man applying mustard to a soft pretzel he'd just purchased from a food cart. I moved the cursor back over to the woman in Tom Promes's arms and zoomed in to the back of her head as close as possible without creating distortion. Just dark hair in a ponytail. Not even a hint of scalp. Promes's hands weren't even visible. He was apparently holding the woman's face as he kissed her. The picture was a bust. It only proved one thing. Tom Promes has a girlfriend.

A light rap on the frame of my open door caused me to look up and see Mandy standing there.

"Good morning," I said.

"You mean, 'Good afternoon,'" she corrected.

I glanced at the upper right-hand corner of the computer screen. Two o'clock already. Where had the day gone?

"I was going to go to that Italian deli in North Beach you like and pick up some sandwiches. Can I bring you something?"

I thought for a moment. I'd been so busy I completely forgot about lunch.

"How about an Italian salad with dressing on the side? No salami or prosciutto."

"Got it," she said. "Whatcha doin'?"

"Looking at a picture from a potential witness. Come here and take a look. Maybe you can spot something I'm missing."

Mandy walked over and stood behind my desk.

I zoomed out and pointed to Bethany Hunt in the foreground.

"That's the witness. She and her boyfriend were on vacation in Monterey about six weeks ago and had this picture taken."

"I love Monterey," she said.

She looked closer.

"Hey, is that . . .?"

"Tom Promes," I said. "And the woman he's kissing is *not* his wife."

Blood suddenly drained from Mandy's face. She was so white she was almost translucent.

"What's the matter?"

"No, it isn't his wife," she said, stunned. "It's my cousin, Julie."

SIXTEEN

MANDY'S LEGS BEGAN to buckle. She grabbed the chair opposite mine and plopped into it.

"Are you okay?"

"Give me a minute," she said as she rubbed her forehead. "Let me see it again."

I swiveled the monitor around so she could see it from her seat. She looked at it for a moment, zoomed in on the back of the woman's ponytail, and then shook her head.

"What makes you so sure it's Julie Wolfer?" I asked. "You can't see her face."

"It's Julie," she said.

"Are you sure?"

"Positive," Mandy replied.

"How can you tell?"

"I told you, we grew up together. I spent my childhood running behind her. You see that little twist at the bottom of the ponytail?"

I looked at the portion of the picture Mandy was now pointing to. The woman's hair had a thin little braid at the bottom of her ponytail. I'd missed it before.

"When we were in sixth grade, we played soccer. Our team was the Stingrays. Julie always wore her hair in a ponytail to keep it out of her face while playing. We both did. She had the habit of twisting a tiny little braid at the end of her ponytail. She called it her tail. Like a stingray has. It was her trademark. I can't believe she's still doing that," Mandy said. "Remember, we couldn't see her hair when we did the interview because of the turban she was wearing."

She let out a long sigh. It seemed to settle her a little bit.

"I'm sorry," I said.

"My God. She's having an affair with the murdered woman's husband."

She put her face in her hands. "Oh, Jules," she said. "What have you gotten yourself into?"

I drew an uncomfortable breath.

"Sleeping with her best friend's husband," she continued, shaking her head. "She's *got* a husband and a little girl, for God's sake. I thought she'd grown up and knocked that crap off."

"What do you mean?"

She closed her eyes, raised her hands to her head, and gently massaged her temples.

"When we were kids, we were kind of tomboys. We rode skateboards and played video games and soccer. We even played on the boys' flag football team in junior high."

"You? Football?" I said with a disbelieving smile.

"Hey, we were good. I was even a quarterback in eighth grade. Julie was a wide receiver. Caught just about every pass I threw to her. And could she run . . ." Mandy said, opening her eyes. "There wasn't a boy in the league who could catch her. The coach called me 'Joe Montana' and Julie, 'Jerry Rice.' Whenever he'd call a play where he wanted me to pass to Jules, he'd say, 'Montana to Rice.'"

She smiled. "That was eighth grade. High school was an entirely different matter."

"How so?"

"Like I said, we were tomboys. Then, over the summer, Julie changed. She 'blossomed,' as they say. She grew about two inches. Her chest grew three. She started wearing makeup and dresses," Mandy said. "I remember the first day of school freshman year, she came dressed to the nines. Short skirt. Halter top. Heels. Tan as a bronze goddess. She was a knockout. As she walked to her locker, every boy's head in the hallway snapped in her direction. She was really something."

"And you?" I asked.

"I showed up in my denim overalls and Chuck Taylors."

I laughed. Mandy smiled.

"It wasn't long before she was the most popular girl in school. Made varsity cheerleader and everything. She was every teenage boy's dream girl. She ate it up, and she took advantage of it. She had smart, nerdy guys doing her algebra homework for her. I don't think she carried her own books to class the entire four years we were there. And the boyfriends . . . She had a different one every two weeks."

"But you told me you were a cheerleader too," I said.

"Yeah. She talked me into trying out, and I made the JV squad. Like I said, Jules was varsity. Bigger deal in the high school hierarchy."

"What did you mean when you said you thought she'd 'stopped that crap'?" I asked.

"Jules and I drifted apart during those four years, and she became one of the 'mean girls.' She knew all the boys wanted her, and she'd steal other girls' boyfriends. Sometimes, she'd do it out of ego. Sometimes, she'd do it out of revenge. Junior year, she got into a snit with Sandy Chessman and decided to get even with her by stealing her boyfriend . . . right before prom. Poor Sandy was so distraught she didn't come to school for three days."

"Wow. Teenage girls can be brutal," I said.

"She even did it to me: Phil Eggleston, my first boyfriend. Julie went after him and stole him right out from under me. No pun intended."

"Why?"

"Because she *could*. It was a game to her," she said. "I punched her in the mouth and gave her a fat lip. Then it was *her* turn to stay out of school for three days while the swelling went down."

She began to massage her temples again.

"I know at brunch, it seemed like we were all chummy, but we were never as close after I hit her. We'd pass each other in the hall at school and nod. We'd be cordial at family gatherings, but that was about it. I was actually surprised when she asked me to be a bridesmaid at her wedding to Jack."

"Tell me about Jack," I said.

"Not much to tell," she replied. "Jules went to college at UC Irvine and met him there. Nice enough guy. Longest relationship she'd ever had. She met him on the first day of classes, and they ended up dating through graduation. They got married the following summer."

"What's he like?"

"Quiet. Reserved. Hard worker. Runs his own company. He developed an app. Maybe you've heard of it? Starfire."

"It has something to do with computer security, right?"

"Yeah. Businesses use it to try to keep the hackers out. He does very well. My mom says he pulls in a high six figures every year. That allows Julie to be a stay-at-home mom. Lucky for her. She got her degree in philosophy. Not real marketable."

"Jack travels a lot?"

"Yeah. He's always jetting off someplace to meet with some corporate bigwig about switching over their computer security software to Starfire," she said. "I guess Jules got bored being home alone all the time and decided to see if she could still steal another woman's man. If she still 'had it.' Jack, Hope, and the soccer mom routine must not have been enough. I thought she'd outgrown that nonsense. Apparently not."

I took a beat.

"Mandy," I said softly, "Julie is the one who lured Kristen Promes out of the house on the day she disappeared. She and Tom . . . They could have been in on it together."

"No!" Mandy snapped. "No! Okay, we now know that she's an adulteress. Make her wear a scarlet A. She's a lot of things, but my cousin is no killer. Kristen Promes never even made it to Jules's house that day. She disappeared en route."

"So, Julie says. The plan could have been for Julie to lure Kristen over and then maybe hide behind the front door or something, invite her in, then catch her by surprise and wrap a wire around her neck."

"Jules would never be involved in something like that," Mandy objected, her face morphing into crimson anger. "There's no reason. She already *had* Tom. As a matter of fact, we don't know if that picture is even real. It could be photoshopped or something."

"It isn't," I said. "I've examined it thoroughly."

"Oh," she said, "like you're a computer expert?"

"The police have people on staff who can verify its authenticity, but you know it's real. Her 'tail.'"

"Okay, so let's assume the picture is real. If she and Tom Promes wanted to be together that badly, they could have gotten divorces. She'd never resort to murder."

I didn't say anything. Denial. A river in Egypt.

"And what about the mutilation? If she'd garroted her in her house, where did she mutilate the body? Where's all the blood that mess would have spilled?"

"Remember," I said, "I've been to her house. She's got a garage."

"So let me get this straight. You think Jules tells Kristen to come over, then when Kristen gets there, she hides behind the door or something, tells her to come in, jumps her, garrotes her, then somehow drags the body all the way into the garage *by herself*, cuts out Kristen's baby, and carves a satanic symbol onto her forehead. All while her daughter is up in her bedroom, by the way, and then she drives Kristen out to Lake Del Valle and buries her in a shallow grave. Give me a break."

"I'd forgotten that her kid was there."

"And Kristen's car was found en route. Not at Jules's house."

"Julie could have driven to Bernal Avenue once the deed was done. Then returned home, called the Promes home, and asked why Kristen hadn't arrived yet," I said.

"She just wouldn't be involved in something like that. We're not as close as we once were, but I know my cousin. She can be catty and manipulative, but murder . . ."

Mandy looked at the floor.

"I need to talk to her," she said.

"You shouldn't right now. Not about this. I'm sure that Chief Lane will put his detectives on her as soon as I tell him we've identified the woman in the picture. I can guarantee he won't want her to know that the police consider her a suspect."

"They don't," she snapped.

"Mandy . . . You know as well as I do that they will. In a murder like this, the partner is *always* suspect number one. If there's an affair, the mistress or boyfriend is number two. It's motive."

"Can you hold off on telling Chief Lane?" she asked. "Just for a day. I'm sorry, but I *have* to talk to her."

"Lane needs to know, Mandy. So does Lynn."

"A day. That's all I'm asking. I want to hear her side of the story," she pleaded.

I stood silent. I just looked at her. In all the time we'd worked together, I'd never seen her like this before. Rattled. Desperate.

"I'm asking you as my friend," she said.

Mandy and I have been through a lot together over the years. I reluctantly acquiesced. Lane wouldn't be happy when he learned we'd given Julie Wolfer a heads-up. I also knew that Lynn was going to kick my ass.

"Two conditions," I said.

"What?"

"You don't wait. You talk to her now. Today. And you *never* tell her she's under suspicion."

"Okay," she said. "What's the second condition?"

"I go with you."

Mandy shook her head. "She'll never open up if you're there."

"She can either talk to me tonight or she can talk to the police," I said. "It's nonnegotiable."

Mandy pursed her lips in frustration. "Fine," she finally said. "I'll call her now."

Mandy pulled out her phone and dialed. She told her cousin we needed to talk to her about something important and that she didn't think the girls should be there. After a few minutes of back-and-forth, she hung up the phone.

"She's going to send the kids to Kristen's parents for the night," Mandy said. "She'll be expecting us around eight."

SEVENTEEN

MANDY WENT TO North Beach and picked up lunch. I ate my salad alone at my desk and thought. The more I pondered the situation, the more apparent it was to me that Julie Wolfer was involved in Kristen Promes's murder. Maybe she did it herself. Maybe she was part of a conspiracy. She was having an affair with the victim's husband. A classic motive. She was the one who got Kristen out of the Promes's home on the day of the barbecue. Kristen coming over to pick up Hope was designed to look like a spur-of-the-moment decision. Julie Wolfer had admitted that. She claimed she "lured" Kristen out of the house so Tom could arrange her surprise Tesla. Who else would have known that Kristen was on her way to Julie's house at that exact time and then intercepted and killed her? Julie had to be involved.

On the other hand, Mandy was right. I couldn't see Julie Wolfer killing the mother of her daughter's best friend with her daughter there in the house. Then, there's the Danica Walker connection. What is it? How does she fit into all of this? Maybe I was reading too much into it all. Mandy was correct in saying that if Julie and Tom had wanted to be together that badly, they could have just divorced their spouses. Why kill Kristen? And what about Jack Wolfer? Were they planning to off him as well? It didn't make sense somehow. Then again, I could be wrong about the whole thing, and we really *are* dealing with a random serial killer. Or killers.

I sat at my desk, running through possible scenarios until around five, when I hopped into the Black Beauty and headed toward the Bay Bridge. I kicked myself for not leaving earlier. The Embarcadero on-ramp to the span converts to a "carpool only" lane at 3:30, which meant I was stuck taking Battery Street through downtown and across Market. It took me almost an hour just to get to the bridge's lower deck.

A little over forty-five minutes later, I pulled into my driveway. It was about 6:30, and the summer sun continued to blaze hot in the sky. The canyon doesn't benefit from the onshore flow that provides the bay breeze, so there was no respite from the heat until I got inside. As I entered my air-conditioned house, Sophie stood at the door, her brown leather leash dangling from her mouth.

"Can I at least change my shoes first?" I asked.

She let out a high-pitched bark. Her tail wagged furiously.

"Two minutes," I said.

The pup followed me into the master bedroom and laid down patiently on the floor as I swapped out the designer footwear I had on for a pair of Nike running shoes. I attached Sophie's leash to her collar and took her for a long walk in the canyon as I continued to ponder possible murder scenarios.

Danica Walker was buried in the city. Kristen Promes, almost sixty miles away in Livermore. Lots of cars and commercial truckers drive through Livermore and over the Altamont Pass to get to the Bay Area. They also drive the opposite way down Interstate 5, headed south to Los Angeles and north to Sacramento. Could the killings have been committed by somebody just passing through? Were murders of opportunity. The killer would do the deed and move on. No one the wiser. Truckers are near the top of the list when it comes to serial murder. They operate in multiple jurisdictions and, yet again, there is minimal coordination between law enforcement agencies.

The more I thought about it, the more I realized that the murders could have been committed by someone from out of the area who makes regular runs up here. Maybe a driver who makes regular runs through Livermore hauling goods to the Bay Area making period homicidal details. It wouldn't be the first time that a trucker was involved in serial homicides. Maybe there was no connection between Danica and Kristen. The killer could have abducted the women, parked someplace out of the way, and killed them in the back of his truck. Plenty of time to commit the murders. No interruptions during the butchery. Then, once everything was done, he could have taken the bodies to their burial spots. Maybe places along his delivery route. Maybe there were other victims yet to be found. Other undiscovered shallow graves in secluded, wooded areas in the region. That's all plausible. But it still doesn't answer the question about the pentacles. A Satan-worshipping, serial-killing trucker? Finding sacrifices along his various routes and offering them up whenever and wherever he can? But my Google search didn't turn up any similar homicides. Could he just be starting? Are we looking at the beginning of a killing spree?

I took Sophie home, fed, and watered her. Mandy would be by to pick me up to go to Julie Wolfer's house soon. We'd decided to drive together. I think Mandy needed the emotional support for what she was about to deal with.

I hopped in the shower and then changed into a light brown, cotton blend Tommy Bahama shirt, tan slacks, and brown leather loafers. I went into the kitchen, mixed some almond milk, protein powder, peanut butter, and berries in the food processor, and made a smoothie for my dinner. I was downing the concoction when I heard the honking horn of Mandy's baby blue VW Bug convertible. I came outside and hopped in. She had the car's light brown convertible top down. Though the temperature was cooling as the sun began to set, it was still unseasonably warm, so she also had the AC up full blast.

"Hey," I said as I slipped into the passenger seat.

Mandy gave me a distracted "hello" and then said nothing as she made her way to I-580 East toward Pleasanton.

We made the fifteen-minute journey in silence. Mandy's mind was clearly someplace else. I think she was going over exactly what she would say to her cousin, writing the script in her head as she drove.

Soon, we pulled into Julie Wolfer's neighborhood. It was quiet, the street deserted. The media throng had finally moved on. I thought about how they'd return once they got wind of the affair.

Mandy pulled the Volkswagen into the driveway behind a gray Porsche Cayenne and turned off the engine.

"You ready?" I asked.

"No," came her terse reply.

I unbuckled my seat belt, leaned over, and hugged her. Her body was limp in my arms, my hug unreciprocated. She was not happy with me.

"You know what has to be done," I said. "If this weren't your cousin and your head was clear, you'd agree with me."

"But it *is* my cousin," she countered.

Mandy unbuckled her seat belt and opened the driver's door. I gently touched her arm. "It'll be okay," I said.

We exited the car and headed up the walkway to the front door. Mandy rang the bell. It was one of those doorbells that played a few notes of a classical piece. I couldn't quite make it out, but it appeared to be strains of a Vivaldi concerto.

"Jeez," Mandy said. "Pretentious much? Typical Jules."

No answer.

"Looks like she's as excited to see you as you are to see her," I said.

Mandy pressed the doorbell again.

More Vivaldi. Still, no answer.

Frustrated, Mandy knocked on the door.

"Jules?" she called.

As she knocked, the door crept open. It apparently hadn't been closed all the way.

"You'd better wait here," I said as I slowly opened the door wider and went inside. I had a bad feeling in the pit of my stomach. Playing the hero wasn't really my forte. That was in Lynn's wheelhouse. I didn't know what the hell I would do if something was indeed wrong. I don't carry a gun. I can't fight. However, I went in anyway. I guess machismo isn't dead in the twenty-first century. It's dumb but still alive.

Once inside, I scanned my surroundings. Everything in the entryway and the living room appeared to be normal. It looked just as it had when we'd been there before. Maybe Julie Wolfer had gone out without closing the front door all the way. Then I remembered the Cayenne in the driveway.

"Ms. Wolfer?" I called out.

Silence.

"Julie?"

I walked through the living room to the kitchen. Although it was twice the size, it reminded me of my own, with shiny oak cabinets and marble countertops. As in the outer area, everything appeared to be in place. Copper cookware hung from a rack up above. Everything was tidy.

"Ms. Wolfer," I called out again.

Still no response.

I walked back out into the living room. A winding staircase with gleaming brown wooden steps led to the second story of the home. I climbed it. Family photos lined the walls as I ascended. Julie Wolfer is in a wedding photo with a man I assumed to be her husband, Jack. Julie in a silky white wedding dress with a laced veil hanging from the back of her head. Jack in a gray tuxedo jacket and starched white shirt accessorized with a gray and black striped ascot stared adoringly into her eyes as she smiled. Two people in love. Their future life together a grand, unexplored adventure.

Next was an eight-by-ten picture of a newborn I assumed to be their daughter, Hope. Wisps of golden hair partially covered a mostly bald pate. Scrunched face. Right eye closed. The left partially opened in a nod to Popeye the Sailor Man. Tiny hands clenched into little fists, ready to take on the world. The baby's mouth was open, revealing pink, toothless gums.

As I neared the top of the stairs, more pictures. Jack's birthday. The family at Disneyland. Julie opening a gift under a Christmas tree. Jack pitching a tent in the wilderness. Hope in a pool with inflatable water wings supporting her little arms. Julie in the backyard pushing Hope on a swing as Jack raked leaves. A happy nuclear family. The stuff of '50s sitcoms.

The hallway at the top of the stairs consisted of burnished hardwood floors, white walls adorned with more photos, and seven white doors—three each on the right and the left of the hall. Double doors stood at the end—the master suite. I decided to start there. I made my way down the hall and tried one of the double doors. I grabbed its gold knob and opened it wide. I rounded a huge closet just past the entryway . . . and I saw her.

Julie Wolfer lay on a California king-sized bed drenched in blood, her arms outstretched wide and her feet crossed. She had been posed to evoke the memory of a crucifixion. A thin, dark brown ring of dried blood circled her neck. A long incision splayed the skin around her stomach. A carefully carved pentacle scarred her forehead. Her eyes were open in a death stare.

I reached into my pocket, pulled out my cell, and was about to give Siri the directive to "call Lynn" when a scream pierced the air—a loud, gut-wrenching wail of pain and anguish.

Mandy dropped to her knees in the doorway and covered her face with her hands.

"Jules," she sobbed. "Oh, Jules."

I went to her and got down on my knees. Mandy buried her face in my chest and cried harder. My Tommy Bahama shirt was a mess of tears and mascara.

"I'm sorry, honey," I whispered. "I'm *so* sorry."

Two hours later, the house was swarming with law enforcement. Evidence techs dusted the house for prints and began collecting anything that might hold DNA. The coroner's van sat in the driveway behind Mandy's Volkswagen. Mandy and I sat on the couch in the living room across from Lynn, Chief Lane, and a Pleasanton homicide detective named Flynn, who was furiously scribbling in a notepad. Mandy had regained her composure somewhat. The large snifter of cognac she sipped from didn't hurt. I held the crystal decanter of liquor and regularly refilled her glass.

"I know it's rough right now, Mandy, but you know how this goes," Lynn said.

Mandy took a large pull from the snifter and nodded. "Yeah," she said after swallowing the drink. "I know the drill."

She took another drink and finished the glass. I refilled it.

"First," Mandy said, "you're sorry for my loss."

"I am," Lynn said softly. "I truly am."

Mandy nodded as she gulped down another big swallow. "You want to know when I last talked to her."

"Yes," Lynn said.

"Early this afternoon," Mandy replied. "Now you want to know what we discussed."

"Right."

"I had just recognized her from that Monterey picture that Topher has. I called and told her that I needed to talk to her."

"Did you tell her about the picture?"

"No. I thought it would be better if we talked about it in person. I just told her that Topher and I had something very important to discuss with her. I knew that she had her daughter and the Promes girl here. I told her that they shouldn't be around when we talked. She said she would send them to Taylor's grandparents so we could have some privacy. She then told me to come around eight. I picked up Topher, and we got here at eight on the button."

Another pull from the snifter.

"So, we know she was alive early this afternoon. Do you know about what time?"

"It was around 2:15, 2:30. Check my cell. You can find the correct time there."

"That gives us approximately a five-and-a-half-hour window," Lynn said. "The coroner will be able to pin it down more precisely after the autopsy."

"Autopsy," Mandy said as her eyes filled with tears. "As if she hasn't been butchered enough already."

Again, she drained the snifter. Again, I refilled it.

A young, uniformed officer, a millennial rookie, entered the room. His face was ashen, and he was breathing through his mouth. I thought he might toss right there on the hardwood floor. The name tag on his chest read "Jenkins."

"First homicide?" I asked.

Jenkins nodded.

"First dead body," he said.

"It gets easier," I told him.

"Sir," Jenkins said, addressing Chief Lane, "may I step outside for a minute and get some air?"

"Of course," Lane said. "You don't need my permission for that, Officer. Take care of yourself. If you don't, you're no good to me."

"Yes, sir," Jenkins said. "Thank you, sir."

Jenkins turned and headed for the front door. Before reaching it, he pivoted and returned to us.

"I almost forgot, sir," he said. "We found the victim's phone."

He'd been holding it in his hand the whole time. He handed it to Lane.

"The techs have already taken prints and tested it for DNA," he said.

Lane opened the phone and pressed a few buttons.

"The call history has been deleted," he said. "I'll get the computer guys to see if anything can be recovered."

Lane headed off in the direction of the stairs. Jenkins walked out the front door. As he opened it, I could hear the din of the media pack. The horde was back. Word of Julie Wolfer's murder was out.

"Great," Mandy said. "Once they figure out I'm her cousin, they'll be on *my* doorstep."

"Let's be fair. If this were somebody else, we'd be doing the same thing, wouldn't we?"

She looked up at me with a knowing glance. We had to be honest. We contributed to that horde. At times, we too could be vampires sucking the blood out of other people's misery for the noble purpose of ratings. We were no different than anybody else now on Julie Wolfer's lawn.

"Why don't you stay in my guest room tonight?" I asked.

"What about my car?"

"It's blocked in the driveway by the coroner's van. I'm sure Chief Lane can have an officer bring it to you later," Lynn said. "In the meantime, I'll drive you to Chris's place. My car is parked a few blocks up the street."

Mandy finished the latest swallow of cognac in her glass, and then, as Julie Wolfer had done, the three of us headed out through the rear garage door and the gate leading to the Montesano house next door. Once inside their yard, we introduced ourselves to Frank Montesano, the family patriarch, and explained our predicament. He helped us surreptitiously escape from his house and up the street to Lynn's car. Apparently, no one in the press had yet discovered Mandy's relationship with Julie Wolfer, and we weren't followed. Soon, we were in Lynn's unmarked, heading up 580 West.

"I'll need some toiletries and things," Mandy said.

Lynn took the Redwood Road exit and drove through the Castro Valley side streets until we reached Mandy's condo building next to All Saints Church in the adjacent city of Hayward. We went inside and took the elevator to the third floor. We walked down the hall to unit 3F and entered to find a cozy, nicely furnished one-bedroom condominium.

"Nice place," Lynn said. "Reminds me of my apartment after I got out of the army."

Lynn's sentence was punctuated by the hourly bells that rang from the church—ten o'clock.

"I always wondered," I said. "Don't the church bells bother you?"

"They ring all day," Mandy replied. "They aren't even real bells. It's a recording they run on the hour until ten. They were a pain at first. Now, I barely notice them."

Mandy went into her bedroom and returned a few minutes later, rolling a small carry-on bag.

"You sure I shouldn't stay here?" she asked.

"You know as well as I do that once the media finds out you're Julie's cousin and that you were at the crime scene, the front of your building will look like Camp Kristen did."

She let out a heavy sigh and followed Lynn and me back to the unmarked. As we pulled away from the curb, Lynn's cell phone rang. She hit a button on her steering wheel to take the call. Hands free. She practiced what she preached. She put the call on speaker.

"Sloan," she said.

"Detective Sloan? This is Inga Swenson at Stanley Crane Jr.'s office . . ."

"It's a little late to be calling, isn't it?"

"Mr. Crane Jr. is working on a case, and we're burning the midnight oil, as they say."

"What can I do for you?" Lynn asked.

"Mr. Crane Jr. can see you tomorrow morning at ten. Is that convenient for you?"

"I'll see you then," Lynn said.

"Wonderful. I'll let Mr. Crane Jr. know that the meeting has been confirmed. Thank you," she said, disconnecting the call.

Lynn looked at me in the passenger seat.

"What are you doing tomorrow at ten?" she asked.

"Paying a visit to Mr. Crane Jr. with you."

EIGHTEEN

AFTER DROPPING ME and my new roommate off at home, Lynn headed out, and I showed Mandy to my guestroom. She unpacked her things, and while I poured her another cognac and a club soda for myself, I took a sip of the bubbly water, thought better of it, and poured myself a cognac as well. When Mandy entered the room, she had changed clothes and put on a pink bathrobe. I handed her a heated snifter and clinked our glasses together.

"To better days," I toasted.

Mandy took a sip from her glass, and I followed suit. The liquor was warm and heated my chest.

"Thought you weren't drinking," she said.

"Rough night, my friend. Rough night."

She nodded in affirmation.

"I can't believe she's gone," Mandy said. "It doesn't feel real."

"I know, kid," I said. "I know."

"All the times I've produced stories on homicides for you, all of the survivors I've coaxed into talking to us about their deceased loved ones . . ."

She took another drink from her glass, then clutched her chest as if to feel the heat resonating from the cognac as it went down.

"I never thought that someday, I'd be one of them. One of the grieving people on the other side of the camera," she said.

"Mandy . . . We don't have to interview you. You don't need to go on camera."

"Yes, I do," she replied. "This is a big story, and now, I'm a part of it. Jules or no Jules . . . I'm going to do my job."

Even in grief, Mandy was a broadcast journalist to the bitter end.

She finished her cognac, and I walked her to the door of her room.

"Funny," I said.

"What?"

"It's been a long time since I've had a guest in this house," I said.

"Breakups are hard," I said, my shoulders hunched and arms outstretched with my palms facing upward in my best "*What? Me worry?*" pose.

Mandy walked inside the room and then stopped. She turned and looked at me. "I don't want to be alone tonight," she whispered.

"Well, you aren't. I'm right down the hall," I said. "And I'll still be here when you wake up in the morning."

"I know," she said. "That's not what I mean."

She came closer, put her arms around my neck, and kissed me. I gently placed my hands on her limbs and parted them from around my neck.

"You're very vulnerable right now. You're grieving," I said. "You don't want this."

A beat.

"I need this right now."

"No, you don't. You just think you do. We're friends," I said. "And let's not even talk about the power differential."

She wrapped her arms around my neck again. "Don't worry," she said. "I won't tell HR if you don't."

She leaned in to kiss me again. I again removed her arms and kissed her in a brotherly way on her forehead.

"Good night, Mandy," I said.

She stood exasperated as I closed the bedroom door.

I awoke early the following day and took Sophie for a three-mile jog. We hadn't done that for a while, and she was happy with the exercise. I was too. I needed to clear my head. Julie Wolfer's murder meant that the killer had some fixation or connection to the Promes family. Why else kill Kristen Promes's best friend? And the murderer switched MOs. Julie wasn't found in a shallow grave like Kristen and Danica were. She was killed in her own home. Julie's stomach had been slashed open like the others. Were we dealing with a copycat? Somebody who wanted the authorities to think that Julie Wolfer's murder was tied to those of Kristen and Danica? But if that were the case, how'd the killer know about the pentacles? That information hadn't been released to the public. And how did the killer know that she was pregnant? Why else slice up her womb? No, it had to be the same murderer.

When I returned to the house, Mandy was scrambling eggs in the kitchen.

"Good morning," I said. "You're up early."

"I've been up most of the night. I hardly slept," she said. "I just called my aunt, Jules' mother, and told her what happened."

Tears filled her eyes.

"Hardest conversation of my life."

"I'll bet. I'm sorry."

"Thanks for letting me stay here. You were right. The press will be all over my condo building, and I just can't handle that right now."

"You're welcome to stay here as long as you'd like," I said.

I looked at the island in the kitchen. Plates of eggs, green, yellow, and red bell peppers, onions, mushrooms, and Havarti cheese spread out.

"Whatcha makin'?"

"Omelets. They won't be as good as Jared's at The Egg, but they'll be edible. Why don't you hop in the shower? Breakfast will be ready in about twenty minutes."

I filled Sophie's bowls with kibble and water and then headed to my bathroom, where I showered and shaved. Twenty minutes later, I reappeared in the kitchen dressed and groomed. Mandy had cleaned up the island and set out napkins, silverware, plates, coffee cups, and saucers. My good china. She slid a yellow omelet flecked with red, green, and gold peppers onto my plate. Gooey cheese leaked from the side where it had been folded. She repeated the process with her own plate. Then she placed triangles of dry rye toast next to the eggs and set small glasses of orange juice beside the meals.

We ate in silence, her mind a million miles away.

"Coffee?" she asked.

"Always."

She grabbed the pot from the coffeemaker and filled the cup adjacent to my plate. I took a sip. Mandy made a darned good cup of coffee. She began filling her cup.

"Listen, about last night . . ." she said, not looking up from her pouring. "You were right. I was vulnerable and grieving. Not to mention all that cognac that went to my head and—"

"I have no idea what you're talking about," I said with a sly smile.

Mandy smiled back in relief.

"Thank you," she said.

"I don't want you to come to work today," I said. "You need time to process what's happened."

"I wasn't planning on it," she said. "My aunt is flying in from Florida today. I told her that I'd pick her up, book a hotel, and start making funeral arrangements."

She took a bite of her omelet and slowly chewed. Her face was expressionless. I couldn't tell if she liked it or not.

"My God," she whispered. "Funeral arrangements. For Jules." She shook her head. "I can't believe this is happening."

I patted her on the back and then took a bite of my omelet. She was right. It wasn't as good as Jared's.

"I think you should stay here for at least a few days. Once the media discovers that you aren't staying at your place, they'll move on."

"You sure it isn't an imposition?"

"I've got this big four-bedroom house that I live in by myself most of the time. Trust me. I welcome the company."

"I guess it's settled then," she said, smiling. "Stu called. He was very sweet. I've got him coming over with his camera, and we will record a piece for the show."

"Again, you don't have to do this," I said.

"And again, I want to," she said. "It's an exclusive." She smiled again.

"Okay, if you're sure you can handle it. Just remember not to give out too much information. Hold back on details and specifics. I'm sure the police don't want everything out there right now since this is an active investigation."

"I'll be careful," she said. "Like I said last night, I know the drill."

"I'm sure you do."

Mandy and I finished breakfast, then I hopped in the Black Beauty and headed for the Bay Bridge. I didn't let the top down. It was already over 80. Another scorcher today.

At ten o'clock sharp, Lynn and I cooled our heels in the reception area of the law offices of Crane, Phelps, and Crane. Inga

Sorenson, apparently Danica Walker's replacement, was a tall, blond, Nordic-looking woman.

Viking blood, I thought. At any moment, I expected her to rape and pillage.

She offered us coffee, and I accepted. Lynn opted for green tea. I was on my third sip of coffee when I heard a voice behind me.

"Back again, I see," Patricia Hart said.

"Yep. Finally getting in to see Mr. Crane Jr.," Lynn replied.

"He's a hard one to pin down," Patricia said.

"I see you're off the desk now. Back to your lawyerly duties?"

"Thank God," she exclaimed. "I think if I'd had to transfer one more call, I would have screamed."

"Well, congrats on your liberation," Lynn said.

"I was sorry to hear about Danica," she stated. "Like I told you before, I didn't know her very well, but she seemed really nice."

"By all accounts, she was," Lynn said. "You haven't, by chance, remembered any more information about her since we last spoke, have you?"

"Nope. Told you everything I know. Not that it was much."

"We appreciate that," I said.

"Any leads on what happened to her?" Patricia asked.

"None that we can discuss," Lynn said.

"I understand. If I think of anything else, I'll let you know. I still have your card."

"Thanks," Lynn replied.

"Well, I'd better get back to it.. Nice seeing you again."

"You too," I said as she walked off.

We sat in the reception area for another fifteen minutes, and I was on my second cup of coffee when Inga Sorenson reappeared.

"Mr. Crane Jr. will see you now," she said.

We followed her around the reception desk and down a narrow, carpeted hallway. The walls were covered with framed copies of old editions of the *San Francisco Chronicle, San Francisco Examiner,* and the long-defunct *San Francisco Call-Bulletin.*

"CRANE EXPOSES CITY HALL GRAFT!" blared one headline in the *Chronicle* from the 1940s.

"PHELPS EXONERATES ALLEGED MURDERESS!" read an old *Examiner.*

"FELTON KILLS SELF AFTER EXPOSURE BY CRANE," read the five-point type of another yellowing page.

It appeared that the firm had quite a storied history.

Ms. Sorenson led us to a heavy wooden door with a gold nameplate that read Stanley Crane Jr. ESQ engraved in bold letters. She knocked lightly.

"It's open," came a voice from inside.

She opened the door to reveal a fifty-something man sitting behind a large oak desk shuffling papers. He was older than his portrait in the lobby, but, with the possible exception of Dorian Gray, who isn't? He was still a good-looking man with wavy black hair and steel-blue eyes. As we entered, he put his papers in a neat stack and stood to greet us. He was a tall man. I put him at six foot two.

"Detective Sloan and Mr. Topher Davis," Ms. Sorenson said, announcing us.

Stanley Crane Jr. extended his hand for me to shake. I grasped it firmly, noticing the shiny gold cuff links glittering in the sunlight that beamed through the window of his corner office. I glanced at Lynn. She saw them too.

"It's a pleasure to meet you, Detective. Mr. Davis, I've admired your work for a long time," he said obsequiously.

"Can I get anyone anything? More coffee, tea, or some water?" Inga said.

Lynn and I declined.

"We're fine," Mr. Crane Jr. said.

"Then I guess I'll head back to the phones," she said. She left the office, shutting the door behind us.

"Please, grab a chair," Crane said, directing us to two brown leather chairs in front of his desk.

We sat. I looked around the office. The walls were bare save a few paintings of various yachts and schooners. Two photos graced the desk. One was Crane on a sailboat, smiling as he leaned on the mast. The other was a studio portrait of Crane with his arm around a smiling blond woman as they stood behind two grinning towheaded girls. The perfect nuclear, *Ozzie and Harriet* family.

Lynn looked at the photograph. "Nice family," she said.

"They're what I work so hard for. At least that's what I tell myself," he said with a chuckle. "That's my wife, Barbara, and our daughters, Maggie and Stephanie."

"Pretty girls," I added.

"That they are," he said. "Maggie, the older one, is nine. Little Stephanie, 'Stevie' as we call her, is seven. Granddad was a little disappointed I didn't have a boy to carry on the family name and take over the firm when I eventually hang it up. C'est la vie."

"Your grandfather founded the firm?"

"Great-grandfather, actually," Crane said. "Granddad started as an associate, and when my great-grandfather retired, he took over the firm and brought in his law school buddy, Phelps, as a partner. My dad was supposed to follow in my grandfather's footsteps, but after I was born, he ditched my mother and got caught up in that whole Haight Ashbury hippie scene, complete with lots of LSD, mushrooms, and Lord knows what else. Haven't heard a peep from him in years. Last I knew, he was living in a commune in Mendocino somewhere. The world's oldest iconoclast."

"So, your mother raised you?" Lynn asked.

"She and Granddad. He groomed me. My given name is actually Stanley Crane III. Granddad pretty much erased my dad. It was my assigned mission in life to make up for the disappointment that was my father. He put me through Cal and USF law school. Like him, I started as an associate. When he and Phelps retired, the torch was passed to me. I guess one of my girls will be sitting in this office someday, although neither shows any inclination of being interested in the law, but they're young yet. Got to carry on the family legacy."

"Three generations," I said. "That's impressive."

"You know what a legacy is?" Crane Jr. asked.

I shook my head.

"A guilt trip laid on you by dead people," he said with another heartier laugh.

"You know," I said, "Danica Walker was raised by a single mom too."

"I know. One of the reasons I hired her. We latchkey kids have to stick together."

"You were a latchkey kid?"

"Granddad helped financially, but Mom still had to work. She was a legal secretary here for thirty years. That meant that after school I was left to my own devices. Danica was too.

Crane shook his head. "That poor kid. I can't believe what's happened. I just can't believe it. To see somebody every day and then, *poof*, they're gone," he said. "It's unfathomable."

"What did you argue about on the day Danica disappeared?" Lynn said, attempting to catch him off guard.

"Who said we argued?" Crane Jr. asked, suddenly flustered.

"You argued that day, and she stormed out of your office."

"I don't remember any argument," he said defensively.

"I can bring in some witnesses who may be able to refresh your memory," Lynn said.

"Witnesses?" he asked.

Crane looked at his desk as if he would find the answer to Lynn's question there among his papers.

"What did you argue about?" she persisted.

"I don't remember," he shot back.

"Come on, Mr. Crane," I said. "Subordinates don't argue with you so frequently that they all blur."

Lynn picked up the family portrait on his desk.

"Maybe Mrs. Crane Jr. could give us some information."

He snatched the photo from her hand.

"All right," he snapped. "We argued."

"Was it about the baby?" Lynn asked.

"How do you know about—" he started to say.

"We know," Lynn said.

"That's impossible. Nobody knew."

"You know the old saying. The only way two people can keep a secret is if one of them is dead," Lynn said. "Is that why you killed her?"

"I didn't kill her!"

"We're not here to cause you any embarrassment, Mr. Crane," I said. "We're just trying to reconstruct Danica Walker's last day. We know you fought. We know she stormed out. We also know about the affair."

Crane looked down at his desk again.

"Okay," he said, defeated. "We had an affair."

"How did it start?" I asked.

Crane let out a heavy sigh. "About six months ago, we were alone in the office one night working late. When we finished, I opened a bottle of wine so we could relax a little before calling it a day. We started drinking and . . . As they say, one thing led to another."

"How long did it go on?" Lynn asked.

"From that night six months ago until she disappeared."

"You've got a wife and family at home," Lynn said. "Where exactly did you conduct these extracurricular activities?"

"Here in the office, late at night. The couch in the reception area was a particular favorite."

Lynn and I looked at each other. We had just sat on that couch. *Ewww.*

"Hotels in the South Bay. You know, off the beaten path," he continued. "About two months ago, I rented an apartment in the Mission District where we'd meet."

"How serious was the relationship?" I asked.

"It was just . . . fun. A harmless fling."

"But Danica didn't know that?" Lynn asked.

"I thought she did, but I was wrong."

"Hence the argument."

"Was the baby yours?" I asked.

"Danica said it was. That day, she was demanding that I leave my wife and marry her, or she'd tell my wife everything. I was trying to convince her to get an abortion. If my wife found out, she'd take everything, including half of this firm. I couldn't let Danica tell her."

"So you killed her," I said.

"No!" Crane Jr. shouted. "I didn't kill her! She was alive when she left this office. Ask your so-called witnesses. We were supposed to resume the conversation after work. After everyone else had gone home, she went out when she got off and didn't return. She never showed up again."

"So, what did you do?" I asked.

"I stayed here in my office and worked. I had a brief due. I was here until around eleven."

"Anybody see you who can vouch for your whereabouts?" I asked.

"The cleaning lady came in around ten like she does every night. She saw me. Plus, this place is surrounded by security cameras. Check the footage. We keep the video for ninety days. I'll make it available to you."

"Thanks," Lynn said.

"Please don't tell my wife," Crane pleaded.

"Provided you're telling me the truth," Lynn said, "she won't hear a word from us."

"Thank you," Crane said, relieved.

Lynn repeated, "Again, provided you're telling the truth."

"On my children," he said.

"Did Danica have any enemies or ex-boyfriends or stalkers? Anybody in her life who might want to hurt her?"

"Not that I'm aware of. Everybody liked Danica. She was young, pretty, smart, ambitious . . ."

"And she was carrying a married man's child," I said.

"She told me that nobody knew that. I only found out on the day she vanished."

"What did you plan to say to her when you talked after work?" Lynn asked.

"I was going to convince her to get an abortion. She already had one kid. She was headed to law school. Two kids, one a newborn, would make the task difficult, if not impossible. It's hard to study for the bar with a baby spitting up on your shoulder."

"She had a mother to help her," Lynn informed him.

"Yeah, but still . . ." he said, running out of excuses. "Look, I was willing to pay for the abortion and everything."

"Big of you," my sister said.

"And if she refused your chivalrous offer?" I asked.

He thought momentarily and then quietly said, "I'd support it and pay her to keep her mouth shut about paternity."

"Blackmail," I said. "For eighteen years."

"No. Not blackmail. She never asked me for any money. She wanted me to get a divorce, marry her, and help her raise the kid. I wasn't going to do that. I've raised my children."

He'd raised his children? They were seven and nine. What planet was this guy living on?

"You'd pay support and hope she'd never tell your wife."

"I guess," he said. "Something like that. Look, she sucker punched me with this. I never saw it coming. I was working in my office. Danica knocks on the door and asks if she can speak to me and *bingo*. She says she's knocked up, and I have to get a divorce and marry her."

"Just like that?" I said.

"Just like that," Crane Jr. repeated.

He looked weary. The color had drained from his face, and he seemed smaller than when we first encountered him—a little boy having to fess up to stealing the class milk money.

"About Barbara . . . There's no chance she'd already found out about the affair? Wives have been known to take out the competition."

"No," Crane said, vigorously shaking his head. "Barbara couldn't hurt a fly. For God's sake, when she sees spiders in the house, instead of killing them, she traps them, takes them outside, and sets them free."

"Spiders aren't sleeping with her husband," I said.

"We were *very* careful. There was no way Barbara could have found out. Danica and I communicated on a pair of burner cells I bought at a gas station. I paid for the hotels and the apartment in cash. Never used my own name. I had a fake ID and credentials made for things like that. The landlord at the apartment wasn't too picky. He didn't care what we did as long as he got his security deposit and the rent was paid on time. There's no way my wife knew."

"Trust me, there is no better detective than a woman who thinks her man is cheating on her," I said. "You'd be surprised what they can uncover."

"Cheaters are never as clever as they think they are," Lynn added.

"You going to talk to her?" Crane asked, his voice quivering.

"I said that we wouldn't, and we won't . . . as long as you're being straight with us."

"I've told you everything I know," he said, slightly relieved.

"We'll need the key to your little love nest," she said. "And your burner cell."

Crane Jr. removed a ring of keys from his pocket, selected one, and used it to unlock the bottom drawer of his desk. He took out the items and handed them to Lynn.

"I'll need the address too."

He tore a piece of paper from a memo pad and scribbled on it with a pen. Then he folded the paper and handed it to Lynn.

"Any idea where Danica kept her burner cell?" Lynn asked.

"Not a clue. Certainly not in her desk. Inga would have found it. She cleaned out everything and boxed it up when she started."

"What did she do with the box?" I asked.

"There was nothing in it of value. Some school supplies. Spiral notebooks with class notes. Stuff like that. I had it sent to her mother over in Oakland," he said. "She's got it."

Lynn scribbled the tidbit in her notebook.

"I guess that's all for now," Lynn said as she turned and headed for the door. I was on her heels.

As she grasped the door's handle, she looked over her shoulder at Crane Jr. "Don't leave town," she said.

Crane nodded, and we walked out into the hallway and shut his office door.

"Don't leave town?"

"They always say that on cop shows," she said. "I wanted to see what it felt like."

NINETEEN

LYNN AND I got in the elevator.

"How's Mandy holding up?" she asked.

"Putting on a brave face but struggling," I said. I pressed the button for the garage.

"She actually made a move on me last night."

"Get out!"

"Seriously," I said. "She was weepy, vulnerable, and in need of comfort."

"And you helped her out with your penis," Lynn said, rolling her eyes.

"What do you think I am?"

"You're a guy. A pretty woman came on to you in your house. Guys are guys."

"I thought you knew me better than that. Of course, I didn't take advantage of the situation. I put her to bed in the guest room and then went to sleep in my own room. *Alone.*"

"Sorry," Lynn said. "So much adultery going around it's tainted my view of men. Tom Promes sleeping with Julie Wolfer. Crane Jr. and Danica. Makes me lose faith in your gender altogether."

"Do you ever worry about Jared cheating? He *is* a good-looking guy."

"When we got married, I made my views on adultery very clear," she said. "I told Jared that I would never need a divorce lawyer. On the other hand, I may need a *defense* lawyer. He got the message."

"Damn," I said, stretching the word into two syllables. "Well, at least you didn't threaten castration. Women always threaten to castrate you if they catch you dipping your pen in somebody else's ink."

"You know me," she said. "A class act to the bitter end."

The elevator door opened on the fifth floor, and a FedEx deliveryman entered. His presence silenced us briefly.

Two floors later, he got out.

Once he'd gone, I turned to Lynn. "What's your impression of Mr. Crane Jr.?"

"Entitled prick."

I nodded in agreement.

"Part of me wants to tell his wife just in the name of karma," she said.

"Why don't you?"

"There are little kids involved. He can destroy his family if he wants to. I'm not going to help."

"One thing bothers me," I said.

"What?"

"He called Danica's baby a 'thing.' Remember he said, 'I'd support the thing.'"

"Why's that under your skin?"

"It's easier to kill a baby if you don't think of it as a baby. If you dehumanize it. It's not an infant, it's a 'thing.'"

"I'd missed that entirely. You might be on to something."

"He *could* be our killer."

"Let me check his alibi," she said.

"Even if his alibi checks out, he's a rich man. He could have paid to have it done. Remember, if his wife found out about his 'harmless little fling,' he'd probably be in a world of hurt. If Danica and her baby are dead . . . problem solved." I shook my head, "People really are capable of some evil shit."

"Don't get ahead of yourself, Big Bro. There's still the Kristen Promes problem. If Crane is our killer, what's his connection to her?"

"You still love knocking over my Lincoln Logs, don't you?"

When we were kids, Auntie, bought me Lincoln Logs for Christmas one year. I'd build these huge towers, and then, just as I was putting the finishing touches on the roof, Lynn would knock the whole thing over and laugh.

"Old habits die hard," she said as the elevator bell dinged, indicating we'd reached the garage.

We exited the elevator and walked to our cars.

"What are you going to do?" I asked.

"I'm going to check on Mr. Crane Jr.'s alibi. Try to track down that cleaning woman. Look over his surveillance footage. I also want to talk to Tom Promes. I think it's about time that we had a discussion with him. I'll ask Chief Lane to set it up."

"I want to be there," I said.

"I wouldn't have it any other way," she stated. "I also want to look at Crane's little bachelor pad in the Mission."

"I want in on that, too," I said.

"Okay," she agreed. "What's on your agenda?"

"I think I'll head over to Josie Walker's and go through that box of things Danica left in her desk when she disappeared. It's probably a waste of time, but . . . You never know. I'll let you know if I turn up anything."

"Ditto," she said before jumping into her unmarked.

"I also want to spend some time with Mandy. Make sure she's hanging in there."

"Give her my love and tell her I'm here if she needs me."

"Will do," I said as Lynn got behind the wheel of her vehicle and sped off.

I got into the Black Beauty and called Josie Walker. I was surprised to get cell reception inside the garage, but it was as clear as it could be. Josie confirmed she had the box and told me to head on over. She had taken off work early. I clicked off, paid my parking fee, and then headed for the Bay Bridge.

TWENTY

AN HOUR LATER, I sat in Josie Walker's kitchen, carefully removing the contents of Danica's cardboard box and setting them on the table. A melodic Brahms's "Lullaby" wafted into the kitchen from the living room. Danica's son, D'Vante, practicing. He was quite good, the music adding a bit of melancholy to the task at hand.

"How's he doing?" I asked, gesturing toward the living room.

"I guess about as well as can be expected. He doesn't say much. He comes home from school, does his homework, and then plays the piano until dinnertime. After dinner, he plays some more. I think it soothes him. His dream is to be a concert pianist."

"I think he's well on his way. Listen," I said with a bit of reluctance, "have you thought about getting him grief counseling of some kind?"

I'll admit that part of my reluctance to pose the question was cultural. Although I've personally spent many hours "on the couch" throughout my life, many African Americans do not subscribe to the idea of professional help for mental distress. I don't know if it comes from a lack of resources or the belief that we take care of our own problems. "Get your black ass up!" as Auntie would often tell us. But even she got my sister and me into therapy after Mom died. She knew that we were too young for self-help, and she was too inexperienced to offer it.

"It helps to have somebody to talk to sometimes," I said.

"Counseling?" She laughed. "On what I make?"

"There are county services."

"The county services aren't worth a shit," she said. "I looked into them. And there's at least a six-month wait."

"I know a few people. Would you mind if I made some calls?"

"I told you, I can't afford it."

"The people I know work on a sliding scale. You pay what you can."

The balance would come from my personal checking account, but she didn't need to know that.

"If you think you can find somebody we can afford, go ahead."

"In the meantime," I said, "maybe I can talk to him. If you want, that is."

"You?" she said incredulously.

"I think I can relate to what he's going through. I lost my mother when I was a child too. Younger than D'Vante."

"I'm sorry," Josie said. "Cancer or something?"

"Murder. Just like him."

"Did they ever catch who did it?"

Silence.

"I see," Josie said. "If you think it'll help for you to talk to D'Vante, it's all right with me."

"Let's finish up here first," I said.

I set the empty box on the floor, its contents now strewn across the kitchen table. Using a pen, I sifted through the remnants of Danica Walker's work life. There was an unopened package of Juicy Fruit gum, a travel-sized pack of Kleenex, half a box of Altoids, pens, pencils, and a pair of spiral notebooks. I paged through them. One contained notes from a communications class.

The other from an introductory course in American jurisprudence. A lawyer in training.

"She sure did keep a lot of junk in her desk," Josie said.

"This is nothing. You should look in my desk drawers."

I kept perusing. A phone number was scrawled on a torn scrap of paper, hastily written in blue ink. I pulled out my phone and dialed it. My call was answered on the third ring.

"Tony's Pizza," came the greeting in a thick Brooklyn accent.

"My name is Topher Davis—"

"You that guy from the tube?"

"Yes."

"I thought I recognized your voice. What can I do you for?"

"Do you know a woman by the name of Danica Walker?"

"Nice kid. Shame what happened to her," Tony said with regret in his voice.

"I found your number on a piece of paper in her desk . . ."

"Yeah. Met her on BART one morning. We struck up a conversation, and I told her about the restaurant and how our delivery territory covers California Street, where her office was. I was out of business cards, so I wrote down my number. She wanted me to put it into her phone, but I'm useless when it comes to this technology stuff. Hell, I'm on a rotary phone right now."

"Did she ever call you?"

"Lots of times. She'd order lunch for the office. Always the same thing. Two large pies. One sausage and pepperoni with extra cheese and sliced tomatoes. The other, a veggie. No anchovies."

"When's the last time you saw her?"

"About a week, maybe a week and a half before she went missing. I'd always deliver her orders personally."

"Did she seem like herself? Was there anything out of the ordinary?"

"Nope. Same as always. I delivered the pies. We made small talk for a few minutes, and then she paid me. Always in cash. Good tipper. Twenty bucks every time."

"You mentioned that you engaged in small talk. About what?"

"The weather. The Giants. How bad the homeless situation was getting. The usual San Francisco stuff. Nothing out of the ordinary."

"What was her demeanor like?"

"Demeanor?"

"Her mood."

"Cheerful," he said. "Same as always."

"Anything else you might be able to tell me?"

"Man, I just delivered pizzas to her office occasionally. That's it."

"If you should think of anything else, will you call me?"

"Sure. Let me get a pen."

I heard him put down the phone. My "on hold" music consisted of the din of diners and the chatter of orders being placed. A few minutes later, he returned to the phone.

"Okay," he said.

I gave him my cell number. "That's my personal number. Call me anytime if you think of anything."

"Will do. And you call me if I can ever deliver a pie to your station."

"Will do."

"One more thing," he said. "That hot anchorwoman you guys have. Katie Robards. Is she married?"

I let him down gently, ended the call, and returned to the task at hand, where I sorted through paperclips, broken bricks of staples, and a staple remover. There were numerous envelopes for monthly credit card and utility bills. The envelopes were all neatly addressed, sealed, and affixed with the appropriate postage. Under one of them, I found a few business cards. Two for *Braids* listing her as a "stylist."

A dry cleaner in downtown Oakland. A dentist on San Francisco's Market Street and a piano tuner. Josie noticed it.

"That reminds me," she said, "I'd better call him. D'Vante has been complaining about his F sharp key sticking."

She took the card and slipped it into her front jeans pocket. "I'll do it today."

I began to put Danica's things back into the cardboard box.

"Nothing?" she asked.

"I'm afraid not," I said. "Another dead end. I'm sorry."

I hadn't meant to give her false hope, but with the amount of help she was getting from local law enforcement, any attention to Danica's case was a reason for her to jump for joy. I made a mental note to be careful to manage her expectations in our future encounters.

"How are *you* doing?" I asked.

"Oh," she said, "I'm getting along. Work helps. They offered me some time off, but I told them no. Spending all day in this house would just make me feel worse. Too much time alone in my head is not the best thing for me right now. I'd rather be occupied."

"You're like me," I said. "Staying busy helps."

She opened a cabinet under the sink and took out a large roll of packing tape to seal Danica's box.

"Thanks for trying," she said.

"Of course. I'll be in touch," I said. "Hang in there."

I was walking through the living room toward the front door when I caught sight of D'Vante sitting at an old Kimball upright piano. He was a thin boy. Skinny, actually. Even seated on the piano bench, I could tell he was tall. His upper body revealed the stature that prompted that annoyingly persistent question posed to all towering boys of color: "Do you play basketball?"

The instrument was walnut brown, and it had clearly seen better days. It was liberally scarred with scratches and scrapes. One of the gold metal knobs used to pull the wooden dustcover over the keys was missing. I'm no music critic, but I thought the young man played beautifully. He had switched to a Chopin *Étude*. His face was expressionless. It was almost like he was in a daze or a dream, carried away by the music emanating from his fingertips. He suddenly saw me and snapped out of his trance.

"I'm sorry," I said. "I didn't mean to interrupt."

"It's okay," he replied, the register of his voice in that odd, transformative place between boyhood and maturity.

"Chopin?"

"*Étude in E Major*," he said. "One of Mom's favorites."

"It's lovely."

"Thank you," he said as he resumed playing. I could tell that he was in his comfort zone—blue jeans. The collar of a blue dress shirt peeked out from under his maroon pullover. Black Converse All Stars with white tips worked the piano's pedals as his long, thin fingers glided effortlessly over the ivory keys.

"You're very good," I said. "How long have you been playing?"

"Since I was three. They say I'm a prodigy. This old piano was my great-grandfather's. I'm told that I climbed up on the bench one day and just started playing. I'd never even had a lesson. Just played melodies that I heard in my head."

"That's amazing."

"My mom started to buy me classical CDs, and I'd mimic them. Note for note. Tchaikovsky, Brahms, Beethoven, Mozart. I hear it, I can play it."

"You're gifted. I don't know how many thousands of dollars my auntie wasted on piano lessons on me before she finally threw in the towel and admitted that I had no musical talent."

His lips curled into a half smile.

"Your grandmother tells me you want to be a concert pianist."

"I want to go to the San Francisco Conservatory of Music. That place costs a fortune. If I can get a scholarship, I figure I can live here at home and commute to the city. Like Mom did . . ." he said, his voice trailing off at the end.

He began to play another piece.

"*Keyboard Concerto Number 5 in F minor.* Another of Mom's favorites."

I watched as he again became lost in his music.

"I don't know what I'd do right now if I couldn't play," he said. "I close my eyes and play my mom's favorite pieces. I hope she can hear me."

"She hears you, son," I said. "She hears you."

It appeared that the young man had found his own therapy.

TWENTY-ONE

I MADE IT HOME around six to find Mandy sitting at my kitchen island on the phone. She was surrounded by scraps of legal papers and notepads. She stared intently at her open laptop as she spoke into her cell.

"Okay," she said on the phone. "I'll take the one on the third page of your website . . . no, the one in the lower right-hand corner. The white one. Yes. I *see* how much it costs. She had insurance to cover any expenses associated with her burial."

A beat.

"I'm sure her husband will cover any costs that the insurance doesn't. You'll get your money."

Another longer beat.

"Look, you aren't the only funeral home in the area. Do you want our business or not?"

More brief silence as Mandy opened the purse hanging on the back of her chair, pulled out her wallet, and extracted a MasterCard.

"I can give you a deposit. Pay attention because I'm only reading this once," she snapped.

She slowly read the card's sixteen digits, expiration date, and three-number code on the back.

"Got it? Good. What's that?"

A beat.

"No, the florist has already been taken care of. Her husband, Jack, will contact you tomorrow with the insurance information. Thank you."

She ended the call.

"Arrangements?" I asked.

"Major hassle is more like it," she said. "Jules was a pain in the ass when she was alive, and she's a pain in the ass now that she's dead."

It was the first time she'd mentioned her cousin's death without tearing up. She had apparently entered the anger stage of the grieving process.

"Come here," I said, walking over to her and hugging her. She hugged me back as if she were hanging on for dear life.

"How about a glass of Chardonnay?" I asked, heading to the little wine fridge I kept in the kitchen.

"Sure," she replied as she began arranging the paperwork in front of her into one big pile that she slipped into a large manila file folder.

I removed two wineglasses from the kitchen cupboard. "When's Jack getting in?" I asked, twisting my butterfly corkscrew into the top of the bottle.

"He lands in Oakland tonight, around eight."

"Would you like me to pick him up?"

"I already offered. He says he'll take an Uber."

"Where's he staying? He can't go home. Not with the press watching the place."

"Taylor's grandparents arranged a room for them at the Hilton Garden Inn on the Peninsula. We figured it's the last place anybody would come looking for them," she said, tucking her work and laptop into her computer bag.

"Has anybody told Hope yet?"

"No. The Duffys, Taylor's grandparents, are keeping the girls away from the TV so they don't pick up anything. Jack's going to tell her when they get to the hotel," she said, shaking her head. "Fathers telling their little girls that Mommy is dead. It's just not right."

"Tom Promes and the Duffys had Kristen cremated as soon as the coroner released the body. They're having a secret, very private service in the Duffy home. Just immediate family. The press won't know."

"And Julie?"

"That one's going to be a shit show, a real madhouse. Jules left explicit instructions that she was to have a big ceremony at St. Catherine's, followed by a procession to the Holy Sepulchre Cemetery in Hayward. She even arranged a goddamned ballroom at the Hyatt in Oakland for the reception."

"Man," I said, exasperated.

"That's my cousin. Showboating until the bitter end."

"She had no way of anticipating the press, though."

"For her, that would have been the icing on the cake. Cameras documenting her send-off for posterity." She rolled her eyes as they filled with tears. "Goddamned pain in the ass," she said, wiping her eyes with her sleeve.

I quickly filled a glass with wine and handed it to her.

"Thanks," she said, taking the glass and then downing its contents. She then held out the empty glass for a refill.

"This isn't tequila, you know?" I said, again filling her glass.

"I'm in mourning. It's how the Irish do it," she said.

"You're not Irish. You're Scottish."

"Close enough," she replied, pounding down the second glass.

"Again," she said, holding the empty glass in my direction.

"Mandy—"

"Again!!" she bellowed.

I complied.

This time, Mandy raised the glass to her lips and sipped.

"Now, *that* is supposed to be how you drink wine."

"I don't want to drink wine like I'm 'supposed to,'" she said. "I want to get drunk."

"You know that isn't going to help anything."

She downed the remainder of her glass and then held it out in my direction again.

By nightfall, Mandy had consumed three bottles of my best Rombauer Chardonnay and passed out on my living room sofa. I took a pillow from the guest room and placed it under her head. Then I covered her with one of Auntie's handmade quilts. She was going to be in a world of hurt when she woke up . . . *if* she woke up.

I was about to begin my own bedtime routine when I remembered the next morning was garbage pickup. I went around back and wheeled the gray can containing refuse to the front of the property. I made a second trip to bring out the yard trimmings cart and a third for the blue recycling bin. I was turning around to head back to the house when the first punch caught me on my left cheekbone. I instinctively grabbed the injured part of my face when another blow caught me in the midsection and took the wind out of me. I fell to my knees.

I looked up from the hard dirt ground to see two men standing over me. They wore black jeans and tee shirts, their faces covered with dark knit ski masks. I somehow recovered enough stamina to charge at the one who'd thrown the first punch. He hit me again, this time in my recently broken right ribs, but not before I grabbed a handful of ski mask and pulled it off his head. It was pitch black outside, and I couldn't see much about his features. What I could tell was that he was a kid. Maybe sixteen or seventeen years old.

Once his mask was off, he turned and ran away before I could get a good look at him.

"Just a reminder from Stanley Crane. Keep your mouth shut," the other one said, shoving me to the ground and kicking me again in the midsection.

I heard his rapid footsteps crunch gravel as I descended into darkness.

TWENTY-TWO

I AWOKE ON THE couch as Lynn wiped my face with a wet washcloth. The cool dampness provided much-needed relief from the sting of my injuries. Mandy appeared from the kitchen, a small icepack firmly in her grip.

"Last time I checked, you were the one lying here," I said.

"You should be more careful taking out the trash," she stated.

I touched my tender cheekbone. I could feel the swelling.

"Actually, I think this time the trash took *me* out. What happened?"

"I dropped in to see how Mandy was doing and found you all battered and bruised in the driveway," Lynn said. "Did you see who did it?"

I began to shake my head, felt the contents of my skull rattle, and thought better of it. "No. It was too dark."

"How many times have I told you to put some damned sensor lights out there? You can't see two inches in front of your face at night," she admonished.

"I did yank the mask off one of them. Couldn't make out his features very well in the darkness, but he looked like a teenager."

"I found the mask outside in the dirt," Lynn said. "I'm going to have it checked for DNA."

"They'll spend money for DNA testing on a simple assault?" I asked.

"A simple assault that may be tied to a triple homicide."

I nodded.

"They also left a message," I told her.

"Message?"

"They said it was from Stanley Crane. It was a warning to keep my mouth shut, presumably about the affair with Danica Walker," I said. "Why'd he pick on me? You know as much about his fling with Danica as I do."

"I'm also a cop carrying a Glock."

I nodded. It hurt. I slowly drew in a deep breath. My diaphragm was sore but not the excruciating pain I'd dealt with a few months earlier when a blast of C4 explosive cracked my ribs. This time around, it looked like I was just bent, not broken. My ribs hurt, but they didn't feel as if they'd been broken again.

It was Mandy's turn to hand me a drink. Johnny Walker Blue. Neat.

"Here," she said. "Drink this."

I took the glass and downed it.

"How are you vertical? You had three bottles of wine."

"I hold my liquor better than you do," she said.

Lynn curled her lips, drew in a deep breath, and then looked at me.

"Listen, Chris—" Lynn began.

"No!" I said. "Don't start."

"You could at least let me finish my sentence."

"You're going to go into your lecture about me keeping Auntie's .38 snub nose here. *No!* No guns in this house! The damned thing almost got me killed the last time."

The last time the gun had been in my house, I was the one on the receiving end of its thirty-eight slugs. I was lucky to still be alive.

"It could save your life one day."

"Like tonight? I should have been packing to take the garbage cans up to the street? I don't think so."

"Forget it, Lynn," Mandy said. "You know how hardheaded he is." She touched my cheekbone.

"Ow!" I yelped.

"Even hardheads can be cracked," my sister said.

"Now what? You gonna sit the Sheriff's Department on my door to babysit me?"

"I don't think so," she said. "This looks like a one-off. Don't talk to Crane Jr.'s wife. Message received."

"So, what are we gonna do?" I asked.

"We're gonna talk to the bastard's wife, of course."

Mandy's cell rang, and she answered it.

"Hi, Jack," she said into her cell. "You get in all right? Do you need anything from . . . okay. Tomorrow then. Good night."

She clicked off.

"Jack all checked in?" I asked.

"Yeah. The Duffys are bringing Hope over in the morning," she said. She then let out a heavy sigh. "He wants me to help him break the news."

Lynn had refilled my scotch glass.

"Looks like you can use this more than I can right now," I said, handing the libation to Mandy.

"Nope," she said. "It's time to put my big girl pants on."

I wasn't quite as sore the following day. What Crane Jr.'s thugs had dished out was hardly a love tap, but it was nothing that ice, time, and ibuprofen wouldn't cure. While my stiffness made maneuvering in and out of the Black Beauty a little tricky, I drove as Mandy sat in the passenger seat, her hair billowing in the wind of the lowered top. Though it was still unseasonably warm, it was a little cooler in this neck of the woods, with the breeze wafting off the bay waters. As she had been on the drive to Julie Wolfer's house the night before, Mandy was quietly going over the script in her head for the coming confrontation.

"Do you know what you're going to say?" I asked as we took the exit from the San Mateo Bridge to Highway 101 North toward the San Francisco Airport.

"I don't suppose it'll be much. I expect Jack to do most of the talking. I'm primarily there for moral support."

We exited the freeway in Burlingame and pulled into the driveway of a conveniently located Hilton Garden Inn across the road from the airport. I spotted a late-model, high-end Mercedes sedan as we entered the parking lot. An older couple stood next to the car. They had aged some since I last saw them at the press conference I had previously attended at the Promes's home. It was as though a weary inevitability had set in. With the string of seemingly relentless tragedies, the ensuing weeks had put a visible strain on the faces of the Duffys. They looked as though they had lived a decade over the previous month. Each was firmly holding one of the hands of a little girl I recognized as Hope Wolfer.

I parked and gently extricated myself from the driver's seat. Hope ran to Mandy as she exited on the passenger side. As soon as Mandy was out of the car, the girl's arms were tightly wrapped around her cousin's waist. As Mandy gently stroked the child's hair, I slowly walked over to the Duffys.

"How much does she know?" I whispered.

"Just that she's meeting her father," Skyler Duffy replied softly.

"This is going to be a rough one," Mason Duffy whispered.

Mandy brought the grinning child over to where we were standing. "Mr. and Mrs. Duffy, I'm Julie's cousin—" she began to say.

"It's nice to meet you, Amanda," Skyler said. "Jack has told us quite a bit about you."

"Nothing good, I'll bet," she said with a crooked smile and a tone that seemed to capture the melancholy of the occasion. "And it's Mandy."

Mason Duffy extended his hand.

"Then you can call us Mason and Skyler," he said. "Jack appreciates that you're doing this."

"Of course," Mandy said, taking Mason Duffy's hand and shaking it. She then resumed stroking Hope's hair. "Which room is it?"

"236," came Skyler's reply.

"Come on, sweetie," Mandy said, taking Hope by the hand. "Let's go see your daddy."

The Duffys and I watched as Mandy led the little girl through automated glass doors and to an elevator in the lobby. Mandy pressed a button, the doors opened, and the pair soon disappeared behind them.

Once they'd gone, I extended my hand to Morgan Duffy.

"I'm—"

"I know who you are, Mr. Davis. Personally, I don't understand why you're here. The press is the last thing that child needs right now," he said, an edge of irritation in his voice.

"I'm not here as media," I replied, holding my palms up in surrender. "I'm here to support Mandy. She's my friend."

"I see," he said.

Mr. Duffy reached into the vest pocket of his blue blazer and removed a shiny, brown wooden pipe. He then took a small plastic bag filled with tobacco from his pants pocket and dipped the pipe inside to fill its bowl. He returned the tobacco to his slacks, pulled out a wooden match, and struck it against the heel of the black-tasseled loafer he wore on his left foot. He was agile for an older man. I was a good quarter-century his junior, and I'd be surprised if I could balance on one leg like that. I could hear Lynn's voice in my head, nagging me yet again to join her yoga class.

"You're not going smoke that smelly thing, are you?" Skyler chastised her husband, waving her hand in front of her face as if fanning away smoke.

"It relaxes me," he said as he puffed and released a small, bluish cloud into the air.

I recognized the aroma as Mild Cavendish. I had a professor at SF State who smoked it in class way back in the Stone Age when it was still legal to smoke indoors.

"I've got to do something to keep from jumping out of my skin," Mason said, blowing another gust of pipe smoke.

"This is just a nightmare," Mrs. Duffy said, shaking her head. "A terrible, never-ending nightmare."

"I'm sorry for your loss," I said.

"*Losses*," she corrected. "Julie and Kristen were so close, she was becoming something of a second daughter to us."

"My condolences," I said.

"Thank you," Mason jumped in as if racing to be the gracious one.

"Where is your granddaughter?"

"We thought it best to leave Taylor at our home for now. Tom was able to evade your colleagues, and he's there with her now," Skyler said. "He's trying again to explain the situation to her in a way that she can understand."

"This is the second time he's had to do this in two weeks," she said. "Now, there are two motherless little girls. Just a nightmare."

"I can only imagine," I said.

"We just want things to return to normal," Mason said. "Well, as normal as they can be with Kristen now ripped out of our lives."

"If you don't mind my unsolicited advice," I said, "staying busy helps."

"I've tried going to work," he said. "Haven't been able to keep my mind on a damned thing. I try to read papers and contracts and just find myself reading the same sentences repeatedly. I have no comprehension of what I've read whatsoever. Thank God for Tom."

"Has Tom been working through all of this?"

"He's been hunkered down in his home office. He's a godsend. More than ready to take over the company."

"He's taking over?"

"That's always been the succession plan," Duffy said. "He's been my right hand for years. Hell, he even met Kristen in my office. He was a new hire. She was answering phones to earn a few bucks during summer vacation from college."

"Vassar," Skyler chimed in.

I thought it was only Harvard people who bragged about their college within the first five minutes of an initial conversation. Then again, I went to a state school. What did I know?

"Tom knows the business inside and out. He'll take over when I retire," Mason continued.

He paused for a moment and then stared at the ground. "Kristen was pregnant with a little boy. The hope was that Tom would pass the company on to him someday," he said.

It seems like there is always more than enough generational wealth to be passed along for white people. Even to their unborn. Not that I had a right to complain. Auntie didn't exactly leave Lynn and me paupers.

Skyler gently touched her husband's back and began to rub it. Marital shorthand for, "It'll be okay."

I wondered how "okay" it would be once the Duffys learned about Tom's affair with Julie Wolfer. What kind of monkey wrench would *that* throw into "the succession plan"? The business was substantial—one of the largest real estate firms in the Tri-Valley area. I couldn't see Mason Duffy handing over his life's work to a man who was cheating on his daughter.

More motive for Tom Promes to want Kristen dead. Kill Kristen, end up with the business *and* the girlfriend. No alimony. No child support for a second kid. No vengeful father-in-law kicking him out of the real estate firm. Tom Promes could get everything he wanted with no loose ends. Yet, it made no sense to kill Julie Wolfer. Why would he off his lover? If he really did do it, Julie would have been the catalyst for the whole thing in the first place. And what would be the reason for killing Danica?

Tom Promes was our most likely suspect. If he didn't kill Kristen Promes, who did? As far as I could surmise, he was the only one with a motive. But how did he pull it off while at a barbecue packed with witnesses? He would have needed a confederate. Julie Wolfer made the most sense. She's the one who got Kristen out of the house in the first place, but now, she's dead. At who's hand and why?

Which brings us back to Danica. The three women were apparently murdered by the same killer. As far as we could tell, there was no connection between Tom Promes and Danica Walker. Crane Jr. was clearly terrified of his wife finding out about his affair. That provides motive in Danica's killing, but what did Crane Jr. have to do with Kristen Promes? We couldn't even prove that Crane knew her, let alone had anything to do with her murder. For a fleeting moment, I thought about the two men "doing each other's murders" before quickly dismissing the *Strangers on a Train* theory.

"Tell me," I said to Mason, "when you were at the barbecue, did you notice anything odd about Kristen's behavior that day? Or Tom's? Or anybody else's, for that matter?"

"I was busy glad-handing," he said. "The real purpose of that event was for Tom and me to schmooze and do some business. Right now, we need a variance to rezone some commercial lots we've optioned as residential so that we can put up a condo development in Pleasanton. The only thing standing in our way right now is Roland Douglas. He's on the planning commission and . . . He owns the lots. Not much of a conflict of interest there, is there?"

He sarcastically chuckled, his laugh quickly turning into a tobacco-fueled coughing fit.

"We've had an option to purchase those lots for five years, and the option's about to run out. If Douglas doesn't approve the rezoning, the property's useless to us. We lose our option money, and Douglas keeps the lots. Tom invited Douglas and his wife in the hope that we could convince him to vote to rezone."

"Isn't there some law or something on the books that would force him to recuse himself from having anything to do with this since he owns the property?"

"You'd think so, wouldn't you?" Mason said. "But there isn't. Unwritten policy is that it's 'recommended' but not required. There are five commissioners on that board, and right now, it's two to two in terms of rezoning. Douglas is the fifth vote. He's our holdout."

"Why?" I asked. "Doesn't he make money once you exercise your option?"

"Two million dollars," Mason said. "Not chump change."

"So why the roadblock?"

"Greed. He figures if he holds out long enough, he can get our firm to raise our price and pay him three or four million dollars. We're already on the hook for seven figures with the option money we've put in. Douglas knows we can't afford to lose that kind of money. If we don't exercise the option, he keeps our cash."

"So, what are you going to do?"

"We've filed suit against him for conflict of interest and not dealing in good faith. We've got a pretty good shot at winning on the 'good faith' issue."

Mason Duffy took another drag from his pipe and noticed it had gone out. He reached back into his pocket, pulled out another wooden match, and repeated his one-legged balancing act, again striking it against the bottom of his shoe. Soon, he was billowing smoke again.

"Tom wanted to see if he could convince him to be reasonable. Change his mind. Stop blocking the project. Vote with us, and let us exercise our option."

"How'd it go?" I asked.

"Tom never got a chance to really work on him because Kristen . . ."

He let out a small sob. His wife resumed rubbing his back.

"Sorry," he said. "Comes and goes."

"It's understandable, sir. No apologies necessary," I said.

He puffed on his pipe and discovered that it had gone out again. This time, he didn't relight it.

"Is there a deadline of some kind on this project?" I asked.

"We're down to four days," he said.

"What are you going to do if Douglas remains intractable?"

"What can I do?" he asked. "Pay him the four million dollars. Bastard."

At that point, my cell buzzed. Lynn.

"I'm sorry," I said. "I need to take this."

"Of course," Mason said.

I clicked on the phone.

"Yeah, Lynn?"

"Ready for this?" she asked.

"What?"

"I just got the autopsy report on Julie Wolfer. You know how her womb was carved out like the others? Fetus removed?"

"Yeah," I said, growing impatient. I saw the elevators inside the hotel, and Mandy stepped out alone.

"Julie Wolfer wasn't pregnant."

TWENTY-THREE

MANDY WALKED OUT of the hotel and into the parking lot. She explained to the Duffys that Hope would spend some time alone with Jack for a while. We said our goodbyes and headed back to the Black Beauty.

"How'd it go?" I asked as we pulled out of the parking lot and headed back to Highway 101.

"Rough," she said. "Very, very rough. Jack told her that the angels missed Jules and wanted her to come and be with them. When she asked him if he meant 'Like Taylor's mommy?' I thought I was going to be sick."

"You okay?"

"As okay as I can be given the circumstances."

"Is there anything I can do?"

"Just drive," she said. "Take me somewhere—anywhere."

I did as she asked, taking Highway 101 to Highway 92 toward Santa Cruz. Didn't feel much like a day at the beach, but all things considered, I figured it couldn't hurt. I debated telling her about Lynn's call but decided to wait. I could tell that, at this point, Mandy was a raw nerve. A live grenade whose pin would elicit an emotional explosion once pulled. It was emotion that she wasn't ready to deal with yet. There would be plenty of time for that later. She needed a few hours to catch her breath and regain her footing.

"Where we going?" she asked as I merged onto Highway 17.

"How long since you rode the Giant Dipper?"

Forty-five minutes later, we stopped at a local Target, swapped our street clothes for shorts, T-shirts, and flip-flops, and walked along the sand at the Santa Cruz Beach Boardwalk. The Boardwalk was busy. Packed as it always was on a warm summer day, with a mix of parents herding young children, teenagers traveling in packs in search of both trouble and adventure, and lovers walking hand in hand as they blocked out the din of the amusement park to focus on the adoration of mutual eyes.

A young boy, maybe fourteen or so, zoomed past us on a skateboard and knocked Mandy off her feet before disappearing into the crowd up ahead. I caught her before she hit the ground.

"Asshole," she muttered under her breath.

"Oh," I said, "like you were never a teenager."

"No, I was an asshole at that age too. It's what gives me carte blanche to call that kid one."

"You're getting old, Lang," I said. "Shall I ask them to turn down their music?"

She playfully flipped me the bird as I righted her on her feet.

"Good thing I didn't break my hip," she said in her best octogenarian voice.

"Want some cotton candy?" I asked as we passed the stand, which offered a variety of sweet treats, caramel corn, and other confections.

"What the hell?" she replied.

I bought a cardboard stick wrapped in layers of pink cotton candy for Mandy and a blue snow cone for myself. Mandy licked her treat, and I watched it dissolve the instant it made contact with saliva. She grimaced.

"Sickeningly sweet," she said, making a face like a six-year-old who'd been force-fed a forkful of liver.

"Well, what do you expect? It's sugar and air."

"I used to love this stuff when I was a kid. Now, it's so sweet I'm gonna hurl if I take another bite."

"See?" I said. "Old."

She tossed the cardboard stick into a nearby trash can.

"Eight bucks down the drain," I said.

"Bill me."

"The roller coaster is over here," I said, gesturing to the long line of patrons waiting patiently for their minute and fifty-two seconds of thrills on the national landmark. A ride on the Giant Dipper was a prerequisite for living in these parts. You had to do it at least once to call yourself a Northern Californian.

"This thing is literally a hundred years old. It's made of wood, for God's sake. You sure it's safe?" she asked.

"Do you know how many thousands of people ride the Giant Dipper in a year? Hell, in a *day*?" I asked. "Nobody gets hurt. It's perfectly safe. When did my daredevil producer become so timid?"

"When her cousin was carved up like a Thanksgiving turkey, and she realized that her boss was withholding information from her," she said.

I looked down at my flip-flops. Why do they always irritate you in the crevice next to the big toe when they're new?

"What is it?" she demanded.

"Nothing. You've just had a rough couple of days, and I thought you could use a few hours of distraction."

"Bullshit," she said. "You act like I don't know you. You're hiding something. What is it? Tell me—now."

"How about we head over to the games, and I win you a stuffed monkey or something? In high school, I was pretty good at that game where you toss the rings over the Coke bottles."

"Topher," she said, a sharp edge creeping into her tone.

I took a deep breath. "Lynn called while you were with Jack and Hope. She got the autopsy report back on Julie."

"And?" she demanded.

"While she was cut open at the womb and given a crude caesarian like the other victims, there's no evidence that she was pregnant. Unlike with Danica Walker and Kristen Promes, there was no fetus to steal."

"Then why . . .?"

"I don't know," I said with as much sympathy as I could muster. "I'm sorry. I didn't want to go into the gruesome details with you today. You've been through enough."

"Let's get the hell out of here," she said.

"Mandy—"

"I want to talk to Lynn. Is she in her office?"

"She should be," I said.

"Call her and let her know we're on our way."

"You sure I can't just buy you a candy apple?"

She turned on her heels and headed toward the parking lot.

After an icy sixty-mile ride back up Highway 101, we were sitting in Lynn's office at 850 Bryant Street in The City. I love how San Francisco is probably the only metropolitan area on earth pretentious enough to call itself "The City."

I'd traded in my flip-flops for a spare pair of running shoes I keep in the trunk of the Beauty in the event I get an uncontrollable urge to sprint someplace. It hasn't happened yet, but it never hurts to be prepared. I'd also changed out of my beach attire and back into my shirt and slacks. Mandy had also resumed her more professional look.

"I'm sorry, Mandy," Lynn said. "I wanted to know more before I went into any more of this stuff with you."

"Stop treating me like a child. I'm a journalist, just like your brother," she snapped.

"A journalist who is too close to this story to be objective. What you are," Lynn said, "is the next of kin."

"I'm a big girl," Mandy said. "What do you know? What's the autopsy say?"

Lynn looked at me. I shrugged.

"While Julie was cut up like the others, unlike those victims, there's no indication she was pregnant," Lynn said. "In the other cases, the women were expecting. The killer murdered them and then took the time to steal their fetuses. In Julie's case, there was no baby to steal."

"So, we're talking about a copycat?" Mandy asked.

"I doubt it. News of the fetal abductions hasn't been released to the public. One of the ways we'll know if we're dealing with the real killer when the time comes."

"Then, it could have been somebody who *thought* Jules was pregnant," Mandy said.

"That is definitely a possibility," Lynn replied.

"Or the killer might have wanted it to look like the other murders," I added. "The fetal abduction is a signature. Maybe he wanted us to know that the murders were connected. Baby or no baby."

"Why?" Mandy asked. "Why would somebody want to do that?"

"Maybe Julie's murder had a different motive than the other slayings. Maybe she was killed in the same way, so authorities would just lump the killings all together. So, they'd think they were dealing with one serial killer with a signature, a victim type, and a single MO. The garroting," I said.

"Working with that theory," Lynn said, "since Julie is the outlier, we need to look closer at her life. Who'd want her dead?"

"Kristen Promes, for one," I said. "Julie was sleeping with the woman's husband."

"Which scratches her off the list," Lynn said. "No better alibi than being dead."

"Then there's Jack Wolfer. If he found out about the affair, that's certainly a motive for murder," I said.

"We need to check and see if he really was in Phoenix at the time of the killing," Lynn stated.

"I can get right on that," Mandy said.

"Mandy, you shouldn't be working on this. You're too close to it," I sternly said.

"I can work with you guys or I can go it alone," she answered. "Either way, I'm finding my cousin's killer."

Lynn and I looked at each other. We'd seen Mandy determined before, but never like this.

"Tom Promes is on the list," Lynn finally said. "Always got to look at the husband or the boyfriend. In these cases, he's both."

"But why would he want Julie dead?" I asked. "If he did have something to do with Kristen's death, then Julie Wolfer would be the prime motive. Kill the wife so you can run off with the girlfriend."

"And then there's the victim everybody still treats like an afterthought: Danica Walker. We still have no connection between her and Kristen Promes, let alone Julie Wolfer. How does she fit in?" I asked.

"I'd suggest we go down the list," Lynn suggested. "Chris, you talk to Josie Walker and the ladies at Braids and see if Jack and Julie Wolfer ring any bells. Mandy, look into Julie's personal life. Who were her friends? Who were the other moms she ran with? Who'd she arrange playdates for her daughter with? As for me, I think it's time that I have another tête-à-tête with Tom Promes himself."

"I want in on that one," I said. "I love doing the 'bad cop, bad cop' routine with you."

"I thought it was 'good cop, bad cop,'" Mandy said.

"Not the way *we* do it," Lynn replied with a smile.

"I want to come too," Mandy said.

"No, Mandy. We don't need an army headed over there. It's intimidating. Too many people rush him, and he'll just clam up," Lynn said. "Let Chris and me take this one. You check into Julie Wolfer's connections. How long had her affair with Tom Promes been going on? Who else knew about it? Did Kristen? And again, follow up on Jack's alibi."

Mandy reluctantly nodded before whispering, "Okay."

"All right," Lynn said. "We've got our marching orders."

"You sure you want to be a part of this?" I asked Mandy. "It's going to get ugly."

"It's already ugly," she said.

TWENTY-FOUR

MT. ZION BAPTIST Church was really more of a chapel than a full-fledged church. Although it was ornate and beautiful with its shiny wood pews and elaborately designed stained-glass windows, I'd have been shocked if a hundred people could have been shoehorned into the little place of worship.

I sat in the back pew closest to the door. I wanted a good look at who came and went as I listened to the reverend go on about everlasting life for those who accepted Jesus Christ as their Lord and Savior. The minister was a short, stout Black man with close-cropped hair seasoned with equal amounts of salt and pepper. Round, wire-rimmed pince-nez glasses rested tightly on the bridge of his nose. Pince-nez? Was it 1910 again already? Despite his diminutive stature, the tenor of his voice was such that it boomed loud enough to rattle the stained-glass depictions of the stages of the Passion. The odd thing was, even though his volume was blaring, his words were calm and soothing.

"Mama is all right," he said, looking at D'Vante, who sat in the left front pew, his arm around Josie's shoulders. From my vantage point, I could see her shoulders rise and fall in periodic

189

spasms of grief. While I could only see her back, I had a good view of her grandson's profile. I could tell that D'Vante was trying his damndest to project stoicism. He was now the man of the house. I knew the feeling well. I was even younger than he when that title was unceremoniously thrust upon me. I was no more ready for it than this somber kid was.

The service, like the chapel, was intimate. There was no press. No cameras or reporters lined up begging for a quote to make their six o'clock broadcasts. No one hiding in the bushes out front trying to catch an emotional picture of the grieving family as they prepared to say their final goodbyes. Even though I'd tried to bring attention to Danica's case with my broadcasts, her death remained a postscript. In the mostly filled little church were Josie, D'Vante, and the stylists from Braids. A small assortment of African American faces I wasn't familiar with dotted the landscape, apparently classmates of Danica's and Josie's friends from her neighborhood who had watched her grow up. Inga Sorenson, the young woman who was Danica's replacement at the reception desk of Crane, Phelps, and Crane, sat in a pew near the rear of the church. I assumed that she'd been conscripted into duty as a firm representative. I knew that Mr. Crane Jr. sure as hell wasn't going to show his face there but sending an employee who'd never even met Danica . . . classy.

An older man sat across the aisle from me. He was conspicuous by being the only white man in the church. He was in his seventies but could easily have passed for being ten years younger. He was fit and trim. You could tell that he regularly went to the gym by the bulging pecs that were apparent through his off-the-rack suit. His skin was flawless and unblemished. A thick shock of snow-white hair covered his head. A matching mustache curled upward at the ends with wax completed the look. I wasn't sure if he was a mourner or a member of a barbershop quartet. Throughout the service, he kept his hands folded reverently in prayer.

While I did need to talk to her, I attended because Josie had asked me to come. She said I was the only person in the press who cared about Danica. As much as I loathed admitting it, she was right. News coverage, especially when it's local, can be a very racist proposition. Most of it isn't intentional. The editorial decisions are made primarily by middle-aged white men like Curt Weil, who, as he said, can see their milky-skinned, blue-eyed daughters in the faces of every young white woman who goes missing. As for lost Black girls with long, beaded African braids, not so much. They cover what they can relate to. They're moved by what strikes them viscerally at their cores. I guess it's human nature. It's also why there is such a desperate need for more people of color to make some of these decisions.

"Danica is with God and the angels for all eternity," the minister continued. "I want you all to close your eyes. Go on, shut them."

The mourners all did as commanded. I followed suit.

"I want you to picture a big sandy beach. One of those beaches where the white sand stretches along the coastline for miles and miles as the crystal blue waters of the ocean lap at its shores. You got that image?"

There was a chorus of "Mmm-hmms" throughout the church.

"Good. Now, think about all the grains of sand that make up that beautiful beach. Millions and millions of grains of sand. Can you see them?"

The mourners repeated their affirmation.

"Now," the minister said, "imagine a little ant trying to move each particle of sand, one grain at a time. Just one solitary little ant trying to move that entire beach grain by grain. Do you see it?"

The crowd murmured, "Yes."

"As long as it takes that one ant to move all the grains of sand on that long, long beach is the length of time that our beloved Danica will be in God's hands," he whispered. "For eternity."

I could see Josie's shoulders bouncing harder and more frequently now. A dry-eyed D'Vante pulled her in closer to him and held her tighter. He was just a boy, but he'd already learned the first rule of being a Black man in America: *never ever let them see you cry.*

D'Vante was the picture of dignity as he later stood at the lectern, eulogizing his mother as a hard worker, a good friend and daughter, and an even better mom. No matter what she was doing or how hard she worked, she was always there for her son as much as possible, both physically and emotionally. The boy swore to be the keeper of his mother's flame and fulfill her dreams. If she couldn't be a lawyer, he would. He'd finish high school, go to college, then law school, and then build the legal practice she would have built.

I've seen it all before. Children taking on the lives of a dead parent. Foregoing their own dreams in the service of existing solely as an instrument perpetuating the legacy of the dearly departed. He was an aspiring concert pianist, and he was good. Yet, he was willing to throw away that dream to do what he thought would make his mother proud. I was sure that she already was.

The service concluded about fifteen minutes later, and six young African American men in dark suits and white gloves took the shiny brass handles of the dark wooden casket sitting in the aisle in front of the altar and carried it to the waiting hearse just outside the entrance. From their ages, I assumed that the pallbearers had been more peers of Danica's from the neighborhood.

I felt myself get emotional as I perused the thin, white program in my hands. Its front filled with a portrait of a smiling Danica. A young woman with years of life ahead of her. It should have been a graduation picture, not the cover of a funeral program. Inside were kind words about Danica's devotion to her son, her strong desire to make something of herself, and her plans for the glorious future that was the Holy Grail of all people of color living in neighborhoods like hers in East Oakland: to enter the middle class.

Now, she was gone. Relegated to photos on the mantle and stories of her various exploits and adventures recounted occasionally. Eventually, the stories from her friends and family would become fewer and fewer, and her name mentioned with less frequency. Time would gradually erase the sound of her voice from the memories of those who loved her. It was how we all eventually ended up. Just a picture on a shelf above the fireplace. The thought brought tears to my eyes. Danica was practically a kid herself. I wouldn't let her be forgotten. I fully committed in that instant to find her killer no matter what I had to do.

***

After the service, people headed to the Walker home for the reception. That's a ritual I've never entirely understood. Personally, the last thing I feel like doing after attending a somber and depressing funeral is to tie on the feedbag. To each his own, I guess.

Josie's little house was filled with people. Most I recognized from the funeral. Some apparently didn't make the service but made an appearance at the reception. I didn't see the new receptionist. I guess that when her primary obligation was met, she headed back across the bridge to her office.

The smells emanating from the kitchen and the buffet table reminded me of my youth. They brought me back to Auntie's Piedmont house on a typical Sunday afternoon after mass. Fried chicken, collard greens with smoked turkey tails, macaroni and cheese (not that boxed stuff but *real* homemade mac and cheese), spiral-sliced ham, candied sweet potatoes, freshly baked icebox rolls, and an array of other culinary delights that I didn't often get the opportunity to partake in, given the world in which I now lived. Lynn was a mediocre cook at best. Jared was a professional chef but knew nothing about preparing a soul food dinner. As for me, I lived alone with a dog. It just wasn't worth the trouble.

Josie Walker sat in a recliner in the corner of the room. Like the Duffys, she too had aged dramatically in the weeks since I first met her. Her eyes were red and puffy as she talked quietly to guests who knelt next to her to offer their condolences. She was gracious in accepting them. The people would say their piece and then head off to the buffet table, where they'd pile sturdy paper plates high with mounds of chicken and collards. D'Vante stood among them, chatting as he held a plate containing just a few perfunctory spoonfuls of various foods. It appeared to be more about having something to do with his hands than sustenance.

I stood in the opposite corner, observing. Like D'Vante, I didn't eat either. Even though everything looked and smelled heavenly, I just wasn't hungry. After about an hour, the man with the waxed mustache who'd sat across from me in church talked to Josie for a few minutes and then knelt and hugged her. He got up and headed for the door and left. Once he was gone, there was a break in the line of mourners, so I walked over. As I approached, Josie dabbed at her eyes with a balled-up Kleenex.

"Who was that?" I asked, my thumb pointing toward the man who had just left.

"Him?" she asked. "An old family friend. A big supporter of D'Vante's music. Nice man."

"How are you holding up?" I asked.

"Oh," she said, "I'm all right."

"Is there anything you need? Anything I can get you?"

"Let's go outside and get some air," she said.

I helped her out of the recliner and followed her past the buffet line, through the kitchen, and into the backyard. It was a neat, well-maintained space with lush, green, neatly trimmed grass and shrubs. The small yard was enclosed behind a six-foot wooden fence with azaleas blooming in the dirt space between where the grass ended and the fencing began.

The only thing out of place was an old, rusty swing set in the middle of the yard. It was your typical Sear's special with two swings, a teeter-totter, and a metal slide whose silver shine had now been discolored by the brown of oxidation. Josie noticed me studying it.

"It was D'Vante's when he was little. Danica worked with me for a whole summer at the store to earn enough money to buy it for him and have it assembled in time for Christmas. Once D'Vante outgrew it, Danica meant to donate it to somebody with a yard and small kids, but she never quite got around to it. It's just rusted metal now. I know I should have the junk man come and haul it away, but I think about Danica working that summer, and I just don't have the heart to. I will, though," she said, apparently trying to convince herself more than me.

"I will," she repeated.

"It was a nice service," I said.

"A lot of people loved Danica. I even got a sympathy card from Rodney, D'Vante's father."

"You did?"

"He wanted me to know how heartbroken he was and that he was sorry he couldn't make it to the funeral. He applied for some kind of bereavement furlough to attend, but it was denied. He expected them to turn him down, but he figured he'd at least try. He never stopped loving Danica. Never. And I don't think she ever stopped loving him.

"You know that man actually sends child support from San Quentin? There's not even a court order in place because he's incarcerated. He's paid pennies a day for his work in the prison kitchen, yet he still tries to help out. It's sporadic. Five dollars here. Ten dollars there," she said. "That boy does not belong where he is. Getting him a new trial was going to be Danica's first order of business once she passed the bar and got herself established in the legal community."

"How much does D'Vante know about his father?"

"Nothing," she said. "We told him that his father was killed in a car crash when he was a baby. Rodney's idea. He didn't want his son to grow up with the stigma of having a convict for a father. There's enough of that in this neighborhood."

"You do know that D'Vante is going to find out one day," I said. "They have this thing called the internet."

Josie Walker cracked a smile. "I'll jump off that bridge when I come to it."

There was an awkward moment of silence as Josie got a faraway look in her eyes, remembering.

"Josie," I said, breaking the spell, "I know it's not the best time, but I need to ask you something."

"About the case?"

"Yes."

"Go on ahead. I buried my baby today, but she won't rest, and neither will I until I know who did this to her and why," she said, again using the ragged tissue she held to absorb the moisture as it returned to her eyes.

"This is very delicate," I said, "but did you know that Josie was . . ."

"Expecting? Yes."

"How'd you find out? Did she tell you?"

She shook her head. "A mother knows these things," she said. "The glow in her face. The sheen in her hair. No appetite at breakfast time. I knew."

"Did you discuss it with her?" I asked.

"I figured she'd tell me when she was ready. I never pried into Danica's business," she said. "I sure wish I'd done that now."

"Does the name Julie Wolfer mean anything to you?"

"Julie Wolfer . . ." she said, tapping her chin with her index finger. "She's that other white girl who got killed, isn't she?"

"Yes."

"I saw it on the news. Your station, actually."

"Her name familiar to you at all?"

"Nope. Never heard of her until I saw the news story."

"So, you don't know if she and Danica knew each other?"

"Not a clue," she said. "Why are you asking me about that girl?"

I thought for a moment. She deserved an answer.

"You have to keep this between us because it's information I shouldn't be sharing with you."

"Okay," she said.

"The police think Kristen Promes's case and Danica's may be connected."

A weathered hand darted over an open mouth.

"Now, Julie Wolfer's too. Nobody outside of my team and the police know, so, again, you *can't* tell anybody. You might jeopardize the investigation, and we'll never get justice for Danica."

"I won't tell a soul," she promised, placing her right hand over her heart as if she were about to begin the Pledge of Allegiance. "How? How are they connected?"

"The police aren't sure. I was hoping maybe you knew something."

"Kristen Promes. Julie Wolfer. I don't recall her ever mentioning either of those names," she said.

She paused for a moment and then asked, "Why do you think they have something to do with Danica's murder?"

"I can't tell you that, Josie. I'm sorry."

"Jeopardizing the investigation. Right," she said. "Don't you worry. I won't do anything that will stop that killer from getting exactly what he's got coming to him."

"I know that you're preoccupied with the funeral and everything. Don't worry about this right now, but in the coming days, can you think of any possible way Danica might have known either Kristen Promes or Julie Wolfer?"

"Of course," she said. "Just let me get through today, and then I'll think on it."

"Thank you," I said, taking her hands in mine. "And again, my deepest sympathies."

Josie Walker let go of my hands, flung her arms around me, and held on like I was a life raft in a raging river.

"It's going to be okay," I said.

Why do people always make that assurance? We have no crystal ball. We can't read tea leaves or any other contrivance that allegedly allows mortals to peer into the future. I didn't have a clue if it was going to be all right or not. What I did know was that I was going to find the killer of this woman's daughter, no matter how long it took or how difficult it turned out to be. I had broken the cardinal rule of journalism. I had allowed this case to become personal.

The phone in my coat pocket began to vibrate.

"Davis," I said into the device.

"This is Tom Promes. I need to talk to you."

TWENTY-FIVE

THE NEXT MORNING, Chief Lane and two of his officers pushed through the throng of media in front of the Promes house and entered, emerging a few moments later with a man in a green golf shirt and brown khakis, his face obscured by a Pleasanton PD cap and windbreaker. The man was not handcuffed, although officers flanked him on both sides, their hands firmly gripping his biceps. The rapid whir of SLRs erupted, capturing every step as the police escorted their subject down the walkway and into a waiting black SUV with dark-tinted windows.

Reporters immediately unleashed a rat-a-tat-tat barrage of questions.

"Chief Lane, is Mr. Promes being taken into custody?"

"Tom, did you murder your wife?"

"Where were you when Julie Wolfer was murdered?"

"Does your daughter know that you killed her mother?"

"Hey, Chief, what are the charges? Murder one or two?"

Lane and his entourage ignored the battery of inquiries, their attention focused squarely on the task at hand, getting the subject into the vehicle. Soon, one officer used gentle force to lower the subject's head into the rear of the SUV before closing the door and hiding him behind the dark glass windows. Once their charge was safely inside the vehicle, Chief Lane addressed the reporters.

"We have no official comment to make at this time. Once we do, you folks will be given a statement at an official press conference," he said, stepping into the passenger side of the SUV and closing the door.

The vehicle sped off, with most of the media quickly packing up their trucks and cameras and following in hot pursuit.

The handful of press that stayed behind noticed a small group of Pleasanton PD officers standing in front of the Promes home as though guarding a crime scene. Soon, a black-and-white department vehicle pulled into the driveway, and two figures emerged wearing black Pleasanton PD windbreakers and dark hats emblazoned with the department logo. One carried a dark leather satchel. They walked past the sentries at the front door and were waved in.

Once inside, we removed our caps and found Tom Promes sitting at the wet bar off the living room.

"Was all this subterfuge really necessary?" he asked.

"We didn't want the horde to know we were talking to you privately. Better they think you're being officially grilled downtown," Lynn said. "By the time they realize that it was one of Lane's guys under that windbreaker and that it's a nonstory, we'll be all done here."

"They already think I'm guilty."

"Are you?" I asked.

"Mr. Davis, I agreed to talk to you, hoping you'd help me get out my side of the story. I even agreed to talk to your sister. Will you help me?" he said, pleading.

"It depends on what you have to say," I replied.

"Well," he said, "if nothing else, at least you got the mob off the porch for a while."

"You can thank Chief Lane for helping us with that."

"Your daughter still with her grandparents?" Lynn asked.

Promes nodded.

"We FaceTime every night before bed. It's for the best right now," he said.

"I understand your intention here," Lynn said, "but to reiterate, you're under no obligation."

"I know," he said.

"So then, we're on the record?" I asked, removing my iPhone from my windbreaker pocket and opening the recording app.

Tom Promes paused for a minute.

"We're on the record. For now," he finally said. "I've got to tell the world *something*."

"I need to warn you that even though this isn't a police interview, and you haven't been Mirandized or taken into custody, anything that you say into that recorder can be used as evidence if there should come a time when there is a trial," Lynn said.

"A trial for what?" Promes askes. "See? Like I said, everybody thinks I killed Kristen."

"Did you?" I asked again.

"No!" he snapped back. "I did *not* kill my wife. Hell, I was right here in a house full of people when it happened. I'm no magician. There's no way I could be in two places simultaneously."

"No, you couldn't be. But you could have hired somebody to do it for you," I said.

"I could have, but I didn't!" he protested.

"How would you describe the state of your marriage to Kristen?" Lynn asked.

"Like any marriage, we had our ups and downs, but . . . We were happy," he said, his eyes suddenly moist.

"Were either of you involved in any . . . extracurricular romantic activities?" I asked.

"No. Of course not. We loved each other," he said. "We had our problems, but we loved each other."

Lynn removed a large manila envelope from the leather satchel she carried and handed it to him.

"Then," she said, "would you mind explaining these?"

"What's this?" he asked, opening the envelope.

He pulled out the photo it contained, and his face went colorless.

"Where'd you get this?" he asked, leafing through the pictures.

"Monterey is lovely this time of year, isn't it?" I asked.

"*Where did you get this?*" he demanded.

"Does it really matter?" Lynn said. "That *is* you, isn't it?"

He said nothing, fixating on the picture. He stared as if it were magically going to change into a photo of a child's birthday party or something.

"Isn't it?" Lynn asked again.

He let out a sharp exhale and then finally a nod.

"I'm sorry," I said. "This is an audio recorder. It can't pick up your gestures. Would you mind answering the detective's question verbally?"

"Yes," he said, defeated. "I am the man in that picture."

"And the woman you're swapping spit with is Julie Wolfer," I said.

"Who else has seen this?" he asked.

"Chief Lane, his detectives working the case, Chief O'Reilly's in Livermore, and a few others," Lynn said.

"And, of course, me," I added. "The rest of the press doesn't have it . . . yet. We thought you might want to get ahead of this."

Tom Promes looked at the print again. "Believe me," I said, "the press and the supermarket tabloids *will* get hold of this. It's not a matter of 'if.' It's 'when.'"

Tom ran his fingers through his hair as he looked at the picture again.

"When did you and Julie Wolfer begin the affair?" Lynn asked.

He paused for a few moments, contemplating. "About six months before she died. Before *they* died," he said, his voice barely above a whisper.

He reached behind the bar and produced a bottle of Jose Cuervo and a shot glass. He raised the glass as an offering.

"A little early for me," I said.

"No, thank you," Lynn said.

Promes filled the shot glass with tequila and downed it like a frat boy on Spring Break. He began to put the liquor bottle away, thought better of it, refilled the shot glass, and repeated the ritual, this time wiping the remnants of liquor from his mouth with his sleeve.

"Sorry," he said. "As you know, it's been a rough couple of weeks."

"It's about to get rougher," I said.

"You were telling us about you and Julie Wolfer," Lynn said.

"One night, I was picking up Taylor from a play date with Hope. Jack was out of town as usual. Julie invited me in for a glass of wine that turned into two. We talked, and . . . One thing led to another," he said, picking up the bottle to pour a third tequila. Lynn's hand darted out and gently touched his.

"You can drink yourself blind after we're gone. In the meantime, let's keep this sober, shall we?"

Promes put down the bottle of Cuervo.

"You started this little romance while your daughters were in the house?" I asked.

"The girls were in Hope's room, asleep. The door was closed. They never heard a thing."

"When did the affair end?" I asked.

"When Kristen went missing," he said. "We knew that as the spouse, I'd be a suspect, so we decided to cool it."

"What was the endgame here? Were you going to divorce your spouses and run away together or something?" Lynn asked.

"No, no. Nothing like that," he said.

I took the photo from his hands and looked at it.

"I don't know," I said. "Looks pretty serious to me. You went away for the weekend, didn't you?"

Promes said nothing.

"Who watched the kids?" I asked. "Kristen?"

Tom Promes looked at the floor.

"So, you're out nailing your mistress while your wife provides childcare. Classy," I said.

"It wasn't like that," he whispered.

"Oh, so Kristen wasn't watching Hope and Taylor while you were out doing the nasty with Julie?" I asked.

"Oh, Big Brother, you make it all sound so tawdry. Can't you see these are two people in love? Where's your sense of romance?" Lynn said, gesturing toward the photo in her hand.

"We weren't in love," Promes said quietly. "We were . . . bored."

"Bored?" Lynn repeated.

"Jack was always gone. Kristen forgot she had a husband once we had Taylor. Every waking moment was about Taylor, which is fine. She's my daughter, and I love her, but . . . I've got needs too. So did Julie," he said. "There was no 'endgame' here. We weren't going to break up our marriages, our families. We were just having a little fun. Is that so wrong?"

"I'm betting Kristen and Jack would think so," I said.

Promes again ran his fingers through his hair. "Look, so I screwed around. That doesn't mean I killed my wife," he said. "Or Julie. My God."

"Where were you the night Julie Wolfer was murdered?" Lynn asked.

"I've barely left this house since Kristen disappeared. I was here in my office working. There are security cameras around the house. You can check the footage if you'd like. I was right here," he sighed. "It's like I'm already in jail."

"Sounds like you're expecting to be arrested, right?" I asked.

"Well, it sure as hell looks like I'll be," he said. "Especially once this picture gets out. The press and the public will crucify me, but I didn't do it, and nobody can prove I did."

I looked at Lynn. She gave me a return glance that seemed to say, "*He's right.*"

"Look, I've been honest. I've been forthright. I even let you record me without a lawyer present. That's enough. I think we're done here. If you have any more questions, please contact my attorney. His name is Paul Wilder. He's in the book."

"The book?" I asked. "What century is this again?"

"You know what I mean," he snapped.

"I guess that means we're off the record. For now," I said, turning off the recording app and putting my phone back in the pocket of my jacket.

"Fair warning," I said. "We won't give this pic to the rest of the media, but once law enforcement gives us the okay, it *will* be on my station."

Tom Promes gave me a resigned look. "Thanks for being straight up," he said.

"One more thing," I added. "What's your connection to Danica Walker?"

"Who?" he asked.

"Another young woman who was killed," I said.

"Never heard of her," Promes said.

Lynn studied him as he issued his denial. It was as if she were looking for a "tell" in a poker game.

"I'll tell you when the story will run," I said.

"Thanks. That's decent of you. It'll at least give me time to get ahead of things with Old Man Duffy."

"Think he'll fire you once this is all public?" Lynn asked.

"Nah. I'm tied up in way too many business deals for that, and he's too old to run that company himself," Promes said. "He won't be happy with me, that's for damned sure, but he won't fire me."

Lynn and I put our Pleasanton PD caps back on to obscure our faces and walked out the door. We nodded at the two officers acting as sentries as we walked around the side of the house to our borrowed Pleasanton PD police vehicle.

"One thing led to another," Lynn said.

"Huh?"

"Tom Promes and Crane Jr. both said the same thing to explain the start of their affairs," she explained. "One thing led to another, and then, *bing, bang, boom.* Why do men always say that to justify their flings? 'One thing led to another.' As if they had no real say in the event. Like it was inertia that drew them to lock organs with these women."

"I guess it's a means of rationalization. How can I be judged based on events I had no control over?"

"Puleeze," Lynn said, her voice dripping with sarcasm. "Poor pitiful men. They just lose their ability to control themselves once a chain of events leading to coitus begins."

"I'm not saying that I agree with it. I'm just giving you my opinion."

"You really gonna broadcast that photo?"

"As soon as Lane says it's okay, and it won't compromise the investigation," I said. "And I need to do it fast. It's now a countdown as to which media outlet releases it first. Not my favorite part of the job, but this is sometimes a dirty business."

TWENTY-SIX

LESS THAN 24 hours after our chat with Tom Promes, the supermarket tabloid, the *National Sun*, printed the Monterey picture under the headline, "GRIEVING HUBBY AND HIS DEAD HONEY." Somebody, presumably tied to Lane's office, had undoubtedly pocketed a pretty penny for leaking the photo. The feeding frenzy began anew, and Camp Kristen had doubled in size as more international press jumped on the bandwagon. Reporters from Hong Kong and the Philippines joined the fray. There was even a news crew from New Zealand.

Since the *National Sun* had already broken the story, I saw no need to wait for an official go-ahead from Lane, and I ran the picture along with snippets of my audio-recorded interview with Tom Promes on our six o'clock show. I didn't feel good about it, though. Promes was right. It did indeed make him look guiltier. Whoever killed Kristen Promes killed Danica Walker. What possible connection could Tom Promes have with Danica?

I had just finished my broadcast when I felt the cell phone in my pocket vibrate.

"Hey," Lynn said as I clicked on the call, "just saw your report. Nice job."

"Thanks. What's up?"

"You free?" she asked.

"Just need to get out of makeup, and I am," I said.

"Swing by 850 Bryant. I've got something here I think you'll want to see," she said, a coy tone in her voice.

"You know how I hate surprises," I said.

"Oh, I think you're gonna *love* this one."

I returned to my dressing room, pulled out my Wet Wipes, and scoured the TV greasepaint from my face. I hate wearing makeup, but having a face that's au naturel for TV news is not done. How you look on television is at least as important as what you say. With the advent of HD and big-screen, 55-inch, 4K televisions, every pore on your face is magnified for public scrutiny. I have freckles around my nose and cheeks I'm not too fond of. Mandy thinks they're cute and says I should let the public see them. I preferred to cover them with a coat of MAC studio foundation.

Once my face was cleansed, I went to the garage and hopped in the Black Beauty. It was a pleasant evening as the ridge of high pressure around the Bay Area was finally starting to move east. I enjoyed the cool breeze on my face as I drove up Bryant Street to The Hall of Justice. San Francisco's one-stop law enforcement shop is located at 850 Bryant Street. It contains the Criminal and Traffic Courts, the county jail, and the headquarters of the San Francisco Police Department. Lynn's office was room 561, the Homicide Detail. I entered to find her pecking away at the keyboard on her desk.

"Perfect timing," she said as she made a final keystroke. "Just typing up some notes. Come with me."

I followed Lynn to the elevator downstairs and down a long hallway. I'd been where we were headed many times before—the Interrogation Room. I stood with her behind a two-way mirror as we looked inside at a Latino man handcuffed to a chair. He was young. I'd put him at about nineteen. He wore blue jeans and a white tank top. A mural of red and green ink covered his arms and neck. Three green teardrops were tatted under his left eye.

"Who's that?" I asked Lynn.

"One of the guys who beat you up."

"How did you . . .?"

"Remember the ski mask you pulled off one of your attackers?"

"Yeah."

"Well," she said, "that ski mask contained a single black hair you yanked out at the root when you pulled it off the attacker's head. It was enough for a DNA test. Turns out that the guy was in the system."

I looked at the kid sitting in the room. I didn't recognize him. It had been pitch black outside that night. He was the right build, though—lean and athletic looking. I can see why he had so much of his flesh covered the night of the beating. If there had been enough light, I'd have been able to identify the art etched into his skin in a heartbeat.

"Who is he?" I asked.

"Jorge Martinez. He's a member of the Joaquin Muriettas in the Mission District. Goes by the street name, Double Eight."

I looked at his right deltoid, where I could see two numeral eights inked alongside the other various works.

"We identified him through DNA for your attack, and when we ran him through the system, we found that he also had a few outstanding warrants—breaking and entering and grand theft auto. Most recently, he was picked up in possession of a trunk-load of stolen catalytic converters. He was released on bond and never showed up for his court date."

"Nothing violent?"

"Not in the system, anyway," Lynn said. "Then again . . . We don't catch everything."

"What's he got to do with me?"

"Well, they said it was a message from Stanley Crane Jr., so let's go in and ask him."

I followed Lynn as she opened the door and entered the Interrogation Room.

Martinez looked up. His expression was almost childlike. Take away the tats, and you'll be left with a naughty little boy who'd been caught cheating on a math test at school.

We pulled out chairs and sat across from him.

"Jorge," Lynn said, "I'm Detective Sloan. This is—"

"I know him," Martinez said in a low growl of a voice. "He's that dude from TV."

"He's also the 'dude' you and your friends beat up across the bay in Castro Valley," she said.

"I don't know what you're talkin' about," he protested. "I don't even know where that Castro place is."

"It's no good, Jorge. We have your DNA from the scene."

"It's a mistake!" he shouted. "I ain't been to no scene."

"DNA doesn't make mistakes. You were there, and we can prove it," she said.

She opened a file folder she had brought with her.

"All of these priors and warrants . . ." She shook her head. "Add assault and battery to all that, and you're looking at some real time, my friend."

Jorge scratched his arm above the tattoo of the two eights.

"Do you know what a quid pro quo is, Jorge?"

He shook his head.

"Help us, and *maybe* we can help you," she said. "Tell us who hired you to attack Mr. Davis."

"I ain't no snitch," he growled.

"We just need a name. No one will know that it came from you."

He said nothing.

Lynn began to look at the contents of the folder. "You've been a very bad boy, Jorge. Or would you prefer Double Eight?"

Silence.

"Okay," Lynn said, closing the folder and rising from her chair. "Don't cooperate. We'll find out what we need to know. And keep in mind, just because you don't help us doesn't mean that the other members of your little social club won't think you did."

"What do you mean?" he said, watching my sister get up from the table.

"We're going to hold you on all this," she said, waving the folder in the air. "I'm going to make sure that the word gets out on the street that you've been talking to us. That you've been an informant."

"You can't do that!" he bellowed.

Lynn's turn to provide the silence.

"They'll kill me," he protested.

"Come on, Chris," Lynn said. "Let's go."

I got up from my chair.

"Good luck to you, Jorge," Lynn said as we headed for the door.

"Wait," he said quickly.

We kept walking.

"I said wait!" he repeated.

Lynn had her hand on the doorknob, then stopped and turned to face him.

"Yes?" she said.

He sighed. "Come back here and sit down," he said. "I'll tell you what I know."

She glanced at me, and a slight smile crossed her lips. We went back to the table and took our seats.

"Okay," she said. "Start talking."

"I don't know who hired us."

"Let's go, Chris," she said to me again, getting up from the table.

"Wait," he protested. "I don't know the kid's name."

"Kid?"

"Sit down and let me tell you."

Lynn sat back down.

"Last week, me and my partners were at the Arco station on Mission, the one by Duboce Street. We were buying some smokes when this teenage kid pulls up, rolls down his car window, and asks us if we want to make some money."

"What did the kid look like?" Lynn asked.

"I don't know. Just some kid. Teenager. Sounded like a white dude. We never saw his face. He was wearing a black Giants' cap, jacket, and dark Ray-Bans," he said. "He never got out of the car."

"What kind of car?"

"Black SUV. Windows were tinted black. Nothing special."

"What happened next," Lynn said.

"Dude said that there was this guy from TV who was hassling his old man. He wanted to make him stop. He said he'd pay us each a thousand dollars if we'd kick his ass," Jorge said.

He looked at me. "*Your* ass," he continued. "Sorry, dude. Nothing personal."

"How'd he pay you?" Lynn asked.

"He gave us each half of the money. Five one-hundred-dollar bills apiece. He gave us an address and said to do the job that night. Then we were supposed to meet him at the Arco station the next day, and he'd pay us the other half."

"What about the message you gave me?" I asked.

"The dude said just to tell you that Stanley Crane Jr. said to keep your mouth shut. Nothing else."

He began to fidget in his seat.

"Either one of you got any smokes?"

"Sorry," Lynn said. "You can't smoke in here."

"Shit," Jorge said, folding his arms in frustration.

"Did you return to the gas station the following day?" Lynn asked.

"Yeah," Jorge Martinez said. "He was there—same car. One of my partners went back and took a picture of you on the ground after we knocked you out. You know, to show that we did the job."

I touched my cheekbone. Even though the bruises and abrasions had healed, it was still a little tender.

"We showed him the picture, and he gave us an envelope. Inside was another fifteen-hundred-bills. After he gave us the money, he took off. We never saw him again," he said.

"So, you expect us to believe that some mysterious teenager you'd never met randomly stopped you at a gas station and hired you to assault Mr. Davis?" Lynn said.

"I swear to God, that's what happened," he said. "I told you everything I know. Don't put the word out that I snitched. You said if I cooperated, nobody would know."

"I'm going to look into your story. If you're telling me the truth—"

"I am. I am!" he said.

"If you're telling me the truth, nobody will hear anything about it from us. But if you're lying . . ."

"I'm not. That's what happened," he said.

"Okay, Jorge. We're still going to have to hold you on these outstanding warrants. I'll be in touch," she said again, picking up her folder and heading for the door.

"How are we going to check out his story?" I asked after we returned to Lynn's office.

"We can see if the gas station has any security footage from the day of your attack and the day after when Jorge and company were allegedly paid," she said.

"I don't get it. What teenage kid would want me to keep Crane Jr.'s affair secret? The woman he was cheating with is dead. Who else would have any kind of a vested interest in this? Do we know if Crane has a teenage kid?"

"No, but I can find out. First, let's see if there's a camera at that Arco station."

TWENTY-SEVEN

IT TURNED OUT that the Arco station had a working security camera, and Lynn got the video. The station owner was cooperative and voluntarily turned over the computer drive containing the footage without a warrant. He was a Sikh who had worked hard with his brothers and sisters to buy the gas station to support their large family. They were tired of the gangbangers congregating there.

Lynn and I watched the video in her office. We looked at the surveillance from the day of my attack. It was silent, black-and-white footage that showed the station's interior, which served as a convenience store, and video from a second camera focused on the pumps. On the day of my attack, we saw Jorge Martinez and two other young Latino men about his age enter the convenience store, buy a pack of cigarettes, and then exit. The outside camera showed them standing in front of the store, talking. One of the young men was about to light a Marlboro (smoking in a gas station . . . not the brightest bulb in the marquee) when a black SUV rolled up. It appeared to be a new car that hadn't received its permanent California license plates yet. A white paper, apparently the temporary California dealers' registration, was taped on the lower right-hand corner of the windshield.

The passenger-side window rolled down, and we could get a glimpse of the person Jorge had described. He wore a San Francisco Giants cap and jacket as well as the dark sunglasses we'd been told about. His build was slim. His skin, wrinkle free and smooth. Consistent with some teens. I say "some teens" because when I was a kid, I had so much acne my face looked like a relief map.

We saw Jorge and his friends approach the window and talk to the driver for a few minutes. Jorge then hopped into the passenger seat. His companions opened the rear door and climbed in. The dark windows on the vehicle then went up. The SUV sat for about ten more minutes before the doors again opened, and Jorge and party got out. The car then drove out of frame.

Footage from the next day showed Jorge's crew hanging out in front of the convenience store. After a few minutes, the same SUV from the previous day rolled into view, and they approached the car as the passenger-side window slid down. The driver appeared to be the same person, in the same attire worn the previous day. The driver handed Jorge a white envelope that he took and examined. He appeared to be counting money. The window then went back up, and the SUV drove out of view. Jorge hands some of the money in the envelope to each of his compatriots. They pocketed it and walked off camera.

"Well, it looks like ol' Double Eight was telling the truth," Lynn said, shutting off the laptop. "Now we need to know who the Giants fan driving that car was."

"Hey!" I protested. "I'm a Giants fan. Don't associate lowlife like that with the real Giants Nation."

"Sorry," she said, rolling her eyes. "I forgot how touchy and protective you guys are. Relax. It's not like I said something good about the Dodgers."

"So, how we gonna find out who was behind the wheel? There are no plates. Where are we going to look for this mysterious teenager? Did you check on Mr. Crane Jr.'s family?"

"Yes. Two young daughters. Just like he told us. It wasn't his progeny."

"You mean it wasn't his *known* progeny. The guy plays around, remember?"

"Good point," she said.

"The fact that the intent of the message was that I should keep my mouth shut about the affair means that Crane Jr. was somehow involved in Danica's murder," I said.

"Or," Lynn said, "somebody wants us to *think* he was."

"You think he's being set up?"

"Crane may be an adulterer, but he's a sharp lawyer. He isn't stupid. Why would you hire somebody to commit an assault and give them the instruction, 'be sure to mention my name'? It looks to me like someone is trying very hard to implicate him."

"Okay, but who?" I asked.

"That's what the taxpayers are paying me to find out," she said. "I want to talk to *Mrs.* Crane Jr."

"That ought to rattle his cage."

"Let's see if anything shakes out."

***

I hopped in the Black Beauty and drove to the Broadcast Center. On the way, I called Josie Walker. I'd been calling her weekly with status updates on the investigation. I told her whatever I could safely reveal.

"So," I said into the phone, "we think whoever had me beaten is tied to Danica's murder."

"I'm so sorry you had to go through that," Josie Walker said in a sympathetic voice.

"All in a day's work. It's not the first time I've been slapped around for working on a story, and I'm sure it won't be the last."

"Please be careful," she said.

"As careful as I can be," I replied.

"I want you to know that I really appreciate all you've done. Thanks for giving a damn."

***

When I returned to my office, I was surprised to find Mandy in one of the editing bays. She was listening to the audio of my interview with Tom Promes.

"I didn't expect to see you here," I said. "I was hoping against hope that you'd change your mind and taken a few days off."

"Work is what I need right now," she said. "It keeps my mind occupied. Without it, I'd just be obsessing about Jules."

"Why are you listening to this?" I asked.

"I saw your report with the audio excerpts. I wanted to hear the whole thing in its entirety. I wanted to know what his demeanor was when you talked to him," she said.

"And . . . ?"

"There's something . . . cagey in the way he talked. He's hiding something. I feel it in my gut."

I told her about my encounter with Jorge Martinez.

She nodded and tapped her index finger against her lips as I spoke, taking it all in.

"So, that leaves us with a reticent, adulterous husband, an adulterous lawyer, and possibly somebody trying to set the adulterous lawyer up as a murder suspect?" she finally said.

"That's about the size of it."

"What's our next move?" she asked.

"Our?"

"You know I'm as much a part of this investigation as you are now."

"Mandy," I said, "you are too close to this. You have no objectivity here."

"I'm sick of having this argument with you, Topher. I'm not going anywhere. I told you that. I want to see this through. I have to. For Jules," she said.

I exhaled a large breath of resignation.

"I have a few updates on the things Lynn asked me to check out," she said.

"Find out anything useful?"

"Jack's alibi checked out. I was able to confirm that he was indeed in Phoenix on the night of Jules's murder. I confirmed a few meetings he had that day and a dinner that night right about the time the coroner thinks Julie was killed. I also talked to several of the moms at Hope's school who knew Julie well. None of them will admit to knowing about her affair. They all say they were shocked when they discovered it in the tabloids. As if anything gossipy can shock upper-class suburban housewives."

"Dead ends," I said.

"Pretty much."

"Lynn wants to talk to Crane Jr.'s wife to see if she knows anything. In the meantime, why don't you see if there are any usable soundbites from that interview I might have missed."

"Would it make sense for me and Stu to try to set up a shoot with this Crane Jr. guy? Grill him on camera? See if I can get anything out of him that he didn't already tell you and Lynn?"

I shook my head.

"Complete waste of time. If he agrees to talk to you, which I highly doubt, he will not tell you anything new. Why don't you go to Oakland and interview Josie Walker's grandson? A victim impact story. I want to keep Danica's name in the public sphere."

"Okay," Mandy said. "I can do that. What are you going to do?"

"Go with Lynn to visit *Mrs.* Crane Jr."

"What good is that going to do?" she asked.

"I'll let you know after we talk to her."

TWENTY-EIGHT

"**I**F YOU'RE ASKING if I knew about my husband's affair, of course I did," Barbara Crane said.

She was an attractive woman in her late thirties with a thick mane of bleached blond hair draped over the shoulders of her white designer jacket. A royal blue blouse, white skirt, and open-toed white Louboutin shoes completed the ensemble. Long, blue-tipped nails tapped the top of her desk as she spoke. We were in her office at the Markus Family Foundation in the Markus Building on Pine Street in San Francisco.

"You knew?" I asked. "How did you find out?"

"Men are so transparent," she laughed. "A little extra attention paid to us out of the blue. A sudden uptick in carnal desire. Flowers and gifts we didn't ask for or expect."

"That could just be a guy appreciating his partner," I said.

She laughed again. It was a lyrical laugh that was a combination of adorable, sexy, carefree, and refined all at the same time. I could see what attracted Crane Jr. to her.

"Please. We know when our man has taken a lover, Mr. Davis. We *always* know," she said. "With Stan, it was long-stemmed roses for no reason, designer perfume, probably the same kind he gave his mistress, and planning a second honeymoon. He's been pushing back on my desire for a trip for over five years now."

"He doesn't know that you're aware of his infidelity?" Lynn asked.

"Of course not," Barbara said. "Men always think that we're oblivious idiots. That they're so much smarter than their wives. Most of the time, in these circumstances, we say nothing. My feeling is that if she keeps him in a good mood and out of my hair so that I can get some peace from time to time, more power to her."

"That's an . . . *enlightened* attitude," Lynn said.

"Detective, I was the only girl in the Markus family. I grew up with five brothers and a very demanding father, yet *I* am the one running the hundred-million-dollar family foundation. I knew how to play the game, and I still do," she said as she began pulling papers from a white leather attaché case and putting them on her desk. "I hope you don't mind. I have to sign off on these grant proposals before lunch today."

"Go right ahead," Lynn said.

"How long have you been married?" I asked.

"Fifteen years," she said, not looking up from her papers. "It was an arranged marriage of sorts. The Markus family media empire and the Crane legal dynasty merging. It was the social event of the season. You must remember, Mr. Davis. We were all over the press. *People* magazine even covered us. A 'fairy-tale romance,' they called us."

She laughed again.

Upon her mention, I vaguely recalled the hoopla of a decade and a half earlier. I never followed much society gossip, but it was on my radar.

"My father got what he wanted. Stan's grandfather got what he wanted. As for my husband and me, we were able to stay in the good graces of those two controlling old goats. Stan ended up with the law firm because of it, and I replaced my father in this chair," she said. "All because we let 'old San Francisco money' remain 'old San Francisco money.' My father is dead now, and Stan's grandfather is in the late stages of dementia, so we can finally do what we want. I expect that I'll divorce him as soon as my girls are of age."

Lynn looked at me and arched an eyebrow. We were thinking the same thing. The 1-percenters definitely *do not* live like the rest of us.

"What do you know about Danica Walker?" Lynn asked.

"Danica Walker?" Mrs. Crane said, looking up from her papers. "The woman from my husband's office who was killed? Not much. I talked to her on the phone several times when she connected me and my husband. That's about it. I never met her. Wait a minute. Is that the woman Stanley was sleeping with?"

Lynn and I said nothing.

"So, that's why you're here? You're investigating the murder of my husband's dead mistress?"

More silence on our part. We let her fill in the dead air.

"So, Stanley screws his receptionist, and she ends up dead. How delicious! Do you think that Stan killed her?"

"Do you?" Lynn asked.

Barbara Crane laughed again.

"Personally, I don't think that my husband has the testicular fortitude to murder anybody. Then again, you know what they say. Desperate people do desperate things."

"And you think that your husband was . . . desperate?" I asked.

"You can't run a large business without a bit of occasional desperation," she said.

"What do you think was making Stanley 'desperate'?" Lynn asked.

"Well," Mrs. Crane said, the baby blue tip of a manicured nail tapping her lower lip, "I know the firm has been having cash flow problems lately."

"Exactly, what kind of cash flow problems?" I asked.

"Billable hours are down. Stanley's firm is legal counsel for several companies and businesses around the Bay Area. They're his bread and butter. In the wake of the pandemic, some of these concerns have been forced into bankruptcy. Several just closed their doors and were never able to reopen."

I knew what she meant. The COVID pandemic had robbed me of my favorite dry cleaner, shoe repair shop, and Italian restaurant.

"How big a hit are we talking about here?" Lynn asked.

"Stanley said that billable hours were down by over 40 percent."

I heard the word "wow" involuntarily come out of my mouth. That's a huge number.

"I know," Mrs. Crane said. "He's been trying to conduct business as usual without laying off any staff, but it's been challenging. He doesn't have office rent, thank God. He'd never be able to cover it at current market rates. He's lucky that his grandfather bought and paid for that building years ago. Things are so bad that he's been considering taking out a mortgage on it."

"It sounds like he's pretty rattled," Lynn said.

"More rattled than I've ever seen him. That's for sure," Mrs. Crane said. "But he's only a 'killer' in court. Outside of the courtroom, he's a garden variety wimp."

As a garden variety wimp, I took personal offense.

"Frankly, other than his family name and money," she continued, "I don't see why a young woman like this Danica would have anything to do with him sexually. I certainly wouldn't."

A short, rapidly repeating buzz filled the room. Mrs. Crane opened her purse, pulled out a shiny new iPhone, and studied it.

"If you'll excuse me, I have to take this," she said, rising from her chair to signal that we should leave.

"Of course," Lynn said. "We appreciate your time."

Mrs. Crane pulled two business cards from a wooden holder on her desk and handed one to each of us.

"If you need anything else, please call my assistant, Shirley."

We took the cards, thanked her, and left the office.

Lynn and I sat in a Starbucks a few blocks from the Markus Building. I had a brewed, black, dark roast. That's what I'm partial to: plain old-fashioned brewed coffee. All of that "medium soy latte with extra foam" crap is just nonsense.

Lynn sat across the table from me, dunking a tea bag into a cardboard cup filled with hot water.

"So, I've been thinking . . ." I said.

"That's always a bad sign."

"Very funny."

"That's what little sisters are for," she said. "Levity."

"So *that's* what you call being a pain in my ass? Levity?"

"Looks like I got all the humor genes in the family."

"Yeah," I said. "You're a real thigh slapper."

Lynn smiled as she raised the cup of tea to her lips.

"Go on," she said. "You've been thinking."

"I've been thinking that maybe we've been wrong about Mr. Crane Jr. If he was involved in Danica's killing, odds are he didn't do it himself. He would have outsourced the murder. If, as his wife would have us believe, he's in dire financial straits, I can't see him paying somebody to do the job. It doesn't make economic sense."

"You can have somebody whacked for a few thousand dollars these days," Lynn said. "I don't care how big a hit his income is taking; he's still a rich man. A few grand is tipping money for him."

She took a sip of her tea.

"You heard Mrs. Crane," she said. "She's already got an exit strategy for the marriage. If I'm her husband, and I'm not aware of her 'enlightened attitude' where my infidelity is concerned, the last thing I would want to do is give her a reason to leave me and take part of the family business with her."

"Well, being rich people," I said, "there's no way that this so-called arranged marriage took place without a prenup in place. We're talking about a family of lawyers here."

"Good point," Lynn said, taking another sip of her tea. "But don't forget, he's got kids. Child support when you're in their tax bracket wouldn't be cheap. If he's already having a bad time with money, that's an added expense he doesn't need."

"So, a hit might actually be a bargain. Okay. But we agree he probably didn't hire Jorge and his buddies to thump me around and name-drop him."

"Yep," Lynn said. "I don't think the man is an idiot. According to Barbara Crane, he's a sharp attorney."

"Right. Somebody is trying to make him look guilty, but who? His wife?"

"She'd certainly have motive. Maybe she's not telling the truth regarding how she really feels about her husband's extracurriculars," Lynn said. "What better revenge than to kill your husband's lover and frame him for the crime? And by professing his inability to harm anyone, she's attempting to camouflage her own involvement in the crimes."

"All right, that makes sense. The wife is definitely a suspect," I said. "But we're convinced that the same person or persons killed Kristen Promes and Danica Walker."

"Same MO, same murderer," Lynn said.

"All right, which brings us back to square one. Where's the link between Kristen and Danica?" I asked.

"And Julie Wolfer. Same problem with Tom Promes as a suspect," Lynn said. "Even if we thought he was good for Kristen's murder, where is the connection to Danica?"

We sat in contemplative silence for a moment. We literally had nothing: a few suspects and possible motives, but nothing that connected our victims or the suspects. My train of thought was interrupted by the "*dum da dum dum*" of the *Dragnet* theme music. I looked at Lynn.

"Seriously?" I asked.

"Hey, you've got *I Love Lucy*," she said, tapping the screen of her iPhone. She put the phone to her ear and spoke. "Sloan."

She sat in stony silence, listening. Whatever she heard made her grimace.

"Okay," she finally said. "We're here in the city. We'll head down there. Give us about half an hour."

She again tapped the screen on her phone, disconnecting the call.

"What is it?"

"Tom Promes," she said. "Somebody reunited him with his wife."

TWENTY-NINE

LYNN AND I drove across town and parked her unmarked on the corner of Bay Street, near San Francisco's Embarcadero. We walked a few blocks, where we found the Tesla that Tom Promes had allegedly purchased for his wife as a surprise on the day of her disappearance, surrounded by yellow crime scene tape. A forensics tech was carefully dusting the car for fingerprints. Another combed the inside of the vehicle for other evidence. Three uniformed officers and one plainclothes detective were also on the scene. One of the uniforms diverted traffic from the scene. The other kept looky-loos away from the vehicle.

The detective was a tall, beefy fellow with a ruddy complexion. His greasy, jet-black hair was a shade that could only be accomplished by dyeing it at home. Furiously scribbling in a notepad, he looked up, spotted Lynn walking in his direction, and his face lit up with recognition.

"Hey, Lynn," he said.

"Jeffrey, I don't think you've met my brother, Chri . . . Topher Davis. Topher," she said, "This is Jeffrey Cromwell. He's a detective in our division."

228

"I like your work, Mr. Davis," he said, extending a hand.

"Much appreciated," I said, taking his hand and firmly shaking it.

"What have we got?" Lynn asked.

"Well," Cromwell said, consulting his notebook. "Tom Promes was expected at his in-laws, the Duffys, last night around seven to visit with his daughter. When the clock struck ten, and he hadn't arrived, they tried to reach him by phone. When he didn't answer after multiple attempts, they called the Pleasanton PD, who put out a BOLO on him."

"Who found him?" I asked.

"An old lady walking her dog around four this morning," Cromwell replied.

"Walking a dog at four a.m. isn't exactly the safest move for a senior citizen in this city," Lynn said.

"She was walking a pit bull," Cromwell said.

I looked inside the vehicle and saw Tom Promes sitting in the driver's seat. His eyes were wide open as if they were watching the road. He appeared to be a typical motorist, save for the dark spot on his forehead dripping the brown stream of dried blood that could only have come from a bullet.

Cromwell removed an evidence bag from his coat pocket and handed it to Lynn.

"Shell casing from a 9-millimeter. Apparently, from the slug that's between his eyes."

"No garroting or mutilation?" Lynn asked.

"There doesn't appear to be, but we'll know more after the autopsy," Cromwell said.

"Just a good, old-fashioned, everyday, run-of-the-mill homicide," I said. "Ah, the good old days."

"Somebody wanted him out of the way and either didn't have the time or lacked the desire to create the show that was staged in the other killings," Lynn said.

"How do we know it's the same killer?" I asked. "Different MO entirely. Plus, all of the other vics were women."

"All of these killings around him, apparently committed by the same perp, and he gets whacked by somebody else? It's possible, but I doubt it," Lynn said. "Remember Occam's Razor, Big Brother. The simplest answer is usually the correct one."

"Has Chief Lane over in Pleasanton made a statement yet?" I asked. "This murder is of a person of interest in multiple homicides in his jurisdiction."

"Nothing yet. Word is that he'll announce a press conference soon," Cromwell replied.

"Any street cam footage?" Lynn asked.

"There's one camera," Cromwell said, pointing to a lamppost in front of Red Jack's, the neighborhood pub. "It's out of order. Budget cuts. Half the street cams in this town are in need of repair."

"Just like Pleasanton," I said. "Must be an epidemic. Why even bother to have the damn things if they aren't going to keep up on the maintenance?"

Lynn walked around the car and peered in the driver's-side window.

"Powder burns around the entrance wound. The shot was fired at close range," Cromwell said. "We figure that the shooter was in the passenger seat, and when he wasn't expecting it, *Bam.*"

"But if that were the case, why isn't the gunshot on the right side of his head?" I asked.

"Maybe he was looking at the shooter directly when he was killed," Cromwell suggested.

"But he's staring straight ahead," I remarked.

"Because the body was posed," Lynn added. "And *that* is definitely the MO of our killer."

"So, you think this is tied to the Kristen Promes case you're working?" Cromwell asked.

"And the Danica Walker case," she replied.

"Wow," Cromwell said. "You're dealing with a lot of bodies here."

"That we are," I said.

Lynn walked around the Tesla and took pictures of the inside and outside of the car with her cell phone.

"Thanks, Jeff," she said. "If you find anything useful, please give me a holler."

"You know I will," he said.

As we returned to Lynn's unmarked, I called Mandy and asked her to grab Stu and get to the scene with a camera immediately.

"Tom Promes?" Mandy said. "First, Jules. Then her lover? Who the hell is doing this?"

"That's what we're trying to figure out," I said.

"Want to do a stand-up at the murder scene for the six o'clock show?"

"Sure. I'll stay here. Can you give me a ride back to Lynn's office to retrieve the Black Beauty when we're done?"

"Of course," Mandy replied. "We'll be there in fifteen minutes."

Lynn headed back to her office, and a few minutes later, Mandy and Stu pulled up in the ENG truck.

"Another corpse. I'm starting to think you're a jinx," Stu said in his Odessa drawl as he looked at the body in the vehicle. He then retrieved his camera from the back of the van. "Julie Wolfer, now Tom Promes. Seems like everybody you talk to ends up in the grave."

"It's sure starting to look that way, isn't it?" I replied.

"Do you think that this is connected to Jules's murder?" Mandy asked as she climbed out of the passenger seat of the ENG truck.

"Lynn seems to think so. The body was apparently staged like your cousin's. As for any other similarities . . . Who knows?"

Mandy handed me a stick mic, and Detective Cromwell was kind enough to give me a soundbite. He didn't give us anything earth-shattering. He only said that the investigation was ongoing. We then got a few interviews from passersby who live in the neighborhood. No one we talked to had witnessed anything. I tried to get our pit bull walker's name and contact info, but Cromwell declined to give it to me because he didn't want us "harassing" a potential witness. I could understand that, but I had to ask just the same.

Once we got all the footage we figured we would get, we were back at the studio in one of the editing bays where Mandy was cutting the day's video into a package. She finished in time to make the broadcast and brushed her sweaty brow with the back of her hand.

"Are you doing okay?" I asked.

"Can I keep staying at your house? I really don't want to be alone."

"Of course," I said. "For as long as you want."

She gave me a melancholic smile.

At six o'clock, I sat alongside Katie Robards and Phil Wagner on the news set and introduced our piece. I withheld any mention of Tom Promes's murder being linked to the others. After the broadcast, Mandy drove me to 850 Bryant, where I picked up my car, then she followed me home.

We went inside, where I fed Sophie and then made the two of us a Caesar salad, which I served with a nice bottle of Sonoma County Chardonnay. We ate and made small talk. I wanted to keep it light. No talk of work. No discussion about murder. After dinner, we watched a silly Adam Sandler movie on Netflix. When it was over, I went to my room, and Mandy retired to the guest room.

At about three in the morning, there was a light knock on my bedroom door.

"Yes," I said, groggy and half-asleep.

The door opened, and Mandy stood there in her pink bathrobe, her face wet with tears.

"Hey," I said, climbing out of bed and moving toward the door. "What's the matter?"

"I'm just having one of those moments," she sobbed. "I had a dream about Jules."

"There, there," I soothed. "It's gonna be okay. It's gonna be all right."

I hugged her and gently rubbed my hand in big circles along the back of her sheer robe.

"It's okay. Let it out," I said.

Her sobs became louder. The flow of tears increased. She lifted her head from my shoulder and wiped her eyes with the ribbon-like sash of the robe.

"Nobody gets it but you," she said, gleaming eyes staring into mine. "You're all I've got."

"Now, you know that's not true," I said. "You've got all of us. Lynn, Stu, Jared . . . We're all with you. We'll all here for you. Every one of us."

I looked into her eyes. They were hazel. Funny, in all the years we'd worked together, I'd never noticed that before.

Before I knew what was happening, she kissed me.

"Whoa. Hold on," I said, trying to push her away.

I was unsuccessful. Her grip around me was too tight, and I was too tired.

"What are you doing?" I asked.

"Look," she said softly, "I know you're my boss and we're friends. Good friends. But tonight, I need you to be something more. I need you. Please. Just for tonight."

The flow of tears again increased. She put her right hand behind my head and pulled me toward her. She kissed me again, her wet face moistening mine. She smelled of scented soap, hair conditioner, and lotion. Her skin was soft. Her short hair, silky. Her lips, sensual. I tried to break free again. This time, I was successful. She looked up at me and pouted.

"Just for tonight," she said.

"We can't," I said. "It's wrong."

"Just for tonight," she repeated. "*Please.*"

THIRTY

I AWOKE AT DAWN with Mandy's head on my chest, our bare legs intertwined. I watched as her head gently rose and fell with each breath I took. Only one thought raced through my mind: what the hell did I just do?

I sighed a heavy sigh, and it was enough to wake her.

"What time is it?" she asked, rubbing her eyes.

I picked up my iPhone from the nightstand and looked at it. "Three thirty," I answered.

"In the morning?"

"Yep."

"Do you have anywhere you have to be today?"

"It's Saturday. I'm free unless another body pops up," I said.

Mandy's lips met mine. I attempted a passionless kiss. I wasn't trying to return her affection. I was too busy trying to figure out how I'd allowed myself to get into this situation in the first place. However, her sultriness won the day.

One thing led to another.

The kiss was slow and sensual. The thing I noticed most was that although she'd just awakened, she didn't have the slightest hint of morning breath. In contrast, my mouth always smelled like something had crawled into it and died before I brushed my teeth and gargled with half a gallon of mouthwash.

Mandy snuggled closer as a million questions bounced around in my head. How do I *really* feel about what just happened? Did I enjoy it? Do I regret it? What do I do now? How do I respond if she wants to do it again? What does this mean for our friendship?

I was saved by the *I Love Lucy* theme coming from the iPhone on my nightstand. Mandy allowed me to extricate myself from her body, and I sat on the corner of the bed with the phone to my ear.

"Why the hell are you calling me at three thirty in the morning? Somebody else dead?" I asked.

"No," Lynn said. "Not as far as I know, anyway."

"What then?"

"I just got the strangest call," she said. "Remember Roland Douglas?"

"The planning commissioner who owns the lots that Mason Duffy and Tom Promes optioned?"

"Right. The option is about to expire, and Douglas, in a blatant conflict of interest, is trying to hold them up for a few extra million . . . if Mason Duffy is to be believed, that is."

"So, why's he calling you in the middle of the night?" I asked.

"I'm not sure," Lynn replied, "but he sounded terrified. Said he needed to meet with us—now."

"*Now?*" I replied.

"Can you be ready in twenty minutes? I'll pick you up."

I looked at Mandy, curled up beside me. She stared at me with sleepy eyes—a sly smirk on her face. Truth be told, it was adorable.

"Can you make it fifteen?" I asked.

"You did *what??*" Lynn said, staring at me in disbelief.

We were headed down Highway 580 in her unmarked. I quickly dressed and then made a hasty retreat from my bedroom as Mandy rolled over and went back to sleep.

"Don't look at me like that," I said.

"You just slept with one of your best friends, who also happens to be your producer, by the way. How am I supposed to look at you?" she snapped.

I was silent. For once, I didn't really have anything witty to say.

"My God. You. Tom Promes. Stanley Crane Jr. Why can't men learn to keep it in their pants?" she said, shaking her head in disgust.

"It wasn't like that," I protested. "She came to me for . . . comfort."

"And being the selfless humanitarian you are, you decided to rain down blessings upon this vulnerable woman by throwing her one. When do you collect your Nobel Peace Prize?"

"Come on. Don't beat me up. I'm doing a fine job of that myself," I said, my eyes cast downward. "I told you what happened because I need your advice."

She shook her head violently.

"Nope. Big Brother, you literally made your bed, and now, you'll have to lie in it. Don't come to me for sympathy. You're on your own."

We drove the next few miles in silence. She was pissed at me. I shouldn't have been surprised. She'd known Mandy for as long as I had. She was always a little protective of her. Almost like a little sister. The sisterhood of professional working women trying to survive in a male-dominated pool of predators. Was I one of them now?

"Tell me about Roland Douglas," I finally said.

"He called SFPD emergency about three this morning and said he needed to talk to me and that it was urgent. He said he had information about the Kristen Promes case and needed to talk to me tonight. Dispatch relayed the message to me, and I called him back."

"What did he have to say?"

"That his life was in danger, and he needed protection. He needed to see me right away," she said. "Like I told you on the phone, he sounded terrified, so I told him I'd meet him."

"Where?" I asked.

"Livermore. Los Positas College in the parking lot in front of the theater."

Los Positas was a sprawling junior college with an excellent reputation for turning out students who, for whatever reason, enrolled because they were unready for a four-year university. By the time they finished the rigorous academic curriculum the school provided, they were more than prepared to seek bachelor's degrees at Cal, UCLA, USF, or just about any other place.

The college had been hit hard during the COVID pandemic, shutting its doors for several months during the yearlong shutdown and then transitioning to online learning. Even though the world had mostly reopened, enrollment was a casualty. The students who remained primarily preferred the convenience of taking their classes on their laptops, so the brick-and-mortar component of the college was more of a ghost town than an institution of higher learning. Meeting there, especially at that hour, made sense if you didn't want to be seen.

We got off the freeway in Livermore and drove through a neighborhood that was a hodge-podge of retail chain stores and restaurants, residential homes, and open grazing land for livestock before finally turning onto the college campus.

"He said to park under the streetlight directly in front of the entrance to the Performing Arts complex," Lynn said. "He said that he'd be watching, and once he saw that we were alone, he'd make his presence known."

"So, he knows I'm with you?" I asked.

"He *requested* your attendance," she said.

We did as instructed and parked under the blaring streetlight. Lynn got out of the car and leaned against the hood. I followed suit. "Did you notify Chief O'Reilly?" I asked. "We *are* in his jurisdiction."

"I figured I could do that later. Why wake him up if this turns out to be a nothing burger."

We had been cooling our heels in the lot for about forty-five minutes when a large, black, turn-of-the-century model Lincoln Town car zoomed into the empty lot and pulled up next to us. A dark-tinted window rolled down on the driver's side. Behind the wheel sat an older white man in his early seventies. His skin was taut from one cosmetic procedure too many. His nose and lips were thin. His head was shaved clean, giving him more of a chemo look than one of fashion.

"Detective Sloan?" he said in a nasally, high-pitched tone.

Lynn nodded.

"Roland Douglas?" she replied.

"Climb in the back," Douglas said.

My sister and I looked at each other, shrugged, opened the rear doors, and got in. Roland rolled up the windows and used a button on the inside driver's door to lock us all in.

"Okay," Lynn said. "We're all nice and secure in a big, abandoned parking lot. What's this all about?"

"My life is in danger," he said, turning around to face us. "I think someone is going to kill me."

"Why do you think that someone wants to harm you, sir?" Lynn asked.

"Because they're killing everyone around me. Everybody who's involved in this rezoning deal."

"The dispute you're having with Mason Duffy and Tom Promes," I said.

"Yes," he replied, making furtive glances out the window.

"Who exactly constitutes 'everyone'?" Lynn asked.

"Tom Promes. His wife. That receptionist from their law firm."

Lynn and I looked at each other.

"What law firm?" she asked.

"The one in the city. The one the other side hired to strong-arm me into going along with their proposal."

"Crane, Phelps, and Crane?" I asked.

"Yeah," Roland Douglas said, growing more jittery by the minute. "That's the one."

"They're representing Promes and Duffy?" Lynn questioned.

"That's what I just said!" he bellowed.

He swallowed a large gulp of air in an attempt to calm himself.

"I'm sorry," he said. "Yes, Crane, Phelps, and Crane. Promes and Duffy are suing to force me to allow them to acquire my land. That's the firm they're using."

"Exactly how far along is this lawsuit?" Lynn asked.

"We're in depositions . . . at least we were scheduled to go into depositions until Kristen Promes disappeared. The plaintiffs had other things on their minds with their wife and daughter missing. I was scheduled to be deposed the week she disappeared. For obvious reasons, it didn't happen."

"Did you ever go into the law office?" I asked.

"No. I had my own lawyers dealing with them. I never met or talked to anybody on the other side. My deposition would have been the first time I met them."

"So, again, why do you think somebody wants to kill you?" Lynn asked.

"Because somebody is knocking off people involved in this case. The plaintiff. His wife. His lawyer's staff. It only makes sense that I would be on that list. I'm the one they're trying to paint as the bad guy here."

"Aren't you?" I asked. "From what I understand, Promes and Duffy made a fair and square deal with you for those lots, and you've used your position on the zoning board to renege and attempt to further enrich yourself."

"It's not like that," Roland Douglas stated. "I made an agreement that was inherently unfair. It was only later that I realized that it was unfair since the value of my property increased dramatically between the time we made the so-called deal and now. I only want what's fair."

"Fair to whom?" I responded.

"All parties concerned," he barked.

"Have you had any direct threat of harm to you or your family?" Lynn asked.

"Well, no. Not really."

"*Not really?*" Lynn said. "Sir, either you have, or you haven't."

"No," he said. "I haven't. That doesn't mean that I'm not on the hit list. I want protection. I want the media on alert. That's why I requested your presence, Mr. Davis. I figure that if this maniac knows I'm being watched by police and the press, it'll make him less likely to try to do something to me."

"Because they all worked out so well for Tom Promes," I said.

"Why call me?" Lynn asked. "I'm SFPD. You live in Pleasanton. Why not call your local PD?"

"Because I read that you were working on the case and the two of you were smart enough to resolve that cop killing thing earlier this year. I figured you must be good. I want the best."

"If you're truly worried about your safety—"

"I am," he interrupted.

"Then call Chief Courtney Lane in Pleasanton. Let him know your concerns. He's in a better position to help you than I am."

"Chief Lane?" he said, fumbling through his glove compartment for a pen and scrap of paper. Upon retrieving the items, he scribbled furiously.

"Yes. You can tell him that I told you to call," Lynn said. "Personally, I don't think you're in any danger at the moment."

"Well, you might not think so, but I'm buying a gun, nonetheless," he announced.

"Before you go arming yourself to the teeth, please, talk to Chief Lane," she said.

"All right," he replied with reluctance, "but I'm taking this seriously."

He unlocked the car's doors, and we got out.

"Well, what do you know? That paranoid son-of-a-bitch just connected Kristen Promes and Danica Walker," my sister said as she took the I-580 on-ramp toward Castro Valley.

"Didn't see that one coming. Danica Walker worked for the law firm repping Promes and Duffy," I said. "As you always say, there are no coincidences."

"So Promes and Duffy are the linchpins here. That explains the tie between Kristen and Danica, but how does Julie Wolfer fit in?"

"More importantly, I'd say that Roland Douglas just put himself at the top of the suspect list. All of our vics are tied to the people suing *him*," I stated.

"You think this whole 'I fear for my life' thing is a red herring?" Lynn asked.

"What better way to throw us off the scent than to claim you're a potential victim too."

"Curiouser and curiouser," she said.

"I suppose you're going to thoroughly examine Mr. Douglas's background?"

"I'll find polyps if he has them."

THIRTY-ONE

WHEN I GOT back home, I found Mandy sound asleep in my bed. The Roland Douglas affair was a nice, albeit brief, distraction. I'd almost forgotten about the mess I'd gotten myself into. Being tired and lacking the desire to complicate things further, I stripped down to my underwear, covered myself with my silk bathrobe, grabbed one of Auntie's handmade quilts, and curled up on the couch. Sleep came in fits and starts as two competing narratives fought for space in my head: the murders and what to do about Mandy. I tried to center my focus on the former.

As I'd mentioned to Lynn, Roland Douglas could have been kicking up dust by claiming that he was an intended victim. If, in fact, the murderer was targeting people involved in the land dispute, thus far, they were all people opposing him in the matter. What would make him think he's a target? He's the primary beneficiary if the plaintiffs simply go away. If this was indeed the motive, it was really Mason Duffy who had reason to fear, not Roland Douglas. Unless, of course, the killings were meant as a warning to Duffy. *I killed your daughter, your son-in-law, his*

mistress, and an employee of your law firm. You can see I'm serious.
Drop the suit and walk away while you still can.

If the property case was the motive, it still left some unanswered questions. First, why mutilate the bodies of the pregnant women? Kristen Promes's pregnancy was known, but Danica Walker's business was kept pretty close to the vest. Few people knew about her condition, so how did the killer? And then there's the matter of Julie Wolfer. She had her womb carved up like the other victims even though she wasn't expecting. Her fling with Tom Promes wasn't exactly public knowledge, either. How did the murderer know?

Then there's the murder of Tom Promes himself. Logic would dictate that he and the women had a common killer, but the MO was completely different. A gunshot wound to the head as opposed to being garroted. Add to that the fact that his was the first male body to pop up in this case. Maybe we were on the wrong track entirely and Tom Promes's murder was just random violence. A carjacking gone bad. Unfortunately, with the easy accessibility to guns in this country, it happens every day.

I had finally closed my eyes and embarked on the beginning of a deep slumber when I was startled awake by the bathroom door closing in the adjacent hallway. Mandy was up. Now what? Do we talk about what had transpired between us the previous night? Do we ignore it? Act like nothing happened and delicately dance around the enormous elephant in the middle of the room? Before I could decide, she stood over me.

"What are you doing out here?" she asked.

"Got back late from my excursion with Lynn. I didn't want to wake you."

"Was the expedition fruitful? Did you find out anything?"

"The law firm where Danica Walker worked represents Tom Promes and Mason Duffy in a land dispute," I said.

She sat on the arm of the couch.

"So, that's how Danica and Kristen Promes are connected," she said with the enthusiasm of a five-year-old who had just correctly added two and two for the first time.

"We think so. They both have Crane, Phelps, and Crane in common."

"But what about Jules?" she asked. "Why did the killer target my cousin?"

"It might have something to do with her affair with Tom Promes . . . We don't know," I said.

Mandy buried her face in her hands and then ran long fingers through her hair.

"Did Julie or her husband have any business dealings with the Promeses or the Duffys?" I asked.

"I can't possibly imagine what it would be. Jules was a stay-at-home mom. Jack is a computer security guy. He has nothing to do with real estate as far as I know," Mandy said.

"No chance he could been working with the Duffy firm on using his software? He and Tom Promes were allegedly close."

"I suppose it's possible," she said. "I doubt it, though. From what I know about Jack, he's pretty conservative when it comes to money. He can pinch a penny until Lincoln has a cerebral hemorrhage. According to Jules, money was always a constant source of arguments in their home. She complained that Jack never gave her the things she wanted."

"Maybe Tom Promes did," I said.

"It wouldn't surprise me one bit if that was one of the catalysts for their fling," Mandy said. "Jules always wanted more than Jack was willing, or able, to give her materially. She always wanted to wear designer this and designer that. Go on expensive vacations. Get a new car every year or two."

"Keeping up with the Joneses?"

"In their circle, they're *all* the Joneses."

"And Tom Promes had plenty of money to do it. The Duffy firm is worth millions," I said.

"So," Mandy said, "what now?"

"We keep digging. At least now, we have an idea of the best place to use the shovel."

An awkward silence filled the room. There was that giant elephant.

"I'm hungry. Want to go to The Egg and have some breakfast?" Mandy said.

"Not just now," I said. "I'm tired. It's been a long night."

"That it has," she said. "That it has."

I slept on the couch until I was awakened by my *I Love Lucy* ringtone.

"Hello," I croaked into the iPhone.

"I'm glad one of us got some sleep today," Lynn said.

"What time is it?"

"It's 2:17 in the afternoon. You've slept most of the day away."

"I guess I was more tired than I thought."

"Philandering will do that to you," she remarked.

"Don't start."

"Well, while you've been off in dreamland, I've been working my investigative skills to the bone."

"What's you find out?"

"On Roland Douglas? Plenty. He's lived in Pleasanton all his life. Fourth-generation resident. His family has been there a hundred years. Great-granddaddy bought a ton of acreage when the city was mostly farmland, and the family holdings increased with each succeeding generation. Roland's father came of age just as the city was morphing into the high-end suburban enclave it is now. He began subdividing the farmland for housing while he was still in high school and made a bundle," she said.

"That he passed on to Roland."

"Ain't white generational wealth grand?"

"If Roland is so well-off, why is he being such a hard ass on the Promes-Duffy option? Sounds like he doesn't need the money," I said.

"Oh, but he does. Turns out he's been speculating heavily in crypto currency. Bitcoin and the like."

"I don't understand how any of that stuff works."

"Apparently, neither does he," she said. "According to his financials, he's lost his ass. His portfolio is down by seven figures and dropping."

"Wow," I said with a whistle.

"Our man Roland needs an influx of cash fast. Otherwise, he risks going under completely."

"Four generations of family money down the toilet, just like that."

"Pretty much," Lynn said. "He's got the proverbial gun to his head financially, and that's why he's been squeezing the Duffy company on the options."

"So, if I have this right, Promes and Duffy are buyers already on the hook. Doesn't it make sense to just sell them the land and cover his losses?"

"He's in deep. From what we can tell, the current option deal won't cover his losses in its present form. If Roland can get Promes and Duffy to renege on the deal, he keeps their option money, and he can then turn around and sell the property at current market price, which is about double what Promes and Duffy contracted for."

"Then getting rid of them does indeed benefit him substantially," I said. "He's got a multimillion-dollar motive for seeing these people dead."

"It certainly seems that way to me."

"Now what?"

"Chief Lane's people have him under surveillance," she said. "We'll see what he decides to do now."

"What if we're wrong? What if Roland Douglas has nothing to do with this?"

"Then, dear brother, we are flat out of suspects," she said.

My phone beeped. I looked at the screen to see another call coming through.

"Sorry, Sis. I need to take this," I said.

"Okay. I'll call you later if anything else comes up," she said, disconnecting the call.

I pressed the icon that connected the new call.

"Hi, Josie."

"Hello, Mr. Davis," came a shaky voice on the other end.

"You sound . . . distressed. Is everything okay?"

"It's D'Vante."

"Is he all right?"

"Physically, he's fine," she said. "He's just having a hard time. You two seemed to hit it off the last time you were here. I was wondering if maybe you could talk to him?"

"Sure," I said without hesitation. "I'd be happy to."

"Thank you," she said, with relief in her voice her voice.

"I'll see you in about an hour," I said.

"Have you eaten?" she asked.

I looked at the clock—almost three in the afternoon and nothing but angst in my stomach all day.

"No. I'm starving," I said.

"Well," she replied, "you're headed to the right place. See you in an hour."

THIRTY-TWO

A NEW RIDGE OF high pressure covered the East Bay, and it was another scorcher as I drove the Black Beauty to Josie Walker's place in East Oakland. I didn't have the top down because the car was cooler with it up. Though the inside temperature was slightly lower, it still felt like I was driving a convection oven as I pulled up in front of the house. The street was packed with cars. Visiting day in the neighborhood. It reminded me of the days Auntie would take me and Lynn to visit friends and relatives after church, all dressed up in our Sunday finery. Black folks in those days took Sunday seriously. It was nice to see the tradition carried on.

I found an open space behind a white van parked directly in front of the Walker home. The name A1 PIANO TUNERS was emblazoned along both sides in large black lettering that was punctuated by a stylish, bold treble clef. I squeezed the T-bird behind the van and a late-model Buick and then got out of the car. Once outside, I noticed that the armpits of the blue dress shirt I wore were ringed with large circles of sweat. I have *got* to either find a way to put modern AC in this car or get a second vehicle that's already equipped with it. This was getting ridiculous.

I opened the trunk and pulled out one of the spare shirts I keep for fashion emergencies. In live television, you never know when something's going to break that puts you on camera unexpectedly. It is for that reason that a good reporter always leaves the house with an extra camera-ready outfit and a makeup kit. I grabbed a lavender dress shirt and removed it from its dry cleaners' plastic bag. I then took some Speed Stick deodorant from the makeup bag, got back in the car, and awkwardly changed. As I stood outside, tucking the shirt into my slacks and furiously swiping deodorant under my arms, the front door to the Walker home opened, and Josie appeared.

"You know you could have come inside to do that," she said.

"And enter your house a sweaty mess on a Sunday? Not a chance."

"Somebody raised you right," she smiled.

I headed up the walkway and into her home. As I entered, I noticed the man from A1 Piano Tuners fiddling with the wires on the family piano. He looked vaguely familiar, but I couldn't place him.

"It must have been rough getting him here on a Sunday," I said to Josie.

"Oh, that's Roy. He's been very good to us for a long time," she said.

My memory banks kicked in and I remembered that he was the white man I'd seen at Danica's funeral.

"He heard D'Vante play at a school recital when he was five or six and said, 'I'm going to support that young man.' He comes by whenever the piano needs tuning or a key gets stuck or something. He does it regardless of whether we can afford to pay for his services or not."

"Sounds like a good guy," I said.

"The best," she replied. "Roy?"

He looked up from his work.

"Roy Carlton, meet Topher Davis," Josie said.

He released a wire he'd been adjusting inside the piano, wiped his hands on the blue jeans he wore, and shook mine.

"It's nice to meet you," he said. "I've been watching you for a long time."

"Thank you," I said. "I appreciate that."

"How's it coming?" Josie asked.

"Fine," Roy Carlton said. "Give me about twenty minutes, and it'll sound like a Steinway."

"You're a saint," she said. "Can you stay for dinner?"

"I'm sorry," he said. "My daughter is making lasagna tonight. I miss it, and I'm a dead man," he replied.

"Another time, perhaps?"

"Definitely," he said, removing a tuning lever from the gray metal toolbox beside him.

"Nice meeting you, Roy," I said.

"Likewise," he replied, returning his attention to the task at hand.

I followed Josie as she walked toward the kitchen. She had done a lot with her little house. It wasn't as large or as grandiose as my place in Castro Valley, but it had a cozy, homey feel . . . something that my place lacked. I felt comfortable in this place. Maybe it was a sign that I needed to hire a decorator and make some changes to my own space.

A teak dining room table stood in a nook next to the kitchen. I could tell that a leaf had been removed to compress it into a dining space for four instead of its maximum seating capacity of six. It was set with fine china, vintage silverware that I'm sure was popular in Josie's grandmother's day, and Depression-era glasses. White people pass along money, businesses, and real estate to their progeny. If African Americans are left anything at all in the area of inheritance, it is generally in the form of material keepsakes like this. Monetarily, it isn't worth much, but it means the world in sentimentality.

The table had all the staples of the Sunday dinners of my youth: baked ham, collard greens, fried okra, corn bread, candied sweet potatoes, and potato salad. Josie donned a pair of potholders, removed a glass baking dish from the oven, and set it on a trivet in the center of the table. Then she turned her head toward the rear of the house.

"D'Vante!" she called. "Supper is on the table."

Silence.

She called out again.

"D'Vante!"

"Whaaat?" came the snotty, teenage reply.

"I said, dinner is ready."

"I'm not hungry," he yelled back at the top of his lungs.

"See what I mean?" Josie said, looking at me.

"Which room is his?" I asked.

"Down the hall. Second door on the right."

I followed her directions, found the appropriate door, and politely knocked.

"D'Vante?" I said softly.

No response.

"D'Vante," I said again.

"What is it?" came the man-child voice on the other side of the door.

"Can I come in?"

Silence.

"Please?"

"Whatever," he said.

I opened the door to find a room that was exceptionally well kept for a teenager. Much to my auntie's consternation, when I was D'Vante's age, my room usually looked like it had been hit by the Loma Prieta earthquake—clothes on the floor. Bed unmade. My study desk was piled high with clutter. Not this kid's room. There was a tan wooden dresser with all the drawers closed and not a hint of clothing peeking out. An open MacBook sat on a desk in the corner next to a neatly stacked pile of manuscript paper for musical compositions. Whereas my teenage walls were covered in posters of Prince, Michael Jackson, and Earth, Wind and Fire, D'Vante's displayed replicas of portraits featuring Beethoven, Mozart, and Brahms.

A twin bed, made of the same wood as the dresser, rested against the wall adjacent to the door, and D'Vante Walker lay stretched out upon it, his hands folded behind his head. His eyes glued to the plain, white ceiling above.

"Hi," I said.

"What are you doing here?"

"Your grandmother invited me for dinner. I was hoping you'd join us."

"I said that I wasn't hungry," he snapped, his eyes still fixed above.

"Okay if I sit down for a minute?"

Silence.

I pulled the chair out from his desk and placed it next to the bed.

"Whatcha doing?"

"What's it look like I'm doing?" he barked. "I'm thinking."

"About?"

"What's it to you?"

"If you're trying to sort out a problem, sometimes it helps to talk to somebody about it. I'm a good listener."

He exhaled in frustration, then turned his back to me and faced the opposite wall.

"Your grandmother tells me you haven't played your piano lately. Why not?"

"What's the point?"

"The point is that you're very gifted. You need to nurture that gift."

"Why? What good is it going to do me?"

"You want to be a concert pianist. With some time and training, I believe you can make it."

"I played for my mother. She's not here anymore."

"Is this what you think she'd want?" I asked. "I heard your eulogy when you said you were going to go to law school in her place. You can't live her life for her, son. You have to be *you*. You can't just throw away your gift and let it whither on the vine. You are a pianist. Embrace it and follow *your* dream."

"Somebody killed her. There's no point to anything anymore."

A beat.

"I know how you feel," I finally said.

"No—you don't!" he shouted.

"Yes, I do. Somebody killed my mother too."

D'Vante Walker rolled over on the bed and faced me.

"You're making that up," he said.

"If only," I replied.

"When?"

"A long time ago. I was just a kid too."

"Who did it?"

"We never found out," I said.

He looked at me with that expression one gets when they don't quite know what to say.

"I wanted to give up too," I told him. "I quit everything for a while. My mother was my world."

"What changed?"

"Before she died, I was living for her. Doing what she wanted me to do. Being what she wanted me to be," I said. "I realized that I had to start living for myself. I had to work to be the best I could be without her. The best I could be for me. We buried her. I couldn't crawl into that grave too. She put too much love and care into me to just toss it all."

He looked down at the bed, taking it all in.

"The good thing was that I wasn't alone. I still had my aunt to guide me. You've got your grandmother."

"She doesn't understand."

"D'Vante, she just lost her only child. If she doesn't understand, who does?"

I rose from my chair and returned it to his desk.

"Think about it," I said. "I'm going to get some of that Sunday dinner she whipped up. You should join us. Everything looks great."

D'Vante looked up, and his gaze followed me as I walked out the door. Upon leaving the room, I found Josie standing outside the door.

"What do you think?" she asked.

"I'm assuming you heard him," I said. "He's angry. Stage of the grief. It will pass. And then it will come back as he cycles through the grief stages again and again until it becomes something that he can find a way to live with."

She nodded.

"It will be the same process for you," I said.

"I know," she said.

"What stage are you in today?"

"I fluctuate between denial, sadness, and anger. Today, it's mostly denial. I pretend that it didn't happen. I need to keep my head on straight for D'Vante."

"You can both use some counseling. I told you that I can recommend somebody who specializes in dealing with grief," I said.

"I don't know . . ."

"Trust me, it'll help."

"I ain't got money for head doctors right now," she said.

"Don't worry about that. My friend works on a sliding scale, remember? You only pay what you can afford."

"I've got a teenage boy to finish raising by myself. I can't afford nothing."

"Then 'nothing' is what she'll charge you," I said.

"Really? Free?" she asked.

"If that's all your budget will allow."

"I still don't know . . ." she said.

"At those prices, what do you have to lose?"

I reached into my pocket and pulled out one of my business cards and a pen. I jotted down a name and number on the back of the card and handed it to her.

"This is the number for Michele Levy. She's excellent. Call her tomorrow. Tell her I sent you."

"Free? You sure?"

"Not a dime if you can't afford it."

She again nodded as she slipped the card into the pocket of her white apron.

"Okay. I guess it can't hurt to at least check her out," she said.

"You'll be glad you did."

I made a mental note to call Michele Levy first thing in the morning to tell her to discreetly forward bills related to the Walkers directly to me.

"Come on," she said. "Let's eat before everything gets cold."

I followed her to the table, where I piled my plate high with way too much food as she filled my glass with Southern-style sweet tea. I ate until I thought my belt would snap. After dinner, Josie cleared the table and brought me a piece of pecan pie from the kitchen.

"You know I'm on TV, right?" I said, holding up my hands. "The camera adds ten pounds."

"After all you ate, what's one piece of pie?" she asked with a smile.

She was right. In for a penny, in for ten pounds.

I took the small plate she handed me, picked up a dessert fork from the table, and dug in. It was heavenly. As I was finishing up, Roy Carlton came into the room.

"All done?" Josie asked.

"I gave her a full tuning and fixed the stuck key. She sounds great," he said.

"I don't know how to thank you."

"Nurturing talent like your grandson's is an honor," he said. "Truly."

"Bless you," she said, handing him a plate wrapped in foil. "I know you said that your daughter is making dinner. At least let me make dessert. It's pecan pie."

Roy Carlton smiled. "Thanks. I'm sure it's great. Enjoy your Sunday," he said as he turned toward the door.

Suddenly, he stopped and turned to Josie.

"Ms. Walker, I want to say again how sorry I am about what happened to your daughter. You and D'Vante have been in my prayers."

"Thank you," she said. "We need all the prayers we can get right now. It's a hard time."

"It's a terrible thing," he said, shaking his head. "Nobody should have to bury a child. Let alone a grandchild," he said. "You take care."

He hugged Josie and then headed out the front door.

"Excuse me a minute," I said, getting up.

I followed Roy Carlton outside, where I found him loading his gear into the back of his van.

"Mr. Carlton," I called.

"Yes?" he replied, turning to face me.

"That was really nice what you said to Josie back there."

"Well, I figure she needs all the support she can get right now," he said.

"May I ask you a question?"

"Sure."

"You mentioned Josie's grandchild. How did you know that Danica was pregnant?" I asked.

"She told me."

THIRTY-THREE

"**W**HEN DID DANICA tell you she was expecting?" I asked.

"The last time I tuned the piano," he said, stroking his chin as he tried to remember. "Maybe two, three months ago."

"She just up and told you? It's my understanding that she was a very private person."

"I don't think she meant to tell me," he said. "We were chatting in the living room one afternoon while I was working on the piano when she had to rush to the bathroom quickly. I followed her to make sure she was okay. Poor thing was puking her guts out. I'm a father. I recognize morning sickness. My wife Marsha, God rest her soul, had it in the worst way. She was as sick as a dog. Couldn't keep breakfast down for the first three weeks she was expecting. I asked Danica how far along she was. She hesitated and then told me around five or six weeks. She asked me to keep it a secret. She wasn't ready to announce it yet. You know how women are about that stuff."

"Sure," I said, even though not being a father, I knew nothing about the situation. "Did she seem happy about the pregnancy?"

"Once she stopped throwing up, she did. Said she hoped it was a little girl. She thought it would be nice for D'Vante to have a sister. Boy," he said, shaking his head. "Both of them gone. My heart breaks for D'Vante and Ms. Walker."

I nodded in agreement.

"She swore you to secrecy. Did you tell anybody she was going to have a baby?"

He stroked his chin again as though it helped him remember.

"I don't think so. I don't know who I would have told about it. We don't really travel in the same circles. Hell, aside from the handful of piano clients I keep, I don't travel in many circles at all. I'm semiretired. Put in thirty years in this business. I met Josie at a music recital my niece was in when she was little. She was playing clarinet. It was dreadful. Thank God she eventually gave it up. D'Vante followed her on the piano. I was blown away by that kid's natural talent. Been helping him out ever since."

"That's very kind of you."

"I've always believed that in my business, when you see an actual virtuoso, you do what you can to support them. My father taught me that. He was a piano tuner too."

He slid the side door on the van shut.

"Well," he said, "lasagna's waiting. Nice meeting you."

"Yeah," I said. "You too."

Roy Carlton climbed into the driver's seat, fired up his van, and drove down the street. I stood on the sidewalk thinking about what I'd just learned. Danica Walker *had* actually told someone else she was pregnant. If she told a casual acquaintance like this piano tuner, who else did she tell? Did she inadvertently spill to her eventual killer?

I took out my cell and called Lynn.

"I was just about to call you."

"Great minds," I said.

"I just finished background on Roland Douglas. As we thought, he has cash flow problems, which is probably why he's taking such a hard stance with Duffy and Promes. I found a couple of speeding tickets but no real brushes with the law. I didn't expect to find anything serious since he's sitting on a city government commission and all."

"So, he's clean. Financially struggling, but other than that, an upstanding citizen."

"Pretty much," Lynn said.

"Family?"

"Here's where it gets interesting. He has a four-year-old girl, Whitney. She goes to preschool with the Promes kid."

"Small world."

"He also has a seventeen-year-old son, Roland Jr. They call him J.R."

"You don't think that—"

"He might be the kid who paid off your attackers."

"Got any proof?"

"Not a shred. But he's the right age. His father is at war with Duffy and Promes, and you're digging into things that could potentially affect Daddy's business."

"It doesn't make sense. Why warn me to leave Crane Jr. alone, then call you for help and beg that I join you?" I asked.

"Maybe Roland Douglas didn't know. The kid just went rogue."

"I suppose that's possible. Douglas's money would eventually wind up in his hands one day. Maybe he was just looking out for the future."

"Then there's the chance that this was all misdirection from Roland Douglas himself. Get us looking closer at Crane Jr. on the one hand while begging for publicity on the other," she said.

"If his kid is the one making the payoff, that also might make Roland Douglas the killer. If he's the murderer, why call you demanding protection?"

"Like you said before, red herring. A little something to throw us off the scent," she said. "I'm gonna sniff around and see what I can find out about Junior."

"Another 'Junior' in this case. What is this propensity that white people have for naming their children after themselves?"

"It's a shot at immortality. A way to ensure their names live on long after they're gone."

"Not me," I said. "Any kid of mine is gonna have enough problems without having to drag my name around too."

"Why'd you call?" she asked.

I told her about Roy Carlton and what I learned about Danica's premature pregnancy announcement.

"So," Lynn said, "there were other people who knew about the baby."

"Apparently so. And if she told the piano tuner, who else did she tell?"

"Not only that, who did this Roy Carlton character tell?"

"He says no one."

"Remember the saying," she said. "The only way two people can keep a secret is if one of them is dead."

"There's an awful lot of that going around with a body count where it is," I said.

"Let's keep doing what we can to keep it from rising."

"Why not start by doing a little background on Roy Carlton too? He says that he and Danica didn't travel in the same circles. What if he's wrong and there is a person they had in common he spilled the pregnancy beans to?"

"Interesting theory," Lynn said. "Let me see what I can find out."

"Okay, I'm headed into the office. Got some thinking to do."

"It's the weekend. Don't you have a perfectly lovely den at home for exercises such as this?"

"I do," I said. "I also have a houseguest I'm not ready to deal with just yet."

"You know," Lynn said, "the situation with Mandy isn't going away. You need to talk to her."

"Thought you were staying out of this."

"I was going to, but you are my brother. You'll find a way to thoroughly mess things up if I don't intervene. It's your gift," she said.

"Thanks, Sis. It's a blessing to know that I inspire such confidence among my nearest and dearest."

"You're the one who slept with her."

"Point taken," I conceded.

"Talk to her," Lynn said.

"And say what?"

"Whatever needs to be said. You're a smart guy. You'll figure it out."

Later that afternoon, I sat with my feet propped up on the desk in my office, looking intently at the photo of Tom Promes and Julie Wolfer taken in Monterey. Something about the picture bothered me, although I couldn't quite put my finger on exactly what it was. The quiet of the station helped. The weekend crew was in, which meant a skeleton staff. It's not the usual noisy hustle and bustle we get on weekdays. Just a single news writer, a weekend producer, and a small on-camera cast featuring Antonio Gutierrez in the anchor chair, Susan Braswell, fresh from her first broadcast gig in Boise, manning the chroma key weather maps, and, in a daring move for a major market television, a woman named Stephanie Flores covering sports. It was good to see the station entering the twenty-first century.

The hum of the janitor's vacuum cleaner outside my office door provided the soundtrack for my contemplation. What was it about this picture that bothered me so much? In the foreground were Tom Promes and Julie Wolfer kissing and canoodling for the camera. The immortalization of illicit, forbidden love, far from home and away from their significant others.

I pinched the screen on my iPhone and closely scrutinized the picture. The background consisted of tourists and vendors. I zoomed in on the faces of the mother and her two sons in their skipper hats as they went into the seashell shop. I took another closer look at the elderly African American couple as they walked hand in hand along the pier. I noticed that the man putting mustard on his soft pretzel was getting more on his fingers than on his snack.

I scanned over to the dark-haired woman surreptitiously entering the Old Fisherman's Grotto restaurant. The picture was grainy due to her distance from the lens, and her face was hard to make out, but it suddenly struck me. The solution to the whole case had been staring me in the face all along.

THIRTY-FOUR

A T TEN ON Monday morning, Lynn and I once again paid an unexpected visit to the offices of Crane, Phelps, and Crane, where we found Patricia Hart answering a feverously overloaded phone bank. She was in midsentence when we entered. She put the caller on hold.

"I thought you folks had hired somebody to do this?" I said.

"Inga is out with COVID. Mild case, but she'll be out at least a week with quarantining and all," a harried Patricia Hart answered. "I did *not* go to law school for this, but team players make partners."

"The boss in?" Lynn asked.

"You're lucky. He's in, and he's free. His morning consultation just got rescheduled."

"Let me guess," I said. "COVID?"

"It never goes away, does it?" she said with a shake of her head.

"Can we see Mr. Crane Jr.?" Lynn asked.

"Sure thing, Detective," she replied with a smile.

She pressed a button on the phone bank, whispered into the receiver, and then hung up.

"Mr. Crane Jr. says to bring you right back."

"Thanks," Lynn said.

"Do you remember the way or need me to take you?"

"I'm lousy with directions," I said. "You'd better lead."

We followed her through a maze of cubicles, down a narrow hallway, and to a closed office door.

"Go on in," Patricia said. "He's waiting for you."

"Why don't you step in too?" Lynn said.

Patricia shrugged, opened the door, and entered. Lynn and I followed.

"Detective Sloan and Mr. Davis," she said, announcing us.

Crane Jr. sat behind his desk, his head buried in paperwork.

"Thanks," he said. "You can go, Patricia."

"They want me to stay," she said, perplexed.

"Oh?" he replied, looking up from his paperwork.

"If it isn't too much trouble," Lynn said.

"What's this all about?" he demanded.

"How and why Patricia killed Danica Walker," I said.

The color drained from Patricia's face. "What are you talking about?" she said, flustered. "You're crazy."

"Your birth name is Patricia Carlton, isn't it?" I asked. "You're divorced."

"It's California," she said with a laugh. "Who isn't? I married Steven Hart when I was twenty-one. It lasted three years. So what?"

"That makes Roy Carlton your father," Lynn said.

"Yes. He's my dad. Again, so what?"

"And you live with him," Lynn continued.

"Yes, I'm a woman in her thirties who lives with her elderly father. Shame me for it."

"Your father tunes the piano at the Walker home in Oakland. He knew Danica was pregnant and that she worked with you.

Maybe he mentioned it in passing or over breakfast, but he told you she was expecting," I said.

Patricia Hart was fidgeting . . . visibly uncomfortable.

"I have no idea what you're talking about," she said, her tone icy.

"Sure, you do," Lynn said. "Your dad told you that Danica was pregnant, and you started to get close to her. Befriend her."

"I try to be friendly with all my colleagues," she snapped.

"Danica Walker was garroted. Her neck wound was consistent with an injury caused by being choked out with a piano wire," I said. "Your dad's stock in trade."

"There are hundreds of piano tuners in the Bay Area, and they all use piano wire. That proves absolutely nothing," Patricia Hart said, turning for the door.

"But they weren't all having an affair with Tom Promes," Lynn added.

Patricia Hart stopped dead in her tracks.

"What the hell are you talking about?" she demanded.

"Mr. Crane, did Tom Promes ever come into this office?" I asked.

"Sure," Crane said. "We had a settlement conference."

"A conference for which Ms. Hart was in attendance," I said.

"Yes. Patricia was at the table. She worked on the case law," Crane Jr. said, confused.

"Yes, I worked on settling the Promes case," she said. "Again, so what? That doesn't mean that we were personally involved. Many people were at that meeting, and it was all totally professional."

I reached into the vest pocket of my sportscoat, pulled out an enhanced copy of the Monterey picture, and thrust it in her face.

"This picture was taken during a romantic getaway between Tom Promes and Julie Wolfer," I said. I pointed to the dark-haired woman darting into the seafood restaurant in the background. "You're clearly wearing a wig, but that *is* you, right?"

She looked at the picture and said nothing.

Crane Jr. reached across his desk, snatched the picture from my hand, and looked at it.

"It *is* you," he said to Patricia. "What's the meaning of this?"

"The meaning," Lynn said, "is that she stalked Tom Promes and Julie Wolfer on their illicit excursion. She'd only do something like that if she and Tom Promes were involved."

"We guess she met Promes during his legal work here, and they began an affair. Patricia thought she was the only one. Turns out she wasn't. She was just the one he was using," I said.

"Using?" Crane Jr. replied.

"To murder his wife," Lynn said.

"I've heard enough of this," Patricia said, heading for the door again.

"Stay right where you are," Crane Jr. demanded.

Patricia stopped, turned, and glared at me.

"Using how?" Crane Jr. asked.

"To do his dirty work," Lynn said.

"In what way?" Crane Jr. demanded.

"We think that Tom Promes seduced her. Probably promised her the world. He'd get her out of her father's house and then marry her. Maybe a few kids. A future together. Kristen was the only thing standing in the way," I told him.

"Then why not just divorce her?" Crane Jr. asked.

"Because Promes had been embezzling from his father-in-law's business to the tune of at least two million dollars. A divorce would inevitably mean an audit. Since he was running this multimillion-dollar real estate firm, there would have been issues as to what, if any, of Promes's contributions to that firm would have constituted community property under California law, and the theft would have been discovered, not to mention the fact that once the affair was exposed, Mason Duffy would surely have kicked him to the curb. The only way to keep his job, his wealth, and his position in the community as an heir apparent to the Duffy real estate empire and hide the theft of the money was if his wife was dead."

"With Kristen Promes dead, wouldn't the company have been left to her daughter?" Crane Jr. asked.

"We were able to get a look at Duffy's will," I said. "Under its provisions, if Kristen died, Taylor Promes would have been next in line to inherit once she reached the age of twenty-five. In the meantime, her father would have been trustee. Taylor is currently a preschooler. That would have given Tom Promes two decades to move and manipulate assets as he saw fit. So again, the simplest form of action was for Kristen Promes to be dead."

"That's where Patricia came in," Lynn added. "Promes conspired with her to murder Kristen using those empty promises of a future together. Maybe he had her hide in the back of Kristen's Rav4 during the barbecue. According to Roy Carlton, Patricia never came home the night before Kristen disappeared, so I'm guessing she spent the night curled up in the back of that vehicle. Promes then arranged for Julie Wolfer, who, incidentally, was the woman he really wanted to be with, to convince Kristen to drive over and pick up her daughter and take her to the party to play with Taylor. At a prearranged spot, Patricia popped out of hiding, probably held her at gunpoint, and forced her to drive to her own car that was parked on Bernal Avenue. After transferring vehicles, she drove her to a storage unit she was renting next door in Dublin, wrapped one of her father's piano wires around the poor woman's neck," Lynn said, "garroted her and cut her baby out of her womb. She then waited until dark and loaded Kristen's dead body into her car before driving down to Lake Del Valle, where she buried her."

"Meanwhile, Tom stayed at the barbecue, giving himself an ironclad alibi while Patricia did his dirty work," I added. "He conned Julie Wolfer into coaxing Kristen out of the house so he could surprise her with a new Tesla when she got back. The problem is that he never took the Tesla out of the garage. The bow for the present was still in the trunk. That's because he knew she wasn't coming back."

"What about the Wolfer woman you mentioned? Was she part of the conspiracy?" Crane Jr. asked, not taking his eyes off of a rapidly shrinking Patricia Hart.

"We don't think so," Lynn said. "We believe that she truly thought she was helping Tom surprise Kristen with a new car to soften her up so that when he divorced her, as he also promised Julie Wolfer he would do, the court proceedings might be a little less contentious. She apparently had no idea she was complicit in a murder."

"Patricia killed Julie after realizing that Tom Promes was having an affair with her. He had made a fool of her by getting her to kill his wife and leaving her holding the bag for homicide while he played house with another woman."

"But . . . What's any of this got to do with Danica Walker?" Crane Jr. asked.

"In a homicide, the spouse is always the main suspect," I said. "Tom, Patricia, or both, figured that the only way to make sure that he truly wasn't a suspect was if it looked like Kristen's murder was committed by somebody else. Somebody with no connection to the victim at all. They settled on making it look like the work of a serial killer. Patricia probably got the idea when she learned of Danica's pregnancy," I said. "Her father inadvertently mentioned it to Patricia when he discovered they were working at the same firm. If there were more than one woman murdered with the same MO, it would look like police were dealing with a homicidal maniac targeting pregnant women and cutting out their fetuses. It also explains why she carved up Julie Wolfer even though she wasn't pregnant. It had to look like the work of the same murderer. By the way, nice touch adding the pentacles. Added a nice 'serial killer' element to the whole scheme."

"When Patricia overheard you and Danica arguing over her pregnancy, Mr. Crane, she realized that you were the father and that it was the perfect time for Danica to disappear and," Lynn said, "cast suspicion on you."

"*Me??*" he exclaimed.

"Back up. In case authorities saw through the serial killer ruse, you got her pregnant, and you were arguing with her in your office about the situation on the day she disappeared," Lynn said. "Video footage from your office building's garage surveillance system shows Patricia leaving with Danica that afternoon. What did you do, Patricia? Offer to give her a lift to BART or something?"

"There were traces of decaf coffee and Benadryl in Danica's toxicology report. What'd you do? Take her to Starbucks on the way home and drug her latte?" I asked.

Patricia Hart stared at the floor. Lynn continued.

"My guess is they got into Patricia's car, Patricia drugged her, then drove her to her kill spot in Dublin where she garroted and mutilated her before burying her body in Golden Gate Park."

"The forensics team found traces of Danica's DNA in your backseat as well," I said. "You really should hire a professional auto detailer."

"And yes, Mr. Crane," Lynn said, "she tried to implicate you. She posed as a teenage boy and hired some gangbangers to attack my brother and throw your name around. Again, if the serial killer angle didn't work, the police still had a viable suspect in you. Danica Walker was just an innocent bystander who fit her needs because she was pregnant, accessible and connected to you. Collateral damage."

"After realizing how she'd been used, Patricia decided to take out the only person who knew what she'd done. The only one standing between her and the rest of her natural life in prison," I added.

"Tom Promes," Crane Jr. said.

"She probably lured him out of the house on the pretext that they needed to talk about the murders. Or was it just a booty call, Patricia?" I asked.

"Fuck you!" she shrieked.

"My, my," I said. "You'll never make partner using language like that."

She folded her arms and glowered at me.

"However, she managed it," I said, "she got him alone in his car and put a bullet in his head, thus using a different MO and making the killings appear unrelated. We knew the shooter was someone he knew because the slug was between his eyes. He was looking at the killer in the passenger seat when the fatal shot was fired."

"You've got *nothing*!" Patricia screamed. "Just a bunch of theories!"

"No," I said. "We have actual evidence. As we mentioned before, there are traces of Kristen Promes's DNA in your car. Danica Walker's too. We also discovered that your father owns a .32-caliber Beretta pistol. That's the same caliber as the gun used to kill Tom Promes. Your father voluntarily handed it over to the authorities, and ballistics is running tests on it as we speak. Thanks for leaving us a shell casing. If it's a match for the murder gun, as we suspect it will be . . . That's game over."

A tear rolled down Patricia's cheek as Crane Jr. glared at her.

"Is all this true?" he asked.

She said nothing.

"Patricia?"

More tears began to roll down her face.

"He said he loved me," she sobbed. "That we'd be together. I just needed to help him make it happen. I did what he wanted.

I followed his instructions to the letter, only to find out he was fucking that Julie Wolfer whore."

There goes the wronged woman tossing around the word, 'whore,' again.

"You were a classic Cat's Paw," I said.

"Shut up!" she screamed, lunging for a sharp silver letter opener on Crane Jr.'s desk. "Shut up!"

She grabbed the instrument and charged at me. It all happened so fast that I didn't have time to react. Catlike reflexes I ain't got. I froze as I awaited the inevitable melding of steel and flesh.

Patricia Hart suddenly began to stumble, losing her balance. It took me a moment to realize that Lynn had kicked her legs out from underneath her and grabbed the wrist of her hand that held the letter opener. Patricia fell backward, knocking Lynn to the floor, her body on top of my sister's. She then jabbed the weapon at Lynn, trying furiously to stab her with it. Patricia was a lot stronger than she looked. I wondered how much of a fight Kristen and Danica had put up.

She jabbed at Lynn's head again and again. My sister somehow had the agility to dodge the strikes. The closeness in the proximity of their bodies must have helped. There wasn't much room for Patricia to maneuver, but she raised the letter opener over her head and prepared to strike at Lynn again. I finally regained my wits enough to reach for the hand holding the letter opener. I reached too high, and the blade sliced the palm of my left hand. The pain was searing as I fell on my behind and used my right hand to grasp my left wrist. The slashed palm was a dripping mess of crimson.

Crane Jr. picked up the phone from the unit on his desk and dialed 911 as Lynn reached for her Glock. Patricia's position on top of her made getting to it next to impossible, but as she writhed on the floor, my sister was able to elbow Patricia in the mouth, drawing blood. I saw her lick a drop from the corner of her mouth as her lips curled into an eerie smile. It was as though the blood had invigorated her. With what appeared to be renewed strength, she forced the blade closer to Lynn's throat. Lynn held the blade hand with both of hers, doing all she could to keep it from entering her windpipe. Then, suddenly, Patricia's body went limp. The letter opener slipped from her hands and clanked on the floor.

Lynn pushed the dead weight off of her and wriggled free, where she saw me standing above them, holding Crane Jr's heavy phone unit in my blood-soaked hands. Lynn caught her breath, stood, pried the adrenaline-glued device from my fingers, and examined my injured palm. Crane Jr. handed her a white handkerchief from his vest pocket, which she used to slow the bleeding.

"Thanks," she said, her attention focused on my wound.

"Hey," I said. "What are big brothers for?"

THIRTY-FIVE

THE POLICE AND the EMTs were on the scene just as Patricia Hart returned to consciousness, Lynn's Glock pointed at her from the safe distance of Crane Jr.'s desk. Once the first responders looked at the bump on the back of her head and laid her on a gurney for the ride to San Francisco General, the room filled with the distinctive clink of handcuffs chaining Patricia's wrists to the metal guardrails of the stretcher. The medical personnel then wheeled her to the elevator, where she soon disappeared behind the closing double doors.

After my hand was properly bandaged, Lynn, Crane Jr., and I spent about two hours filling in the SFPD officers on the scene about what had transpired. Lynn laid out the whole story just as it would be presented to the district attorney for prosecution. I filled in what blanks I could while Crane Jr. told what he knew about Patricia as an employee and . . . his affair with Danica and her pregnancy. Once he finished, he hurried down to his car to rush home and tell his wife about the affair and pregnancy before it made the news. I didn't have the heart to tell him that she already knew. Oh, what a tangled web we weave . . .

I called Mandy and Stu, who came to the office building to shoot B-roll footage for the six o'clock show. Lynn gave them an on-camera soundbite. It was the least she could do. I had just saved her life by knocking out Patricia Hart. Well, right after Lynn saved me from the letter opener, but who's counting? Lynn returned to 850 Bryant to be present for Patricia Hart's processing and to take care of administrative issues dealing with the arrest. Stu drove the ENG truck back to the station. Mandy rode with me in the Black Beauty. I told her what I could.

"So, Jules wasn't a part of it?"

"Not knowingly," I said. "In the end, she was just another of Tom Promes's pawns."

"Do you think he really loved her?"

"With a guy like that, who knows?" I replied. "From what I've learned about him, he was a user. People were only as valuable to him for what he could get from them."

Mandy shook her head.

"Well, she wasn't an active participant in a murder. That's something," she said. "What tipped you off about Patricia Hart?"

"The Monterey picture," I said. "Once I recognized her in the background, I figured there could be no legitimate reason for her presence other than spying on Tom Promes. I had Lynn run a check on her, and once we discovered that her father was the Walker's piano tuner and that he was one of the few people who knew Danica was pregnant, it all started to fall into place."

"What about hiring the gangbangers to slap you around? How'd she pull that off?"

"She's a slight woman. Small. Youthful in appearance. Wash off the makeup. Put on a baseball cap and shades. Stay in the car. Not hard to pass for a teenage boy. The area around that Arco is known for gang activity. Finding someone there to enlist for a battery wasn't hard."

"Where'd she get the truck?" Mandy asked. "The black SUV?"

"We learned from Roy Carlton that his work van needed service for a few days. The dealer gave him the SUV as a loaner. Patricia simply borrowed it."

Mandy shook her head again.

"Those poor kids," she said. "Taylor Promes without a mother or a father. And Jules's little girl, Hope, now motherless."

"It's incredibly sad," I said. "The upside is that I'm sure that Kristen's parents, the Duffys, will give Taylor the best, most privileged childhood anybody could possibly ask for."

Mandy nodded.

"As for Hope . . . Well, she has her father. And she has you."

Mandy's eyes had begun to moisten.

"You bet she does," Mandy said.

We got to the station, and I quickly hammered out some notes for the teleprompter to use on air. Just bullet points with the pertinent facts I would ad-lib—no time to write a full script, not that my now gauze-covered hand would let me. The show was starting soon, and I had to make a call before we went on air.

I caught Josie Walker at home. Usually, she would have been at work this time of day, but as the pain of Danica's death began to take hold, she finally decided that she needed to take more time to be home with D'Vante and to try to heal.

"Mr. Davis," she said. "This is a surprise."

"I have some news."

"Oh?" she said. "Sounds like I need to sit down for this."

"It would be a good idea," I responded.

I heard the sound of a kitchen chair scraping against linoleum.

"Okay," she said. "What is it?"

I told her the whole story as Lynn and I understood it. When I finished, there was a long silence.

"Josie? Josie, are you still there?"

"Mr. Carlton. He didn't know, did he?"

"Roy Carlton didn't have a clue. He had no idea what his daughter was up to. They lived in the same house but were virtually strangers when all was said and done. Worse, he blames himself for tipping Patricia off about Danica's pregnancy."

"It's not his fault," she said. "I'll call him. It looks like we both lost children."

She was right. They had.

"How's D'Vante doing?"

"What you said to him helped. He's back to the piano and taking out his frustrations and grief by playing all his mother's favorite pieces."

"That's wonderful," I said.

"He's also talking about attending that music school in San Francisco again. The odds are long, but he says he'll go if he can get in and get a scholarship to pay for it. It's what Danica would have wanted."

"With his natural abilities, I don't think getting in will be a problem," I said.

A few weeks later, D'Vante was notified that he had received a full, four-year scholarship to the San Francisco Conservatory of Music upon graduation. It covered tuition, books, supplies, and a stipend for room and board. The only conditions were that he attended his classes regularly and maintained at least a 3.0 GPA.

The scholarship came from an anonymous donor who wrote that he had been touched by hearing D'Vante play and wanted to help him reach his full potential. That was true. I *was* touched by how the kid tickled the ivories. I considered my contribution an investment. I'd made worse ones.

The scheduled A Block segment for the top of the six o'clock show was thrown out to make room for my exclusive. Mandy did a quick and masterful job editing our new footage, weaving in some existing soundbites we'd previously run before in our coverage and telling the complicated story in pictures that were easily consumable by a television audience. When we broke for commercial, the anchors and crew erupted into a spontaneous round of applause.

"Brilliant!" Kurt Weil said, calling down from his office. "Just brilliant. We've got the jump on every station in town. Nice job."

"Thanks, Kurt," I said.

Compliments and accolades are nice, but I was uncomfortable accepting them for this story. There was so much wreckage in its wake. A single mother had lost her only child. A couple buried their daughter—two little girls without mothers. One missing a father too. A piano prodigy had lost his mother, both his North Star and the source of his inspiration. And Mandy had lost her cousin. No. I didn't feel like taking bows for helping Lynn untangle this one.

Once the broadcast wrapped and I'd gotten out of makeup, tie, and jacket, I headed for the garage, where I found Mandy standing next to the Black Beauty.

"Give a girl a lift?" she asked.

"Which way you headed?"

"Let's just drive for a while."

The heatwave roasting the Bay Area had finally broken, and the weather was beautiful and mild. I let the top down on the car, drove out of the Broadcast Center lot, and headed for the Bay Bridge. We'd missed the worst part of the afternoon commute, and it was clear sailing into the East Bay. We rode in silence as I took the Broadway exit in Oakland and headed for Jack London Square. As I drove, Mandy just stared out the open-air car.

"You okay?" I finally asked.

"I will be," she said.

"Feel like a walk?"

"Sure," she said. "Why not?"

I drove along the water and then past stores and shops as the setting sun gave birth to Oakland nightlife. Waterfront restaurants were bustling as hostesses escorted lines of patrons inside. Packs of millennials and Gen Zers poured into the trendy bars and night spots that were springing up in the area. Yoshi's jazz club had a line that stretched around the block as people crowded in to hear the newest saxophone sensation. I imagined a crowd like that one day turning out to experience the musical stylings of D'Vante Walker.

I pulled into the lot for Kincaid's restaurant and gave the valet the keys to the Beauty. The young kid looked like he should still be practicing with his learner's permit. I sucked it up and let the wide-eyed youngster take my prized classic.

"This car is rad!" he said, hopping behind the wheel.

"Just make sure that it's still 'rad' when you bring it back to me," I said, slipping him a twenty-dollar bill.

"Yes, sir!" he said as he pocketed the portrait of Andrew Jackson before speeding off for the garage.

I pointed toward the shoreline, and Mandy and I headed in that direction. It was shaping up to be a beautiful night as we watched couples walk hand in hand along the water as the sun morphed into an amber glow that glistened on the waves.

"I guess we should talk, huh?" she asked.

"I think it would help."

"I was a mess when I came to your room that night. I was sad, scared, angry, hurt . . . You name it. A million emotions were swimming in my head. I couldn't handle them and felt like I was falling apart. Hell, I *was* falling apart. I couldn't handle what was going on inside of me, and I needed . . ."

"Comfort," I interjected.

"Yes," she said, her eyes downcast.

"And I just happened to be there," I said.

She looked up at me. "Yes."

"I see."

"I wasn't using you. I swear I wasn't. I just needed to feel safe. To be in arms I knew would protect me. Make me feel secure. Yours did that."

"Are you saying you're sorry?"

"Oh no," she said. "I'm not sorry at all. You gave me just what I needed."

My turn to cast my eyes downward.

"Are *you* sorry?" she asked.

"Mandy, we've been friends for a long time . . ."

"Are you sorry?" she persisted.

"Truth? No. No, I'm not sorry. Not at all."

"So where does that leave us?" she asked.

"Have you got a date for the Emmys yet?"

ACKNOWLEDGMENTS

The completion of this work would not have been possible without the village that supported me during the writing process.

Thank you to Shawanda Williams and Kreceda Tyler of Black Odyssey Media for their belief in me and my vision.

Thanks to my intrepid "title queen" agent, Kimberley Cameron, who believed in me and helped me bring Topher and Lynn to life in the first place.

Thanks to my dear friend Pam Jones and my sister Heather Copeland Freeman for reading the bad drafts and helping me make them better.

Thanks to Rick and Cindy Simons for always being in my corner.

Much gratitude to Amy Henderson for being a cheerleader when I get stuck.

Thank you to my friends and mentors, Jesse Kellerman and Jonathan Kellerman. I couldn't have done it without you, amigos.

A special thank you to Elaine Petrocelli at Book Passage in Corte Madera, California, for supporting me and my work.

Much gratitude to David Ivester and Karin Conn, who helped present this work to the world.

Last, but certainly not least, thanks to my beautiful family: my sisters—Tracie Copeland Stafford, Delisa Copeland Peterson, and Tonya Copeland—and my children—Adam Copeland, Casey Copeland, and Carolyn Copeland McKinney—for their love and support.

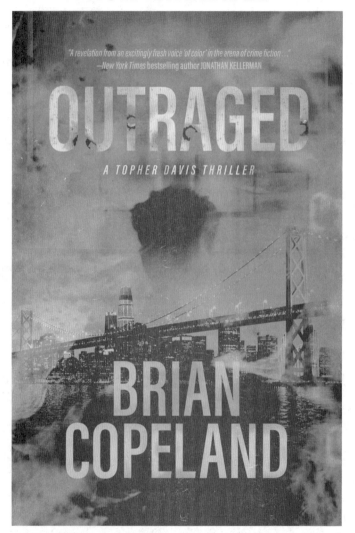